Bill Bailey

Bill Bailey

a novel by
CATHERINE COOKSON

BOOK CLUB ASSOCIATES LONDON

This edition published 1987 by
Book Club Associates
by arrangement with William Heinemann Ltd

Printed and bound by
Richard Clay Ltd, Bungay, Suffolk

This is a story for young women
disillusioned with boyfriends and looking
out for a more stable companion;
For young widows with children,
and those without;
For widows not so young;
For a one parent family;
For divorcees with children;
For those on the loose;
And for dream-shattered women of
all ages with hope springing eternal who long
to meet up with an ordinary bloke like
Bill Bailey.

1

❧

"A paying guest?"

"No, Mother; a lodger. As I said, he works on the buildings
. . . he's a lodger."

"You're getting coarse. And what do you think people will
say in the avenue?"

"They'll say, Mother, they wish they'd had the chance to take
. . . a lodger. I know of three redundant managers in the street,
and their wives are scraping for jobs."

"Well, far better go out to work again than take in a person
like that."

"Perhaps you've forgotten, Mother, we've had all this out
before: I have three small children and it was costing me practically all I worked for in paying someone to look after them,
and travelling expenses. Anyway, since that do in hospital, I
haven't felt up to standing all day smiling and saying, 'Yes,
madam; that was made for you', and generally to old bags who
still don't know how the other half lives."

"You needn't have paid anyone to look after them; I offered,
didn't I?"

"Yes, Mother, you did. But look what happened when I was
in hospital. There was chaos. I was hardly round from the anaesthetic when you told me you were on the verge of a nervous
breakdown, and you listed all the things Mark had said and
done. Anyway, don't let's go on: I am taking a lodger because I
cannot make ends meet otherwise."

"Well, you know who's to blame for that. And I'll say it
again: if he had been any kind of a husband he would have seen
that you were properly cared for by taking out an insurance."

"He did take out an insurance, Mother. I have the house."

"Yes; and nothing with which to keep it up. He was irre-
sponsible right from the beginning. A freelance journalist!

I

Huh! he should have got a proper job. Your father provided for me."

"But only just, as you often tell me, Mother. Only just."

At this point the kitchen door was thrust open and a blond nine-year-old boy cried, "He's here! He's here, Mam. In a whopping big car," then turned about and disappeared.

As though caught up in the boy's excitement, Fiona Nelson and her mother went to the window and looked down the long narrow garden towards the gate, where a man was taking luggage from the boot of a car. He had placed two cases inside the gate on the pathway when the boy reached him and attempted to pick up one of the cases. They saw the man rumple the boy's hair, at the same time apparently turning him towards the car for, together, they went back to it.

"Well, he's a good age."

Fiona glanced at her mother, saying, "That at least should put your mind at rest."

"Well, it hasn't. The whole idea's obnoxious. And look." She pointed. "Golf clubs!" Mrs Vidler's voice held a note of utter disbelief. "You said he worked on the buildings, a bricklayer."

"I said no such thing; I didn't specify what he worked at. You made up your own mind about that after I said he worked on the buildings. And that's what he does, so he told me, along with his men."

"*His men?*"

"Yes. He's a builder, Mother. He's building those detached houses above the park."

"*What!* . . . *Really!* They're expensive."

"Yes, Mother; they're expensive."

Fiona watched her mother's countenance alter. It was as if her face was changing its skin. She had seen that look before. It meant, the chase had begun, for under that refined exterior was the hunter. But that she had never chased a quarry like this one approaching the front door now Fiona would have been willing to bet.

There was a tight smile on her face as she left her mother arranging her hair and hurriedly nipping at her lips. She crossed the small hall towards the open door to greet her future companion by saying, "Well, you've got here, then?"

And the man, dropping the cases just inside the door,

answered, "Yes, I've got here, in the flesh. And don't attempt to move those." He indicated the two big cases with his foot.

"I had no intention of doing so."

"Huh!" He was looking her straight in the face, as he added, "No; you wouldn't, would you?"

Fiona felt herself rearing slightly. She wanted to step back from him, but she didn't; she returned his stare, thinking that she had never been able to stand men with sideboards, even short ones like this; and they were grey, and yet his hair was still dark, in fact mostly black. He was only slightly taller than her, and she was five foot seven; what was more, he was thickset. She had never liked thickset men. His whole appearance, like his voice, had a roughness to it. If there had been any romance left in her, she told herself, she would have said he looked rugged; but no, he was rough, all rough; and loud, as he proclaimed now by yelling down the garden, "Hi! laddie; don't attempt to carry those."

He left her side and hurried down towards the boy, and took the golf bag from him; brought it swiftly back, dropped it near his cases, then went back to the car again. He hadn't even glanced at her this time.

When Mark came into the hall she put a hand on his shoulder, and he looked up and said, "It's a Volvo, Mam, the car."

She did not remark on this, but watched her future lodger-cum-paying-guest place one more case on the drive, then lock the car door, after which she turned her son about and pressed him towards the far door, saying, "Go on into the garden; Katie and Willie are in the playhouse. Stay with them until I call.'

"But, Mam."

"Do as I say, Mark, please."

The boy lifted his shoulders in protest, but did as he was bidden.

Then there was the man again placing another large case against the other two, and she knew she should say to him, "You'd like to get unpacked, I'm sure." But she told herself she might as well get the family introduction over because her mother, in her present mood, would stay on until she did meet him.

"Would you like to meet my mother? She's in the sitting-room."

"Anything you say." His tone implied, I'm in your hands, so

she led the way into the sitting-room where, looking from one to the other, she said, "This is Mr Bailey, Mother. My mother, Mrs Vidler."

Fiona watched her mother move slowly towards him, her hand outstretched, and in her most refined tone say, "How do you do?"

She also watched the man hesitate a moment, seeming to take her mother in one hard blue glance; then taking the outstretched hand, he said, "I do very well, ma'am. How do *you* do?"

Fiona had to turn her head away. The chase was on, but the scent was misleading.

"I'm so pleased my daughter has decided to take a paying guest. . . ."

"Paying guest?" His head turned sharply towards the young woman who was now his landlady, and he said, "That's what I am then, a paying guest? Does that mean it will cost more than being a lodger, or are the rates the same?" His blue eyes were twinkling and for a moment she imagined that he winked. "Your advert said lodger."

He turned quickly again to Mrs Vidler when she said on a light laugh, "Oh, that was Mrs Green's doing in the paper shop. She's a very . . . well, ordinary person; her trade is mostly with the council house estate. . . ."

"Oh, aye, I see. I see." He was nodding. "And they are a *very ordinary lot*, *very* ordinary that lot." And he drew in his lips and knobbled his chin to emphasise how ordinary the council house lot were.

Fiona closed her eyes for a moment. Her mother wasn't stupid; no, so couldn't she tell she was on the wrong scent? It seemed not.

In an effort to save the situation she said, "Would you like a cup of coffee? I've just made it."

"No. Thanks all the same. I had a pint or two before I landed."

"You like a drink?"

Her mother's tone was one of polite enquiry, and the answer came, "Oh, yes, ma'am; I have the same intake as a whale."

"You're joking, Mr Bailey. . . . Are you married?"

William Bailey looked at the well-preserved, once pretty woman. She was kicking sixty if he knew anything. But they never let up, did they, her sort? He allowed a pause to ensue, then a sad note in his voice, he said, "Four times, ma'am. And four divorces. I made the mistake in each case marryin' a woman older than meself. I did it because I wanted to steer clear of the young 'uns, you know, like your good-looking daughter here." He now thumbed towards Fiona, then ended, "I run along the middle track of the jungle now, ma'am, well away from the hunters on both sides."

"Four times divorced!"

"'Struth, ma'am. Sad but true. Four times divorced." And now pulling a wry face, he said, "If you don't mind, I'll sit down. I stand most of the day, and so when I can I always take a pew." And he lowered himself into an easy chair whilst looking across at the open-mouthed woman and saying, "I'd get me legs up an' all, if I was you, ma'am, for there's nothing brings on varicose veins in advancing years like standin' about."

Fiona daren't look at her mother whose face was almost purple now. And her mother was right; she had made a mistake in thinking that this lodger business would solve her problems, for this one was going to be a problem in himself.

She now followed her mother as she made her stiff-backed exit from the sitting-room without wishing the paying guest goodbye, and she made sure that she closed the sitting-room door behind her, for she knew what would happen in the hall.

"He's impossible, dreadful. Get rid of him. Tell him you've changed your mind."

"Mother, I . . . I have a notion he was just pulling your leg."

"Pulling my leg indeed! Varicose veins, and indicating that I was an old woman! He's dreadful, coarse, ignorant, the worst of his class I've ever come across. You simply can't let him stay."

"He has paid a month in advance, Mother, and I've already spent a third of it in stocking up the freezer, et cetera."

"I'll make it good, I'll do without my holiday."

"Mother" – she pressed her towards the front door – "leave it for the time being. If I find him impossible, he'll go. Believe me."

"And this business that he doesn't like young women, that's all my eye."

Fiona smiled primly now as she said, "You're using a common expression, Mother."

"Oh, girl! don't you start. Now look, get on that phone if he starts any funny business. Do you hear me? Get on that phone."

"I hear you, Mother. And the minute he starts any funny business I'll shout for help."

Her mother had taken three steps from the front door when she turned about and came back, saying in a stage whisper, "It isn't right, you being in this house alone with him."

"Hardly alone, Mother, with three children. And I have a son who will guard me, never fear."

"*Fiona*." The finger was wagging now. "There's nothing funny about this business. I wouldn't trust that man as far as I could toss him."

Her mother was indeed worried, as her speaking in the vernacular proved. And she herself wasn't seeing anything funny about this business, either; for at this moment she was wishing that she hadn't spent so much of his advance payment, for she still retained enough of her mother's character to admit she didn't really know how she was going to put up with him.

And a moment later when she entered the sitting-room she was startled by his first words: "I know. I know. You don't know how you're gona put up with me. I'm brash, loud, vulgar, the lot. Well, that's me. But not as bad as I have just portrayed meself to your mother. Sit down and let's talk this out."

"I haven't time to sit down, Mr Bailey."

"Oh, then that means me gettin' to me feet. Well now, here I am on me pins, standing trial, and I'm going to add to me brashness by telling you straightaway I could see what your mother was after as soon as I set eyes on her. And the reason why I'm here at all is that I have just escaped from a similar type. They're the very devil, you know, women like your mother."

"You put a high value on yourself, don't you, Mr Bailey? How do you know my mother isn't married and has no need of . . . er . . . another man?"

"Oh, I learnt that from Mrs Green; she gave me the rough details. You have been widowed for three years, your mother for four. Would you like to know her recommendation in her own words?"

"Not necessarily, thank you."

"Well, I'll give them to you, necessarily or not. The old 'un, Mrs Green said, is a bit of an upstart. But the young one's all right. She couldn't have been fairer than that, could she?"

They stared at each other; and then he, laughing, said, "Let's

6

clear the air a bit further eh? I'm not after anybody's blood, young or old. As I said, I steer a middle course; I value me freedom. And that was a lot of polony about me being married an' divorced four times. It was once. And that was more than enough. Not that I don't enjoy meself, mind." His chin was knobbled again. "But if I have a love, it's me work." He leaned towards her now, saying, "You were surprised the other day, weren't you, to know I was the boss of the show? Thought I was a brickie, didn't you?"

"I had no thoughts about you at all, Mr Bailey. We were discussing a business deal, and as you are a businessman you will know that it is wise to keep personalities in their place."

"Oh, come off it. Sayin' that proves you know nothing about business, and once you tell them to keep their place that's when you have trouble. Like now, with the strikes. But speaking of places, the way you meant it, don't worry, I know me place, and I like it, and I mean to stick to it. So now, if you will excuse me" – his voice changed into one of pseudo-refinement – "I'll go and see if my valet has unpacked. What time is dinner?"

She had to force herself to say, "I'll make it for whatever time is convenient to you."

"Well say, it being Saturday, make it for five; I like a long Saturday night out."

He was walking away from her when he turned his head towards her and added, "On the tiles."

He was hardly out of the room before she flopped into a chair and, resting her elbow on the arm and her head in the palm of her hand, she swayed herself slightly and muttered as she did so, "Oh, my God! What an individual!"

2

"Are the children ready?"

"Yes, they're in the sitting-room waiting."

"It wouldn't do any harm for you to come to church this morning. . . . And washing on a Sunday! You never had to do anything like this before. Are you giving him notice now his month's up?"

"No, Mother. He has already paid another month in advance."

"You're asking for trouble; you know that. I saw Minnie Hatton the other day, and she says he's got a name."

"Oh, Minnie Ha-Ha says more than her prayers, and she whistles them."

"*What!* The way you talk. I suppose you've got that from him. And where is he today? Still in bed?"

"No, Mother; he's in Liverpool, visiting his father."

"Liverpool? Is that where he comes from? Well, what can you expect, coming from a place like that?"

"Mother, let up for goodness sake! . . . I'll call the children."

At this Fiona marched from the kitchen, banging the door after her.

In the sitting-room, she said, "Come on. . . . And I told you to sit up straight, Katie, and not lie about on that dress."

"I don't want to go, Mam; I don't like going to church with Grandma."

"When's Mr Bill coming back? He said he might be earlier."

"When did he tell you that, Mark?"

"Just before he left. He's going to get us tin whistles and we're going to practise 'Bill Bailey'."

"You're going to practise no such thing. . . . And stand up straight, Katie."

"I want to go to the toilet."

8

"You've had plenty of time to go to the toilet, Willie. Now all of you get yourselves out, your grandmother's waiting. And behave yourselves; I want no bad reports."

When, standing together, the three of them all looked up at her, she made a sudden dive for them and put her arms around them. And they clung to her and laughed.

"Be good," she said softly. "It isn't for long, only an hour. And I'm making you a chocolate mousse for your lunch."

"Oh, goodie!" They were all about to make a rush for the door when her voice checked them in a harsh whisper: "Walk!"

As if governed by the one set of muscles, their faces dropped into a blank mould, and, forming into a line, Mark first, followed by Katie, and then Willie, they fell into step and marched from the room.

Fiona did not immediately follow them to hear the reception they would get from their grandmother when they entered the kitchen doing their turn, as they called it; but leaning her hips against the back of the couch, she drew in a long breath as she muttered, "The little devils!" Then she almost sprang into the middle of the room as her mother's voice came from the hall, crying, "Fiona! Fiona!"

"Yes? What is it?"

"I've told them they're coming back with me for lunch, but they have informed me in one voice that they are coming straight home. Will you please tell them that they are to do what they're told? I've already prepared the lunch; and I'm doing this to give you a break. So will you please tell them what they've got to do?"

Fiona told her small brood what they had to do, and promised them she'd keep the chocolate mousse intact for when they came home. Then she watched them walking dejectedly down the pathway behind her mother: Katie as if she had a hump on her back, Mark dragging his feet, and Willie aiming to kick the toes out of his best shoes.

Returning to the kitchen, she emptied the washing-machine into the dryer; then made herself a cup of coffee, sat down by the table that overlooked the back garden, and told herself she should now mow the lawn, then start on the weeding of the vegetable patch at the bottom. But she also told herself she was going to do none of these things, she was going upstairs, take a bath, give her face a do, and that definitely needed it,

9

then put on a decent dress and sit in the garden and have a read.

She looked at the clock. It was half-past ten. Take all in all, she would have at least three hours to herself, which didn't often happen on a Sunday.

The hall clock was striking twelve when she came downstairs; and going into the small room that had been her husband's study, she took a book from the shelf, then stood looking around her as she thought, Why can't I let him use this to do his paper work. I never liked the room when Ray was here, because he was always shut away in it, it was forbidden territory to both me and the children. So why . . .? Oh! She jerked her chin up, then went out, took a deck-chair from the outside store and placed it under the silver birch, the one big tree in the garden, and settled down to read.

But she hadn't read the first chapter of the book when she dropped it into her lap and, leaning back, let her thoughts wander over the happenings of the past few weeks, which weren't all unpleasant, and a restful form of sleep was about to overcome her when the voice hit her.

"So this is what you do when you're left on your own!"

She pulled herself up so quickly that she almost toppled sideways out of the chair.

"I . . . I didn't expect you back until this evening. You said. . . ."

"Yes, yes, I know what I said. But here I am. Where's everybody? Where's the kids?"

"At church."

When she made an effort to rise his hand came out, the palm vertical like that of a policeman on point duty, and he said, "Stay where you are. I'll get another chair."

She watched him stride across the lawn towards the shed. He looked smart. His clothes were always good, well-fitting. There was something different about him, though she couldn't put a finger on it at the moment.

He placed the chair at an angle to her own, and then she saw the difference: his sideburns were gone, and his hair was cut much shorter.

During the few weeks they had been together he had developed the unfortunate knack of picking up her thoughts, as he did now, saying, "Yes you see, they're gone." He rubbed his forefingers up each side of his face. "Think you'll be able to tolerate me better now? Oh, don't get on your high horse." His hand was out again, flapping towards her now. "Anyway, you didn't like them."

"What do you mean, I didn't like them? It's of no interest to me how you wear your hair: clean-shaven, or bearded, or. . . ."

"Well, why did you say you couldn't stand men with sideburns?"

"Me say that! I never. . . ."

"Well, your daughter must be tellin' lies."

Oh, Katie. Katie. She turned her head to the side.

"Anyway, I feel I look better scraped and scalped."

She was looking at him again, saying now, "You're such a modest man, aren't you, Mr Bailey?"

"Yes, Mrs N. That's one of my virtues, no vanity about me." He grinned. Then looking around the gardens, he said, "The place is dead without the kids. And this lawn wants a cut. We'll have a bite, and then I'll do it."

"There's no need; I always see to the lawn."

"Yes, you see to everything, don't you? Bloody little wonder, you are. Oh, I'm sorry." He pursed his lips. "But you know, you would make a saint swear at times. Here I've been in the same house with you for four and a half weeks, and you're still Mrs N and I'm still Mr Bailey. Look" – he leant towards her – "I'm not after anything. I've told you not once but a dozen times since I came here, I'm a middle-of-the-road man."

"Please. Please." She looked over her shoulder. "There's people in the garden next door."

"Well, it'll give them something to talk about, pass their time. And I'm not far wrong in thinkin' that they're interested already in the goings on in number sixteen; the one, two doors down" – he thumbed over his shoulder – "always manages to be at the gate when I draw up. And she seems very interested in the weather. She asked me yesterday if I thought it was going to rain."

Fiona lowered her head. There was a gurgle in her stomach; it was rising up to her breastbone. She mustn't laugh at him, because what would happen if he were given encouragement she didn't know. He was leaning towards her again, his voice low now as he went on, "'How long is the heat goin' to last?' she said. And I answered, 'Oh, as long as the weather does, ma'am.'

And then she asked if I was going away for the week-end. And I said, 'Aye, ma'am; yes, I am. I'm going to Greenham Common to keep the lasses company because they couldn't have seen a good looking fella like me for a long time, and I bet some of them need more than the weather to warm them up.' "

"You didn't!" The words came out almost on a hiss. And he hissed back at her? "I did! And then, you know what she did?"

She waited.

"She flounced. That's a Victorian word, you know; the ladies flounced about then. Well, she turned and she *flounced* up her drive. I think, in future, when she wants to know about the weather she'll turn on the television."

"You're impossible!" She was gulping in her throat now and her eyes were moist.

"I know. And now do you think I could have a bite of something, I'm starvin'?"

"Yes, of course."

He put out his hand and helped her to her feet. And they went into the kitchen together. And as she took the cold chicken from the fridge, she said, "How did you find your father?"

"I didn't find the old . . . budgerigar, he had gone off to Morecambe with his girl friend, and had never let me know. I had left him this telephone number an' all."

"Your father . . . had gone off with . . .?"

"Yes, that's what I said, his girl friend. And don't look so surprised. He's seventy-four, but he doesn't look his age; he could pass for sixty any day, and he acts fifty. And she's just on that. Look, the way you're holding that knife, you'll cut yourself."

She said now slowly, "You must take after your father."

"Aye, I do. And I couldn't have a better pattern. He's been a good father to me. And I had a good mum an' all. She was a gentle woman, in the real sense of the word, except for her hands. She had a hand like a steel brush and she laid it across me at least once a week. But mind, I deserved it. You know, it's funny, they say men usually marry women that represent their mothers, like. You know? But in my case I went and married one that was exactly the replica of meself, brash and bouncy. I never knew what it was to live with meself until I woke up one morning an' discovered that that was what I was doing. It's all right for a man to be loud-mouthed. Well, it all depends upon how he uses it. If it's with panache – that's a good word, isn't it – like I do . . . well! But with a woman it's different, gets on your nerves. I can't stand a brash woman. Of course, I had to learn that. I also had to learn that you can't change people. Rub off some edges here and there, but you don't really change them. . . . Here, give me the knife; or that poor chicken'll wish it was dead."

She handed him the knife; then dropping into a chair, she folded her arms on the table, bent her head over them, and began to laugh. Her body shook. The tears ran from her eyes; and all the while he stood at the opposite side of the table, the knife in his hand, making no attempt to carve the chicken. He just stood looking down on her, and when, gasping, she raised her head, he said quietly, "That's the best sound I've heard you make since I came into this house, and it was a belly laugh, no refined giggle. An' you know what? I'm goin' to look upon it as a start. And now the next thing you must do is get yourself out."

She was sitting back in the chair, wiping her face, and she blinked her wet eyelids as she looked up at him and said, "Out? What do you mean, out?"

"Just out. Out to enjoy yourself. Oh, I'm not askin' to be your escort, so don't let your face drop to your bust; what I'm sayin' is, I'll stay in some night and see to the kids, if you want to go to a dinner or something. I haven't seen any men around; but that's not sayin' you haven't got a boyfriend somewhere?"

"*Really!*"

"All right. All right, I won't go on. But you've surely got some woman friend you could do a show with, or something. . . . Anyway, if you are stuck for some place to spend an evenin' there's always your mother's."

She got to her feet now, saying, "You're impossible, you know that? But nevertheless, thanks for the offer. I might take you up on it some night."

"Bikini or bones?"

"What!"

He dug his finger down to the chicken. "Do you like breast or leg?"

"Anything. Oh, the top part of the leg."

"The top part of the leg it is, madam. By the way, I've

promised to take the kids in the car to the fun fair at Whitley Bay sometime, if that's all right with you."

"Oh, the fun fair? Oh ... well, I think they're much too young. ..."

"Young for a fun fair? Don't be daft, woman. Kids are never too young for fun. But if you feel worried about their safety you come along an' all."

"I've never been partial to fun fairs."

"Eeh, by! You know at times you sound just like your mother. You're not, but you sound like her." He pushed the plate towards her, saying, "Not much salad for me." Then added, "Well, if the fun fair's out, what about Whitley Bay sands?"

"Yes. Yes, I'm sure they'd like that."

"And you?"

"We'll see."

"Negotiations pending."

She bit on her lip, and again she was laughing, but silently now. And she kept her head down as she put a small cloth on one end of the table and set it for their lunch.

They were sitting opposite each other, but she hadn't swallowed her first bite and he was on the point of saying something further when there was a commotion in the hall, and the children burst into the kitchen, only to stop for a moment before exclaiming excitedly, "Oh! Mr Bailey. You're back, Mr Bailey."

He was standing up now, and they were gathered round him, all talking at once.

"Did you bring us the tin whistles?"

"You said you wouldn't be back till tonight."

"I can sing that song, Mr Bill."

"Can you, Willie? Well, I'll have to hear it."

"*Fiona!*"

Fiona looked at her mother who had appeared, standing in the doorway, every part of her bristling with indignation.

"Yes, Mother?" Fiona went towards her and actually pressed her back into the hall.

"Well! What is this? You knew he was coming back early."

"I did nothing of the sort, Mother."

"Then why are you all dolled up?"

"Dolled up? I've had a bath and put on a clean dress. If you call that dolling up. ..."

"Look at your face, all made up."

"If you recall, Mother, I used to make up every day."

"There was need of it then; you were going out to work. There's something going on here."

"*Mother!*" The word was ground out. "There is nothing going on here but what's in your mind. And I would thank you not to suggest there is. And now listen to me." She actually pushed her astonished parent in the shoulder. "I'm a married woman with three children. I'm twenty-eight years old. I've been on my own for three years, and you haven't been much help except to criticise. Now I'm going to tell you this. If you want to keep in touch with me you'll stop treating me as if I were a fifteen-year-old."

"How . . . how dare you!"

"I dare, Mother. And I should have dared a long time ago. And now I'm going to tell you something else: I'm going to give you something to talk about, you and Mrs Minnie Hatton, and the rest of your clique. I'm going to Whitley Bay with him this afternoon. It's supposed to be a treat he's giving the children, but it's really for me, because he's sorry for me and the nun's life I live in this house, dominated by you."

"*I . . . I can't believe it.*"

"No, I don't suppose you can, Mother. Now will you kindly go because I have to get ready."

For a moment Fiona thought that her mother was about to faint; but her next words proved that she was far from fainting when she said, "It's a long time since I used my hand on you, but at this moment I have the greatest desire to slap your face."

"No doubt, Mother. But you remember the last time you slapped my face and in such a way that I fell onto the stone hearth and Father told you, should you do it again, he would do the same to you? . . . You didn't know I knew that, did you? Now Mother, will you please go home!" She went to the door and pulled it open.

Mrs Vidler's plump body looked as if it was about to burst, and saying, "I'll never forgive you for this, never!" she marched out of the house.

As Fiona slowly closed the door and stood with her back to it, the kitchen door opened, and although she had her head bent she knew he was coming towards her.

He stood in front of her for some seconds before he said, "Well, that's a battle you've won. And not afore time I should say. Now go upstairs and get yourself ready. . . . Yes. Yes, I listened in; we all did. And those kids have got her measure. And they're all right. They're digging into the chocolate mousse, so come on."

He now drew her gently from the door, turned her about and pressed her towards the stairs, saying, "She beat me to it in one way: I should have told you you look different, smashing in fact. . . . Now, don't turn round; keep on going, up . . . them stairs, and tell yourself you're starting a new life."

A few seconds later she entered her bedroom, and again she stood with her back to the door and what she exclaimed to herself now was, "That man!" but she didn't explain to herself the meaning the words now conveyed.

3

He stood in the kitchen dressed in a dinner jacket; the dress shirt, no big frills just small pleats, was topped with a narrow black tie. His face, well shaved, showed no blue haze and his hair was meticulously brushed.

"I might be a bit late; you know how these things go on, once a year do's that seem to last a year. . . . What you lookin' like that for?"

"Like what? I . . . I was just thinking you look very . . . smart."

"Thank you. You're surprised, I suppose, to see me wearing a dinner jacket?"

"No, not at all."

"You should see me in grey tails an' topper. Oh aye, yes" – he nodded at her – "by courtesy of Moss Brothers. I was invited to a wedding last year, one of the County nobs. I'd just done a good job for him. It was Sir Charles Kingdom. I'd made good an old part of his house. It was more like gutting it and starting from scratch. But anyway, the old boy was pleased. And so was his daughter. And they asked me to the wedding. It was a great do. Talk about knees-up among the top people; that lot could show you a thing or two, apart from wearing kilts. But as the night wore on some of them were missing an' all. Oh! Oh, I'm sorry." He flapped a hand at her. "But these things happen."

He now stood looking at his finger nails and saying, "It's a devil of a job to get these clean for the occasions like this; I've scraped them until all the enamel's gone off the inside."

"You could put some nailwhite on."

"What's that?"

"Oh, it's for making the nails look white underneath. Hang on; I'll get some."

"No, no." He put out a hand and stopped her. "Sounds pansyish to me. I'll sit on me hands, eh?"

She smiled at him now, saying, "Nobody would notice your hands."

"Think not?" His voice was quiet; his blue gaze deep; and she said, "No; of course not, because, as you frequently point out, you're a very presentable fellow."

"Aah! You're getting your own back now, are you?" He slanted his gaze at her before saying, "Always hitting below the belt. Anyway, I must be off; and I promise you I'll come in quietly, no mattter what the hour. And I'll try not to sing."

Taking up his mood, she said, "Do that. But if you cannot overcome the urge, please make it a different tune, because I am heartily sick of 'Won't You Come Home Bill Bailey', both verbally and as demonstrated on tin whistles."

He laughed now, saying, "But they love it though, don't they? And let me tell you, they're learnin' to play those whistles properly. They could move from them to flutes, you know. That's how things start. Things have always got to have a start. Like me from tea-boy to tycoon. Well, not quite a tycoon yet, but I will be one day. I must tell you about me rise sometime. Yes, yes, I must. . . . Well, good-night Mrs N."

"Good-night, Mr Bailey. Have a good time."

She followed him into the hall, and as he lifted a black coat from off a chair and went to put it on, a chorus of voices from the stairhead called, "Good-night, Mr Bill. Good-night, Mr Bill." And a female voice piped, "You do look pretty."

He walked to the bottom of the stairs and, looking up, he said, "Thanks, Katie, my love. Good-night, Mark. Good-night, Willie."

"Will you come and sing to us when you come in, Mr Bill?"

"Yes, Katie yes; I'll come and sing to you when I come in. Go on now, off to bed. Good-night."

As he turned towards the door he muttered under his breath, "You won't blame me, will you, if I keep me promise?"

Her voice as low as his, she replied, "I would prefer that you broke it."

He paused now as he murmured, "Do you think I'm pretty?" and when for answer he got a bleak stare, he laughed, saying now, "Do as I always tell you, mind, don't answer the door to anybody. There's some nasty types about, including your mother. By the way, have you heard from her this past week?"

"No."

"Good."

Hastily she closed the door on him; then went into the sitting-room and dropped onto the couch. But she did not switch on the television, which had been her intention; instead, she sat looking at the artificial flames coming from the electric fire and she tried to recall what her life had been like before this middle-of-the-road man had come into it.

4

He had been with them for ten weeks now and it was the first time he had been so late coming in for his meal. It was half-past seven when he entered by the back way, and she was ready to say, "If you are going to be as late as this you should at least let me know," but at the sight of his face, she said, "Is anything the matter?"

"I've lost a mate."

"Oh!" was all she could find to say.

He took off his coat and sat down at the corner of the table, "He was comin' back from visiting his wife's people in Wales; a lorry ran into them. His wife and four-year-old boy went with him; there's a little girl of three in hospital. I had to see to . . . to things. God, you wouldn't believe. . . ." He dropped his head onto his hands. "Three miles outside the town it happened. Can you imagine it? Practically on the doorstep. And he wouldn't have gone if I hadn't said, 'Take your last week's holiday now; if not, you won't get it afore Christmas as we are up to the eyes.' "

She felt helpless as she watched him now join his hands and bang them hard on the table.

"Can I get you anything? A drink? Something to eat?"

He straightened up and leant back in the chair; then after a moment he said, "Nothing to eat, but a strong coffee please. I'm going to slip out again, call at the hospital to see how the child is. Then I want a drink. By God! yes, I want a drink. . . . Is there any hot water?"

"Yes, plenty."

"Then I'll have a quick sluice. Don't make the coffee yet."

When he went from the kitchen she hurried after him and up the stairs and into the attic playroom, just in time to stop her small brood from engulfing him as they usually did. Then she returned downstairs, and waited. Twenty minutes later, he was in the kitchen again, shaved and looking spruce, as he usually did, except that his face was grim. He gulped at the coffee, gave her a brief, "So long!" and went out. . . .

She busied herself for the most part of the evening; then sat in the sitting-room awaiting his return.

It was half-past eleven when she heard the key in the door. She didn't leave the room, thinking he would go straight upstairs, but within a minute or so the sitting-room door opened and he entered saying, "Saw the light."

She could see immediately that he had been drinking, and more than usual, but he was steady on his feet and his speech was only slightly slurred.

"Still up?" he said.

"Yes."

"Got any of that inferior coffee of yours waitin' to be golloped?"

"I think I might manage a cup." She passed him, but as she opened the door she turned and said, "Don't talk, please, until we get into the kitchen. Mark's been restless; he's just gone to sleep."

With exaggerated steps now, he tiptoed across the hall and followed her into the kitchen, and sitting down by the table, he said, "I like this. Best room in the house." Then added immediately, "You've got your stiff neck on again 'cos I'm tight."

She did not answer, and he said, "So would you be if you had gone through what I have the day. You know something? I looked on him almost as a son, because I started him the same way as I'd been started, tea-boy, everybody's dog's-body. I made him do all the things I'd done. My dad was a brickie, you know, and I couldn't wait to get on the buildings with him. Played the nick most of my last year at school. Well" – he tossed his head – "nearly all my time at school I played the nick. But what d'you think? He wouldn't ask for me to be taken on with his lot, putting up skyscraper flats. Muck, he called them. But he got me set on with a small man, Carter. Funny that, you know. Dad seemed a funny man to me then, but he was right. Oh yes, he was right. Mr Carter had six blokes working for him. The same six had been with him twelve years, and what those blokes didn't know about building wasn't worth knowing. And I watched them. I copied them, and each of them let me into his own private tricks. I was fifteen when I started, and I was thirty when old Carter died. And his wife said to me, 'You've been a good lad, Bill. He thought the best of you. I've had offers for the business, but you go to the bank and get a loan, and it's yours.' And that's what I did. There's none of those six alive now. But I gradually picked me own team, kicking out the scum on the way an' them that say, what's yours is mine, and what's mine's me own. There's a lot a bloody double dealin' scroungers in this business, you know, selling your stuff on the side, under your bloody nose. Anyway—" He took a sip of the coffee, and, looking across the table at her, he said, "You know, you make rotten coffee, Mrs N. Do you know that?"

She gave a tight smile as she answered, "I'm so glad you like it, Mr Bailey."

"You're all right. You know that?"

"Yes, yes, I'm very much aware that I'm all right."

"You're laughing at me behind that face of yours, aren't you?"

"Yes, Mr Bailey, I'll agree with everything you say tonight."

He bowed his head now, saying softly, "I'm in a hell of a stew. You see, he was fifteen an' all when I took him on, an' just like I'd been, full of tongue and backchat. He thought he was the bloody cat's pyjamas, good as the next an' better than most, and he was an' all. And like me, he was a worker, an' wanted to learn. I made him go to night school like I did. . . . Oh, that's stretched your face a bit, Mrs N, hasn't it? Me goin' to night school. Well you see it was all right being able to do every job on the site, but there was a business side to it; things had advanced in that way since I ran round with the tea can. And I was out to learn. Still am. But you wouldn't believe that, would you? No; no, you wouldn't. By the way, how's your mother these days? You don't mention her. She comes up, I suppose, when I'm out of the way?"

"No; I haven't seen her; but she's started to phone, in order, you understand, to tell me what a dreadful daughter I am. But. . . ."

"So, you haven't seen her? My! My!"

"No; but I understand she's not too well and I've promised to go across tomorrow afternoon." She smiled now, adding, "I'll have to put my armour on, though."

"Aye. Aye; that'll be necessary." He now looked down on his joined hands. And he remained like that for some moments; and then he said vehemently, "I'd gaol every mother's son of them that pass on a hill. There's a type of driver whose one aim in life seems to be to get in front and stick there. They don't give a damn what they pass, from a kid on a tricycle to a thirty-five articulated tonner. That type wouldn't take any notice if it was the Pope escorted by a bloody chorus of archangels."

She bit tightly on her lip, as she too now bowed her head. Even in his sorrowing he was himself.

When his hand came out and caught hers, she jerked her head up as he said, "I wasn't intending to be funny; that's just me, 'cos I'm not in a laughin' mood."

"I . . . I understand." She did not withdraw her hand; and now he said softly, "It's a long time since I felt het up like this inside. I'll never forget the sight of them lying there in the hospital. They phoned me straightaway, the police. You know why? Because he had me name in his wallet! I was the one he'd chosen to be informed if anything happened. He thought as much about me as I did of him, you know. He was almost half my age, but we were close. More than mates; like father and son."

They both turned now when a small cough came from the direction of the open door, there to see Mark standing.

"I've got a pain in my tummy, Mam."

As Mark came towards them she withdrew her hand, then rose from the table, saying, "Come along. I'll make you a hot drink."

"I'll be going up." He had risen from the table and she looked towards him now and said, "I'm sorry I can't be of any help."

"That's all right. Nobody can help much in a situation like this. Good-night. Good-night, laddie." He ruffled Mark's hair as he passed, and the boy turned round and watched him leave the room. Then sitting down on a stool by the stove, he said, "Mam."

"Yes, dear?"

"Are you going to marry Mr Bill?"

"What! Marry Mr Bill? Whatever put that into your head? No, of course not."

"Well, you were holding hands."

"Oh, that was because a friend of his has . . . is ill, and he's rather worried about him. Is that what's been worrying you, about me marrying?"

"Well, no; but I think about it."

"Well, don't think about it any more because I shall never marry Mr Bill."

"Would you be his girl friend?"

"What! No, I certainly would not; never be his girl friend. What makes you say such a thing?"

"Well, people have girl friends and boy friends."

"Well, I'll certainly never be Mr Bill's girl friend. A friend, yes, but not . . . well, his girl friend. Do you understand?"

The boy did not indicate whether he understood or not but when a few minutes later she handed him the hot drink, he said, "I like Mr Bill. It . . . it would be nice if you married him."

"Mark." She pulled a chair forward and sat down near him; and bending until her face was close to his, she said, "You're nine years old; you won't understand this, but Mr Bill is not the marrying kind, he doesn't want to marry; he is what he calls a middle-of-the-road man. You won't understand that either, as yet, but it means that he neither wants to marry, on the one hand, nor be entangled with . . . girl friends on the other. Do you understand that at all?"

He screwed up his face, then took another drink and said, "Katie says you'll marry him; she bet me ten pence; but then she's reading this story about a princess and them living happy ever after."

"Oh, my dear." She put her arm around him and pressed him to her, saying softly, "Why would I want to marry anyone when I have you and Katie and Willie. Come along now, and finish that drink, then up to bed."

A short time later, when she put out the light in her room she turned her face into the pillow, saying as she had done once before, "Oh my God!"

It was four o'clock the following afternoon when she returned home from a visit to her mother. She was feeling worn out. Her armour had been dented in several places: she had listened to a tirade against . . . that man; she had heard of all the things her mother had sacrificed on her behalf, to send her to a private school, dressing her in the best, then for her to marry a freelance writer who would have left her roofless when he died but for her insistence that he take out an insurance.

She had expected a greeting from the children en masse as she entered the house. It being half term, she had left Mark in charge, instructing them that no one must go out until she returned. But there was no sound from the sitting-room or the kitchen or the study, and the only light showing was in the hall.

She ran upstairs, calling, "Mark! Katie!"

She opened the playroom door in some anxiety, then heaved a sigh as she saw them all sitting on the old couch.

"What's this? What's the matter with you?"

It was Katie who answered, her voice breaking, saying, "He's gone. Mr Bill's gone."

"What! What are you talking about?"

Mark got up from the couch. His eyelids were blinking rapidly, and his lips trembled before he said, "He . . . he came this afternoon and took his cases . . . and his golf clubs."

She put her hand out against the stanchion of the door, and her voice croaked as she said, "Did he say anything? Leave a message?"

"No. I asked him where he was going, and he said that he might be going into an hotel for the time being, and he left you a letter. It's on the desk in the study."

She seemed to slide down the stairs; and there was the letter lying on the pad.

Tearing it open, she read:

I've had enough, Mrs N. I'm not one for suffering for suffering's sake; and yesterday was a bad enough day. And I knew that sometime, my lugs being what they are, ever at the ready, I was likely to hear something that would knock the stuffing out of me, and I did just that, for I happened to step back towards the kitchen to tell you that I'd be going out early this morning when I heard the lad's question. And if anything sounded final and underlined, your answer did.

Enclosed is a couple of months' pay in lieu of notice. And it's funny, isn't it? This is the first time I've written at this desk. Such is the irony of life. . . . Anyway, I'll get to sleep now nights instead of wanting to come along the landing and bash your door down. You can tell your mother she was right. That'll make her happy.

Bill.

She put one hand tightly over her mouth, the other hugged her waist, and like this she walked up and down the narrow room half a dozen times. Then she stopped abruptly before rushing from the room and into the hall and to the telephone table and grabbing the yellow pages directory from its drawer. There were two hotels in the centre of the town: The Grange, and The Palace. There were three others, but they'd be further from his work.

She rang The Grange.

"Can you please tell me if a Mr Bailey has booked in this afternoon?"

"I'll enquire, madam."

She kept tapping her teeth with her finger nails while staring at the mouthpiece.

"No; there is no such name on the register, madam."

"Thank you."

She rang The Palace. "Can you please tell me if a Mr Bailey has booked in this afternoon?"

"Hang on. I'll enquire." The voice sounded chummy.

"A Mr William Bailey?"

"Yes."

"Yes, he booked in just a short while ago."

"Is he still in the hotel?"

There was a pause before the voice said, "Yes; he must be; his key isn't here."

"Is there a phone in his room?"

"Yes, of course, madam."

"Would you put me through, please?"

There was another pause before the voice said, "Yes, right."

She had the feeling that everything inside her head had come loose.'

"Hello. Yes?"

"Bill."

There was a long pause.

"Oh, you've done a bit of detective work? And quick at that. It's all right; you don't need to apologise."

"*Bill.*" She had yelled his name. "Listen to me. If you had let those . . . lugs of yours remain just a little longer outside the kitchen door you would have heard why I gave my son the answer that I did, when I went on to explain to a nine-year-old in the best way I could that you are not the marrying kind of man, but a middle-of-the-road one. That's what you have impressed upon me, isn't it, since the day you came into this house? You know what you are. . . . You are a big loud-mouthed egotist. You consider no one's feelings but your own. How do you know I haven't been waiting for you coming along the landing and bashing my door in? But I had to tell myself it was something that a middle-of-the-road man wouldn't do. Now you've booked in, haven't you? Well, you can book out just as quick again and get yourself home. Do your hear me?. . . . Are you there?"

"Aye. . . . Aye, I'm here."

"Well then what do you want me to do? Sing, 'Won't You Come Home, Bill Bailey?'"

There came a rumbling chuckle from the earpiece; then his voice quiet, he said, "I'll be back there, lass, in quicker time than it took me to come. But that's if I can get past the receptionist; she's had her eye on me from I came in. She doesn't know I'm a middle-of-the-road man."

When she heard the click of the phone, she thrust the receiver back on the stand; and once more she was holding her mouth tightly with her hand; then again she was running up the stairs.

They were waiting for her, all standing facing the door. And going to them she gathered them into her arms and almost spluttered, "He's coming back."

"Oh, Mam! Mam!"

"Now listen." She pushed them away from her. "I want you to stay up here and be quiet for a time. Now you will, won't you? You may have a picnic. I'll . . . I'll bring your tea up. And there's jelly and blancmange."

"Oh, goodie!" Katie was now dancing from one foot to the other. . . .

Ten minutes later they were settled: and now she dashed into her room, dabbed at her face in the mirror, combed her hair, took in several deep breaths in an effort to compose herself; then went downstairs.

When she reached the foot of the stairs, the phone rang. She ran to it.

"Fiona?"

"Yes, Mother."

"He's gone then?"

"Who's gone?"

"Don't be obtuse, girl. Mrs Quinn phoned me from two doors down. She knew I'd be pleased to hear that he had gone, bags and baggage this afternoon."

Fiona gritted her teeth before she said in the softest tone she could muster at the moment, "Mother, she must have made a mistake; Bill and I are going to be married . . . or live together. We haven't decided yet."

"What!"

"I think you heard; marriage or sin. Whatever suits us both."

"You wouldn't! Not with that man."

"I would, Mother; and am. And I'm only too pleased to be doing so. Now phone Mrs Quinn and tell her to keep you informed of the proceedings." She forced herself to put the phone gently down. Then she went into the kitchen.

The daylight had gone. She drew the curtains; then looked at the clock. It was twenty minutes since she had phoned. It shouldn't take him five minutes by car from the town centre, but he would have had to do some repacking.

Her heart hit her ribs as she heard the sound of the car drawing up at the gate.

She made herself go to the sink and turn on the taps ready for washing up dishes that weren't there.

When the back door opened she had to force herself to turn round. She picked up the tea towel and dried her hands; then looked at him standing within the doorway.

He came slowly towards her; took the tea towel from her hand; then holding her gaze, he put his arms about her and, his voice husky, he said, "You mean all that you said on the phone?"

She had to swallow deeply before she could answer: "Every word."

She was being kissed as she couldn't remember ever being kissed, and it seemed never ending. When eventually he released her, he said, "I've got a lot of time to make up, because I've wanted to do that since the minute I stepped into this house. You know that?"

"No: I don't know that, Bill Bailey. I only know that you're an idiot to have played the game you have."

"What . . . well, what else could I do? What would have been your answer if, within the first week or two, I, in my polite refined way, had said, 'What about it, Mrs N? What about us two gettin' hitched?' You were as prickly as Margaret would be at the Labour Conference. And of course, don't forget, there was your mother. . . . Anyway, my question to you is" – he paused – "Do you think you could ever *really* love me, not just take me on?"

She pursed her lips and wagged her head as she said, "I could try."

"Enough to marry me?"

"Oh Bill." Her voice was soft, her whole expression was soft. "I love you enough to do whatever you want."

"No, no!" He made pretence of pushing her away. "'Cos that's temptin'. You know what you said last night? . . . Not his girl friend." Then his tone becoming serious, he said, "I don't want you for a girl friend, Fiona; I want you for a wife."

Slowly she put her arms around his neck and laid her lips gently on his; then, her voice a whisper, she said, "You're the best thing that's ever happened to me, Bill Bailey."

His throat swelled, his eyelids blinked, and he turned his head to the side for a moment, and no words came. But when they did, they were in the form of his usual cover-up: "But mind," he said, "I'm not taking you on simply because of yourself, it's because I want charge of those three kids in order to further their education and grammar like, and their usual musical instruction."

They were clinging together now, and almost between laughter and tears she said, "Never change, Bill Bailey. Promise me you'll never change."

5

"Get on with your tea. I've told you, it's no use lingering; he won't be back for a long time yet."

Fiona looked impatiently down on the three of them sitting round the kitchen table: Mark was slowly munching his last piece of cake, Katie was doing a tattoo with a spoon on an empty jelly dish, while Willie was picking at a spot on the back of his hand.

Fiona now gently smacked at Willie's hand, saying, "You'll make it bleed again. Leave it alone."

"Mam."

"Yes, Katie?"

"After the funeral will Mr Bill's friends go straight to a house in Heaven?"

Fiona turned helplessly towards the stove, as if to find an answer there. But she was saved by Mark saying scornfully, "There are no houses in Heaven; people just float about."

"They don't! There are houses, big houses, mansions. 'Twas in the hymn."

"Don't be silly."

"I'm not being silly, our Mark. They've got to have a house; they can't fly about all the time. Anyway, I'm going to have a bungalow when I die, a nice little one, all to myself. And. . . ."

"When I go to Heaven, I'm going to play marbles all the time."

Fiona, Mark and Katie now turned their full attention on Willie; and he stared back at them and emphasised, "I am."

Katie sniffed, then said disdainfully, "That's daft; there'll be no marbles in Heaven."

"There will! There are!" The statement was firm and defiant. 'The minister said so, the black one."

When Fiona said, "Who?" Mark explained, "He was from the

monastery, Mam. He comes some Sundays for the children's service."

"Oh. Oh." She nodded her head. And now her young son, looking up at her, said, "And Danger House . . . and com . . . muter games."

"You mean computer games." Mark was quick to contradict him; and Willie was about to retort when Fiona picked him up from his seat and hugged him for a moment before putting him on the floor again, saying now, "Upstairs with you all!"

Katie, however, was slow to rise from her seat, and she looked up at her mother and, her face heavy-laden with the importance of her question, said, "When is Mr Bill going to be our father?"

Fiona's answer was interrupted this time by her son's saying, "Who art in sixteen Woodland Avenue."

Fiona brought her lips tightly together in an effort to prevent herself from laughing outright. Mark was clever at catching and turning a phrase, but she pretended to ignore him. And so, looking down at Katie, she answered her, "I'm not sure yet; but sometime soon."

"Then he won't be a lodger any more, will he?"

That thin resemblance to her mother was about to retort, "He is not a lodger, he is a paying guest," but she thrust it aside, saying, "No; you're right, he won't be a lodger any more."

"What'll we call him?"

"Father Bill . . . Poppa Bill . . . Daddy Bill," sang Mark now, as he marched towards the door; and his sister, taking up his mood, followed after him, chanting, "Mr Bill went up the hill to get a pail of water," and Willie, as usual coming up in their train, took up the marching routine, and Fiona's voice followed them as she cried, "Get on with your homework, Mark. And you, Kate and Willie, you have an hour in the playroom before bed. And don't dare come downstairs any of you." And she was about to turn and clear the dirty dishes from the table when their concerted voices hit her, "Well, tell Mr Bill to come up and see us, else we will."

"*Get!*"

As she heard their footsteps scrambling up the stairs and the thumping of their running feet across the landing, she looked up towards the ceiling and sighed.

She couldn't remember feeling so happy ever before; the only thing that was marring her present state was the fact that Bill was very cut up about the young fellow and his family dying like that, and the little girl in hospital.

She stopped in her clearing and now asked herself if she had said there was only one thing that was marring her happiness; she was forgetting her mother. . . . Oh! her mother . . .

It was almost four hours later when she heard the car draw up at the gate, and she hurried from the sitting-room to open the door.

A few minutes later he was in the hall, and she was in his arms, her slim body seeming to be lost in the bulk of him.

As he took off his overcoat and dropped in onto a chair, she said, "You hungry?"

"No. No. I'll have a cup of tea; but not yet awhile. Come in here." He put his arm about her and led her into the sitting-room, and when they were seated on the couch before the electric fire, he pointed to the artificial logs, saying characteristically, "We'll have that out of that; I can't stand make-believe things. We'll have an open fire put in there, eh?"

"I like my artificial logs."

He pulled her tightly to him, saying, "You'll like what I like or else." Then his mood changing suddenly, he lay back against the couch and became silent; and after a while she said, "Been a bad day?"

"Horrible. I knew I'd miss him, but God! when it came to the final act I nearly howled aloud. As I said, lass, he was like a son, the one I always wanted and never had. I love kids. Well, you know that. By the way, they're quiet." He looked upwards.

"They've been in bed for some time now, and don't you go in to them tonight."

"Oh no. You needn't stress the point, I haven't a joke in me tonight. You know something, lass?"

"No; what?"

"They say blood is thicker than water . . . that's all in me eye and Betty Martin. Those two, Dan's parents and the pair they had with them . . . I can't get over it. All right; his mother's crippled with arthritis, but she's not yet sixty. And his dad's had two slight heart turns. But nevertheless, that little lass in hospital is their grandchild. But they were adamant they couldn't take her on. Get a kind of housekeeper in, I said, and I'll stand half the racket; 'cos they're not without money. I know that. But no, no. And then there was his cousin and his piece, both in their thirities. But no, no; again no; they couldn't have the child. They were both in business, you see. And what was more, they had made up their minds when they married they didn't want children. What they should have said was that they are a couple of upstarts, too big for their bloody boots, moving into a bigger house in the Welsh upper belt. . . . And talking about houses. The old man might have a dicky heart, but he hasn't got a dicky head. You know what he's been up to over the last three or four days? He's made arrangements for all the furniture to go to the sale, and he's put the house in the hands of an estate agent. You know, Fiona' – his voice was grim now – 'if it hadn't been I'd just come back from the funeral, I would have shot me mouth off, because they didn't give a damn about that child lying there. The only thing I got out of him was that he'd come back within a week or two when her arm was properly fixed and she was fit to leave hospital and decide then what was to be done with her. And I'll tell you what they'll do, I know it, they'll have her adopted. You'll see, they'll have her adopted. But whatever happens to her, I'll damn well see that what is made out of the house and furniture and insurance goes into trust for her."

She held his hand tightly, but could find nothing to say, and after a moment, he went on, "It came to me today why Dan and Susie only went up once a year to see them. Sometimes, they'd stay a week, but more often only two or three days; and before he got married he made just flying visits. Somehow he didn't seem to belong to them. I could recognise nothing in either of them that was in him. I suppose he missed something right from the start and that's why he cottoned on to me. And I was ready for a son." He now turned his face fully towards her and, lowering his voice, he said, "And I'm ready for a wife, lass. I asked meself the day, if I hadn't you to come back to what would I have done? Oh, I know" – he tossed his head – "got blued, really stinkingly blued. And now we're on the subject of you and me, it's gettin' harder each night not to come along that landing and bash your door down, as I've said afore; and I nearly did last night; you know that?"

She made a small motion with her head.

"Well, you were lucky you have three kids; I somehow couldn't do it with them scattered about. I imagined just as we'd be gettin' down to it Katie would put her head round the door and say, 'What you doin', Mr Bill?' "

She choked and gulped; then dropped her head onto his shoulder, saying, "Oh, Bill." And he, his voice now almost a broken whisper, said, "But there's no fear of that happening the night, lass. Put your arms around me and hold me tight because all I want at the moment is a mother."

They got out of the car in the hospital car park, and once again Fiona asked in an undertone, "Are you sure it's all right to take the three of them in there?"

"Woman, I've told you, there were squads in there yesterday."

She now looked down at the three pairs of eyes staring up at her, and after drawing in a sharp breath she muttered, "I've told you now, behave yourselves."

"They always behave themselves. Come on." He held out his hand to Katie, adding, "What does she think you're going to get up to in there, coup your creels? That's what the Geordies say, don't they?"

Katie, glancing mischeviously over her shoulder at her mother, said, "She thinks we might all sing, 'Won't You Come Home, Bill Bailey?'"

He, too, now glanced at Fiona; then looking from Willie to Mark, he said, "That's a good idea, isn't it?" and they both laughed, while Willie piped up, "We didn't bring our tin whistles."

"Oh, what a pity! Why didn't you think of it beforehand?" And at this Willie, now hanging on to his other hand, grinned up at him knowingly.

A few minutes later, after walking along two corridors, they entered a wide room with beds and cots along both side walls. Every cot had a child in it and with the exception of one all were surrounded by people and toys, some of the latter almost as big as the children.

Bill led the way to the cot where the child was sitting with her head lowered as if looking at the plastered arm lying on the coverlet.

"Hello, there, Mamie. Look who I've brought to see you."

The child raised her head and there was a dazed look in her eyes for a second; then her face brightened and she said, "Oh! Uncle Bill."

"Look who's here!"

Katie was now standing wide-eyed and wide-mouthed and hugging a small box of sweets to her breast, and Bill had to tug her towards him by the arm while saying to the child in the bed, "Look! this is Katie. And you're nearly as big as her and you just turned three and she all of seven. My! My!"

There was no response from either child, and now Bill, turning his head to the side and speaking into the back of Katie's neck, said, "Say hello to her."

Katie made an effort: she closed her mouth, then opened it, then shut it again while she stared at the bandaged head and discoloured chin; then she acted uncharacteristically, she burst into tears.

Taking the box from her, Fiona lifted her into her arms and, smothering her head against her shoulder, whispered, "There now. There now. She's all right, she's all right. Now look! if you don't stop you'll have to go outside."

Bill now took the box from Fiona's hand and gave it to Willie, saying, "You give it to her." And on this Willie, utterly composed, moved up by the bedside, grinned at the small occupant and, handing her the box, said, "They're mixed, some's got chocolate on, t'others just toffee. There's half a pound."

It was some seconds before the small hand came out and took the box from Willie. But when she made no verbal response Bill leant over her, saying gently, "What did you say to Willie for those nice sweets?"

The child looked up into Bill's face and her lips trembled, and her eyelids blinked, and she said, "Uncle Bill, I want my mammy."

Bill now turned quickly from the bed, muttering softly, "Oh God!"

Fiona had put Katie down on the floor again and she now stared at this man who, she imagined, could never be lost for words on any occasion: he was the quick thinker with a ready rejoinder, the man who could take the words out of your mouth and make them funny. She looked from him to the pathetic figure of the child in the bed, and now pushing him to one side, together with Willie and Katie, she drew a chair towards the head of the bed and, sitting down, she took the hand from the box and stroked it gently whilst saying, "It's all right, my dear, your mammy has . . . has gone on a little holiday."

The round red-rimmed eyes looked into hers and the quivering mouth said one word now, "Daddy."

"Well" – Fiona swallowed deeply – "he's with your mammy. She's . . . she's not very well." There was a break in her own voice now and she turned a desperate glance onto Bill. But she got no help from him for he was still standing with his back to the bed and stroking Katie's hair with quick movements of his fingers as if endeavouring to brush something from it.

"When you are better you can come to our house."

They all looked at Mark now who was standing at the other side of the bed.

He had caught the child's attention. Her face seemed to brighten for a moment, and when she said, "And Johnny?" Mark said quietly, "Yes, and Johnny. And Katie's got a doll's house and it's got six rooms, and I've got a rocking-horse, it's called Horace."

Fiona stared at her son. There had always been something different about Mark since he was quite young. She recalled the times when his father and she would be arguing, especially if the children had been making a noise and he couldn't get on with his writing which, as he would inform her loudly, was their livelihood. At these times Mark was apt to come between them and ask some irrelevant question but one that needed an answer. She recognised, as time went on, that he was trying to divert their attention from each other and onto himself.

She was smiling her approval across the bed at him when Willie burst in with, " 'Orace's not yours now, he's mine. I scratched my name on his belly."

"Willie!"

"Well I did, Mam." He looked up at Fiona.

"She means you should say, stomach." It was Katie now, tears forgotten, and at this Willie grinned.

Then all their attention again was drawn to the child in the bed for she had put her hand to her head and, her small face screwing up, she began to cry.

Bill immediately drew the attention of a nurse, and when she came to the bed she said quietly, "Head aching, dear? Oh, we'll soon give you something to ease that." Then turning to Fiona she made a gesture that they should all move away and when they were in the aisle she said, "She'll have a drink then she'll go to sleep. She sleeps a lot; her head was badly bruised."

"Seriously?" Fiona spoke the word gently, and the nurse said, "No, not as far as we know. There was no visible damage, only grazing and cuts, but mainly on the scalp. She'll be all right." She nodded reassuringly.

Fiona moved towards the door, but Bill did not immediately follow; he stood at the foot of the bed gazing at the child whose face was now awash with tears. Then he turned abruptly and joined the others; but he didn't speak.

Not until he was seated in the car and with his hands on the wheel and his head bent over it were his feelings expressed in the word, *"Hell!"*

"Eeh! Mr Bill. He swored."

"Be quiet! Willie."

"Well he did, he said. . . ."

"Willie!"

Fiona was looking straight ahead through the windscreen as she said now, "I feel like an afternoon out. Would you like to take us all to tea somewhere?"

Bill slowly straightened himself, turned his gaze on her; then slowly he said, "Yes, woman. Yes, that's what we'll do." And leaning his head back, he said, "Right kids?" And after a small pause they all answered as in one voice, "Right, Mr Bill."

They had driven to the coast; they had walked along a cold and windy beach and for a time the children had joined in a game with others and a dog and a ball; then they'd had tea in an hotel where Katie had caused a stir among the occupants of the room by remarking, and none too quietly, "They've got real table-cloths on here."

At home they'd had another tea, followed by the usual routine that led to the children's going to bed. And so it was some time before Fiona and Bill went into the sitting-room, where Bill, dropping onto the couch, said, "You know what I'd like to do?"

"Yes."

"You don't, 'cos I'd like to get really bottled up."

"I know that."

"You do?"

"Yes, because every time there's a crisis your reaction is to go and get bottled up."

"But I've only been bottled up once since I came here, the night of the accident."

"Yes, that's right, but the urge has been on you at other times too."

"You see too bloomin' much, woman."

"I don't mind if you go and get bottled up" – she sat down close to him – "the only thing I would object to, even if I hadn't to stay back and see to the children, would be if you expected me to accompany you."

He gave a short laugh, saying, "That'll be the day when I see you bottled up. I'll know then that the last vestige of your mother has been wiped out. . . . By the way, did you see your mother's stooge from two doors down" – he thumbed towards the street – "in the ward when we were there?"

"You mean Mrs Quinn? No, I didn't notice her."

"Well, she noticed you, she noticed us. And she was there when we came out an' all. I bet by now the jungle wires have been singing."

"Well, she couldn't make much out of that, could she, visiting a childrens' ward?"

"Well, we were together, and if we're together so much in the day, we will definitely be together much more in the night, will be the general opinion if I know anything. Anyway I want to talk to you about that. When are we going to make our wicked thoughts respectable? Do you want it done in church or . . .?"

"Oh, no!" She held up her hand. "Not in church, not in our church anyway. Mother would have a protest meeting outside. No, I wouldn't do that. And you being a divorced man, and an agnostic into the bargain. . . ."

"I'm a what!"

"You know what I mean, neither one thing nor the other."

"That's wrong. I have me own ideas of why, seeing that He's built us as we are, we've got to do nothing about it, until we sign our names."

She laughed gently as she pushed him away from her saying,

"That's like a current; it's running through your mind all the time."

"Aye, you're right, and it's a wonder it hasn't given you an electric shock before now." And in his turn he pushed her, and they both leant against each other laughing gently.

Releasing herself from his embrace, she said, "All this is sidetracking the main issue, isn't it?"

He thrust out his lower lip, then ran his hand through his hair before he said, "The bairn, aye, I can't get her out of me mind. You see, I saw her soon after she was born, before Dan even. And later when he saw her the tears ran down his face: he loved his boy but he always wanted a girl. I've watched her grow. She was chatting before she could walk. She took after her mother in that way, 'cos Susan was a chatterer." And his voice now rising almost to a shout he demanded of her, "Can you understand those grandparents? Can you?"

"Shh! You'll have the lot of them downstairs in a minute."

"I'm sorry. But can you?" His voice had dropped to a mere whisper, and she said, "Yes, in a way; they are ill and they're old. But not the cousin and his wife. Tell me" – she took his hand now – "if you hadn't come here and things hadn't turned out as they have done, what would you have done about her? The truth now."

He turned his head away, saying, "Well, the truth is, I would have tried to adopt her in some way."

"And that's what you would like to do now?"

He looked at her, and after a pause he said, "I wouldn't ask it of you; you've got enough on your plate in bringing up those." He raised his eyes to the ceiling.

"What if I want to do it?"

"It would just be to please me and that would make me feel under a sort of . . . oh, I don't know, taking advantage. No. It's no go."

"Would you allow me to have some thoughts on the matter and to tell you that my mind was already made up when I saw that child in that bed today? Of course, too, it was how you felt about her, but I knew as soon as I saw her. And then when she asked about her mother, that settled it completely. Now what's the alternative? If we don't take her, she will be put into care somewhere. And" – she raised her eyebrows now and poked her head towards him – "what kind of a life would I have with you

39

after that? You would become unbearable; you'd go on the razzle, and I would then have to admit my mother was right, I must have been blind. She took your measure, you know, the minute you stepped in the door, the middle-of-the-road man. . . ."

His arms were tight about her, his mouth was equally tight on hers; then when at last they drew apart he said, "Polony! She thought I was right for her, the old bag. But lass" – his voice dropped to a tender note – "I've got no words to tell you what I'm feeling at this minute: I'd only make a hash of it and come out with something brash, in tune with my character. Yet I'll manage this, but don't expect me to repeat it." He tweaked her nose gently with his finger. "I've thought about you as a lady from the first minute I set eyes on you, a real lady every inch of you, inside an' all. I pass women in the street every day and I'm comparing them with you, and if we never married, if nothing ever happened after this moment, I'd know that me life had been worthwhile in just meeting you."

"Oh, Bill. Bill."

When she laid her head gently on his shoulder he held her for a moment; then reverting to his usual self, he said, "Oh, for God's sake! woman, don't start bubbling. I've had enough of it today. Come on; let's have some of your horrible coffee . . . or tea." And lifting her head up, he held her face between his hands, ending with, "And let's discuss the day I can make an honest woman out of you. And it's got to be soon, or else this town'll experience something that'll put the rape of the Sabine women into the shade."

6

❧❧

She was singing, her voice rising above the sound of the hoover, when the phone rang. She was still smiling when she picked it up; then the smile slid from her face as the voice came over the wire saying, *"Fiona."*

"Yes, Mother."

"I suppose you're going to tell me you've been too busy, that's why you couldn't come round to see me."

"Yes, Mother, I have been busy. But even so, I can see no point in coming to see you when we do nothing but fight."

"I do not fight, girl: I have never fought; I merely state facts and point out things that you should see yourself if you weren't at the moment hypnotized by that awful man."

"Well, Mother, your facts are wasted. And let me tell you I'm very happy to be hypnotized by that awful man whom I intend to marry."

There was a long pause, and she was about to put the phone down when the voice came again, saying, "The minister won't allow it, he's divorced."

Smirking now, she gave the reply that Bill himself would assuredly have given: "Oh, we don't mind the minister's being divorced."

"Fiona." The word seemed to make the wires ring in her ears.

"All right, Mother. But we are not going to trouble the minister."

"Girl, you wouldn't go to a registry office?"

"We'll go to a voodoo man, Mother, if we want to."

"Really! I don't know what to make of you, Fiona. You never came out with things like that before. Voodoo man indeed! You're getting almost as common as him, if that's possible."

"It's a nice feeling. And I'm busy, Mother; have you finished?"

"No, I haven't, and I can tell you this: you're getting your name up in another quarter."

"Really? That sounds interesting."

"You may take it lightly but imagine how I feel when I'm told that men, workmen, are coming to your house at all hours and staying all hours. Talk about having an affair with the milkman. I'm telling you, girl, you're the talk of the street. And what's more. . . ."

Fiona banged down the phone and stepped back from the hall table and stared at it. That woman! What was she to do with her? And that Mrs Quinn. She must be ever on the watch. Of course she had nothing else to do: she didn't go out to work and her husband was abroad most of the time. But what would the new people next door think if they listened to her? She had always considered herself fortunate that this house was the end of the avenue and there wasn't another Mrs Quinn to the right of her.

She went into the kitchen and stood leaning with her hands on the sink looking through the window down the garden. Her teeth were tight together. Women like her mother and Mrs Quinn were the very devil.

She recalled the incident that her mother was referring to. It happened only two days ago when Mr Ormesby, one of Bill's men, called with a message from him to say that he had been trying to get through to her all afternoon from Newcastle but the line seemed dead; and so he had phoned the works and asked Bert Ormesby to call in and tell her he was being held up and to test the telephone to see if it was all right.

It had been pouring with rain and she had invited Mr Ormesby in; and she had made him a cup of tea and they had sat at the table talking, mostly about Bill and how, if he brought off this deal he was after, which was the building of a small estate at the top of Brampton Hill in the best part of town, it would be a good thing for them all for the next year or two.

She knew quite a bit about Mr Bert Ormesby; in fact she knew quite a bit about his eleven men, the permanent ones, because, in a way, he considered them his family. Bert, she knew, was the only bachelor among them and he was the butt of the gang because, not only was he teetotal, but also he didn't smoke and he attended church. Result of his father running a pub and his mother being a Presbyterian Bill said; and guess who won.

The children had come into the kitchen and he had talked and laughed with them. He had surprised her further by telling her he was also a Sunday School teacher. His visit had lasted over an hour, during which time he had gone through three cups of tea and two teacakes.

She wanted to cry but she wasn't going to. She wouldn't allow her mother to mar her happiness. Nevertheless, the brightness had gone out of the day. . . .

At half-past three she picked up Willie from nursery school and was thankful that his stay there was drawing to a close and that his next school would be nearer to Katie's and Mark's. Then she drove half-way across the town to collect them, and as usual, having tumbled into the back of the car, they all talked at once, telling her the happenings of the day; and to each she made the appropriate sounds, until Katie remarked, "I smacked Josie Morgan's face."

"You what! Why did you do that?"

"'Cos she said I couldn't be a bridesmaid at a Registry Office; they didn't have bridesmaids at Registry Offices."

The car wobbled just the slightest, and Fiona's hands on the wheel tightened before she said, "Katie. Haven't I told you not to talk in school about anything that happens at home?"

"I didn't, Mam."

"You must have."

"Well, I only told her last week that when you got married to Mr Bill I'd be a bridesmaid, and she said her mother said you couldn't be bridesmaids at Registry Offices. But Anna said you could."

"Anna?"

"Yes, Anna Steele, she's my new friend. I've picked her instead of Josie because Josie swanks about their car and says it's a better one than Mr Bill's Volvo."

Mark now said, "Your big mouth'll open so far it'll swallow you one of these days." And for answer, he was told vehemently, "Well, far better have a big mouth than a big nose that could poke a drain."

"Stop it! both of you."

Except for the hum of the car there was silence for some minutes; and then it was broken by Willie saying, "I wish I was old and six."

Her eyelids blinked. She pressed her lips tightly together. She wanted to laugh and at the same time she wanted to cry. It was one of those days. . . .

Bill came in at his usual time; he took her in his arms, kissed her hand, then said, "Hello, Mrs N."

"Hello, Mr Bailey," she said.

Holding her away from him, he said, "What's the matter with your face, Mrs N? Something happened?"

"Only Mother . . . and Katie, and oh" – she shrugged her shoulders – "one of those days."

"Oh God. Not your mother again. What is it now?"

"I'm having it off with one of your men."

"No! Where is the . . . bugger? I'll break his bloody neck. How long has this been goin' on? I knew I should never have come to this house. I knew you would let me down."

"Shut up! And that language; they'll hear you upstairs." She was smiling now.

"What happened? What vitriol has she been pouring over the wires now?"

"Get your wash and have your meal and then I'll tell you."

He had his wash; he had his meal; he had romped with the children upstairs for half an hour; then got changed; and now they were in the kitchen. And when she told him, he didn't laugh or joke, as she might have expected; what he said was, "I'm sorry to say this, Fiona, but your mother is dangerous."

"I know that, Bill. I've known it for a long time. And, lately, things that my father said to me that I didn't really comprehend years ago have a real meaning now. Once, I recall, she had been to his office and when he came in there were words; and later he said to me apropos of nothing that had gone before, 'Men can be vile and cruel but they don't create as much harm as women who are sweet and poisonous.' I know now he had his reasons because there are people who still think she is sweet, such a nice lady, so refined."

"Yes, so refined. That's the worst sort; you know where you are with slack gobs. . . . Well, Mrs N, I can tell you, it's been one of those days for me an' all. I had a phone call from the old man about the child. Oh, of course, he said, they agreed that we should adopt her. Oh yes. But there was the question of the money. What money? I said. Well, the company that was liable for the accident would have to provide for her until she came of age. Hadn't she lost all her family at

44

one go? She had to be compensated. What were my thoughts on the subject? he said.

"Well, right away I told him what my thoughts were on the subject; I didn't want any of the money; if I was going to adopt her I would work for her and whatever money there was should be banked, together with the money from the house and furniture – I got that in – in a kind of trust in her name for whatever she needed later on.

"Yes, yes; he said he agreed with that wholeheartedly, but there should be a proviso, he thought, that if she went away on a holiday or to a private school she should be allowed to draw on it to meet expenses.

"You know, Fiona" – he wagged his finger at her – "I may be wrong, but I think I'm right when I tell you what was in the old boy's mind: they'd be willing to have her for her holidays and things as long as she was provided for. You see, they wouldn't expect, they wouldn't have the bare face to ask, me to pay for her when she went to stay with them, but a trust is a kind of an inanimate thing, it doesn't argue or feel, it just pays out."

"Oh no, Bill."

"But oh yes, Mrs N. You don't know that old boy like I've come to know him. He's been on the phone nearly every day. He would have signed her away to a workhouse in the old days rather than have the responsibility of her, he's that kind. And his wife an' all must be of the same calibre. Oh aye, there'a a lot of odd bods in the world, Mrs N, and it's been my misfortune to meet a number of them, all types and from all classes, you wouldn't believe." He now shook his head as if in perplexity, saying, "Can you understand anybody not wanting a lovable bairn like that? And . . . and isn't it wonderful that she's taken to us. Which reminds me, if I want to slip along there I'd better go and get changed." He pulled her to him. "I hate this business of going out on my own at night now. Once we're made respectable we're going to have a baby-sitter and a full-time daily help for you."

"No, thank you. I don't want full-time daily help. Baby-sitter, yes, and someone for a few hours in the morning. . . ."

"When you become Mrs Bailey, Mrs N, you're going to have someone to do the chores. I'm not going to have my wife taking in washing."

45

"Go on, get yourself away." She went to push him, but then said, "About the estate deal, has it come off?"

"No, not yet. I'll know tomorrow, but I think it's nearly sure, and if it is, I've got ideas for the chaps. It'll be a big thing and they've got to be in on it. They're all good lads, and they work like hell – an' – be merry for me. I know they lose nothing by it, but if this estate business comes my way, I'm going to form a kind of . . . well board, something like that, and they'll have a percentage of the profits at the end of the year. That's for the eleven permanent ones. Of course I'll have to take on a good few besides and you never know what you're gettin' these days: joiners who think a dovetail is something that comes out of a pigeon-loft; and painters who've never used a brush, just one of those rollers. Boy, I've had 'em all. Well, here I go, off to see . . . our younger daughter." He gripped her chin between his large hard hands now and, shaking it, he said, "What with the six I'm going to give you you'll be the finest mother of the ten best bairns in the world."

The thrust she gave him sent him out laughing, and she stood looking towards the door through which he had passed. What on earth had she done before he came into her life? What? She couldn't recall; she only knew that from the first sight of him her world had changed.

7

It was two days later when, at four o'clock in the afternoon he literally bounced into the kitchen, pulled her floured hands from a bowl and waltzed her round the room, singing, "There is a happy land far, far away." And then he cried, "And it's not so far away the day, Mrs N," and he gave her a smacking kiss before drawing in a long breath and adding, "I've got it! And not only the estate but two superior dwellings for the gentlemen on the finance board." His voice had assumed a high and mighty air. "'We are very impressed with your work, Bailey.' But Sir Kingdom Come, as I call him, you know from Brookley Manor, you know what he said?"

"No. What did he say, Sir Kingdom Come from Brookley Manor?" She was smiling widely at him.

"Well, he said, and in a very ordinary voice, 'I'm glad you've got it, Mr Bailey. I've seen your work and I would have been surprised if they had given it to anyone else.' And he held out his hand to me and shook it hard. . . . You know, there's nowt as funny as folk, is there, dear? The old boy can trace his line back to when one of his ancestors put a chastity belt on his wife and went off to the Crusades. By, I've often thought those lasses must have had an awful time of it. . . . Don't choke." He thumped her on the back. "And Mr Ramshaw and Angus Riddle and Arthur Pilby, well, they all spoke highly too. But there was one exception, Brown. To my mind he's the only fly in that financial company, a tsetse fly at that, poisonous individual, and compared to any of the others he's got as much breeding as a runt sow in a pigsty."

"Oh! Bill . . . You are the crudest, rawest individual."

"Aye, yes, I know what I am, but you love me, don't you?" He was kissing her again. "And look at me! I'm all flour."

"Serve you right. Are you home for good?"

"No, I just dropped in to tell you . . . no to see, ma'am" – he pulled at his forelock – "if it would be all right to bring half a dozen or so workmen around the night, the ones that have hankies and don't spit."

"Bill!" she protested, slapping him, the while still laughing, "don't be vulgar."

"Well, it's those that have been with me longest," he said. "I want to talk this thing out, tell them where they stand. Anyway, as I said, ma'am, with your leave." He again touched his forelock, and she said, "What for, tea, a meal or what?"

"No, nothing like that, they'll want to have a wash and brush up first. They'll come about half-past seven or eight, and you, Mrs N, can put on your best bib and tucker; I don't want to let them think I've been shootin' me mouth off for nothing."

He kissed her yet again, and was making for the door, humming, "There is a happy land," when she stoppped him by hissing, "About this happy land, when I can get a word in, you've got to be more careful with your translations. They did their marching bit down the path this morning to the car, singing it and in no small voice."

"They didn't!" There was a large grin on his face. "The lot?"

"Yes, the lot."

"Well, if they say nothing worse than bum you won't have any need to worry."

"You've forgotten about our neighbour but one."

"Oh, I hope she heard them." Then poking his head towards her, he said, "She saw me coming in, Lady Quinn, and if she's still at the gate I'll sing it to her."

"Don't you dare."

"I dare, Mrs N," and on this he banged the door.

Quickly, she opened it again, and watched him walk down the path; then she drew in a breath of relief when she saw him getting straight into the car.

They came in a bunch at a quarter to eight. Bill introduced them, seemingly in seniority of age: Barney McGuire, a sort of foreman, Harry Newton, Tommy Turnbull, Bert Tinsley, Bert

Ormesby, Dave McRae, Jack Mowbray, Alec Finlay, Morris Fenwick, and Jos Wright. They all said either, "How d'you do, ma'am?" or, "Pleased to meet you."

She had placed extra chairs around the dining-room table, and it looked like a board room. They filed in; an hour and ten minutes later they filed out again and into the sitting-room where she had sandwiches and coffee and tea ready. She had, in a way, expected some quip from Bill about her not supplying any beer or hard stuff, but no, he did not make one joke about her but treated her with a dignity she found quite new to his character. He joked with the men, and they gave him as much as he sent. The chipping was mostly about the work, what he expected them to do and what they had decided not to do; but not once did he allude to her in any jocular way.

She was pleased by his attitude, yet at the same time it constricted her conversation with his men.

Five of them had come in their cars and had given the others a lift and, as it was a fine windless night, she walked with Bill down the pathway and onto the pavement, and there, they once again shook hands with her and thanked her for her hospitality. And as they got into their cars Bill chipped them about what would happen if they were late for work in the morning. This he emphasized loudly to three of them who had openly arranged to go to a certain pub and have a drink before it closed.

She and Bill stood close together on the pavement and waited until the last car moved away; then arm in arm they went up the pathway and into the house. And in the sitting-room once more he looked at her and said, "What d'you think about them as a bunch?"

"They're very nice fellows, and they think a lot of you."

"Aye, sometimes; but you should hear what they say behind me back. They're going to tell me to go to blazes and as far beyond. I hear them and when I face them and say, 'What now?' all they come back with is, 'One of these days I'll walk out.' I'd like a pound for every time Jack Mowbray has said that. And you know something? He did walk out once, but he was back the next week. I hadn't got anybody in his place because I knew what would happen. 'What's brought you back?' I said. 'I didn't like the boss,' he said; 'he had a bigger mouth than yours.'"

She shook her head slowly, saying, "Well, in that case the man must have been quite unbearable."

"Watch it. Watch it, woman." He was about to grab her when a thin voice penetrated their preoccupation, calling from the stairway, "Mam, I want a drink; my throat's dry."

She clicked her tongue.

"Katie! I bet she's been awake all this time, in fact, all of them. I warned them they hadn't to come downstairs, so you had better go up and tell them what it was all about else there'll be no peace. Make it short and snappy."

"Yes, ma'am." And turning from her, he called, "Get back to that bed this minute else I'll give you a drink all right." . . .

The scrambling she now heard overhead confirmed that they were all up and waiting.

Life was good.

At least that's how she felt until half past eleven the next morning when the phone rang.

"*Fiona!*"

"Yes, Mother?" She closed her eyes, drew in a long breath and waited.

"You are determined to disgrace yourself, aren't you?"

She opened her eyes and stared at the mouthpiece, then replied, "Yes, Mother, if you say so. But what have I done now to disgrace myself?"

"Holding drunken parties. I couldn't believe it. But then I could. What that man has brought you to and what you seem to forget is that you've got three children to bring up. And what an example you are showing them: cars lined up outside, and the street raised as they piled into them late at night."

"*Shut up!*"

"What did you say?"

"You heard me, and I'll say it again, *shut up!* The drunken orgy to which you are referring was come by with tea and coffee, and the men were all gentlemen . . . yes gentlemen, having a board meeting to discuss a big new venture. Do you hear that, Mother? A big new venture, which spells money, big money . . . *great big money*. That should impress you. And the next time we have a board meeting here I'll invite Mrs Quinn in and from then on you'll hear no more gossip from her, because, Mother, she is like you, she is jealous and would give her eye teeth to have a man of her own. Again like you, Mother. . . ."

"How dare . . .!"

"I haven't finished, so shut up. And I'll say this, and it's been in my mind for a long time, if you had looked after Father and treated him as you should he might have been here today. But when he was ill and needed comfort, where were you? At your meetings, terrified, if you missed one, you wouldn't be the next chairwoman; and running after the Reverend Cottsmore, much to the annoyance of his wife. Now there you have it."

The perspiration was running from her brow into her eyes; her hand was trembling as she held the phone. She waited for the torrent of abuse but it did not come.

She replaced the receiver, then leant back with both hands on the small table and for a moment she felt she was going to pass out.

Her step was erratic as she walked towards the kitchen, and there, sitting down, she dropped her head onto her hands and started to cry, not because of what her mother had said to her but because of what she had said to her mother. She felt full of remorse, telling herself she should not have brought that up. She knew her father had been aware of her mother's feelings for the Reverend Cottsmore and that it had hurt him, but he himself had done nothing about it. But she recalled one thing he said and that was the day before her wedding. He was sitting in the little summerhouse at the bottom of the garden.

They had the place to themselves and on that very day her mother had been out arranging the flowers in the church. He had taken her hand and said something she considered very odd at the time. "One day, my dear," he said, "you'll reach what is called the change. You've likely heard all about it. With some it lasts for years, all depending on the person's constitution. But during it never think of divorcing your man."

He had laughed, and she had laughed with him, but she knew now that he was telling her that her mother was experiencing the change and that she wasn't accountable for her instability. But if she remembered rightly, her mother's instability must have preceded the change for a long time. Yet this knowledge did not lessen her feeling of guilt, and she felt that her father, had he been alive, would certainly not have applauded her outburst.

She rose from the table, thinking she would go and have a sherry to help pull herself together; but almost aloud, she said, "No! Don't start that." Her girlhood friend, who was two years her senior, had begun with an early sherry when they moved to London six years ago, and what was she doing now? Attending Alcoholics Anonymous, and with a divorce on her hands. And so she made a strong cup of coffee.

But this didn't help and an hour later she lifted the phone again.

When a small voice said, "Hello," she said, "I'm sorry, Mother."

There was no reply, and so she went on, "I shouldn't have said what I did, but I was so upset because, as I said, it was just a business meeting and . . . and they only had tea and coffee." She was feeling like a child trying to explain some misdemeanour.

The voice came pitifully small now, saying, "You hurt me, very deeply. You hurt me so much, Fiona."

"I'm . . . I'm sorry, Mother. I really am. And . . . and I'll call in sometime, sometime soon."

"Very well. Very well."

There was a pause and then the click of the receiver being put down. . . .

She felt miserable all day, so much so that after picking up the children from school she had to make an effort to be interested in their chatter. And Mark, always sensitive to her change of moods, asked, "You got a headache Mam?"

She replied. "Yes, rather a bad one." And later she gave the same excuse to Bill because she didn't want him to think worse of her mother than he already did.

It was exactly seven days later, however, that all the feelings of remorse and guilt towards her mother were swept clean away.

She should have been prepared for her mother's visit because two days previously, when picking up Katie from school, the child had informed her that her grandmother had been to the school and talked to her at dinner-time. Apparently she had questioned her about the child she had visited in hospital, and Katie had told her that it was Mr Bill's and they were going to adopt it.

She had stopped the car and looked at Katie and said, "Is that what you said, exactly? Try to think."

So Katie thought; then she said, "I said its mother and father had died in a car accident and now it was Mr Bill's."

She had stared at her daughter's apprehensive face, then smiled and said, "That's all right then." Yet for the remainder of the journey she had continued to ask heself why her mother should go to the school, if not to find out something to add to what she already knew.

It was known in the ward that negotiations were going on about the adoption of the child; so some talk may have filtered from there to her mother through Mrs Quinn, whom she herself had seen on two occasions visiting another child in the ward. It would also be known that they were bringing Mamie home in a fortnight's time. But what was not widely known was that she and Bill were to be married in a fortnight's time. . . .

It had rained almost incessantly for three days, and because of it the work on the clearing of the new site had been held up, and this had brought Bill home at half-past three this afternoon. And he was now in what was to be his study going over papers and plans.

She had picked up the children from school, settled them with their tea in the kitchen, taken Bill a cup of tea, and was crossing the hall when the front door bell rang. And there, under an umbrella, stood her mother. She felt her mouth drop open as she watched her close the umbrella, shake it, then lean it against the wall under the small porch.

"I've got to talk to you. . . . The children in?"

"Yes; they're in the kitchen having their tea." She watched her mother look round the hall, then march towards the sitting-room; and she herself followed, yet not before casting her glance towards the study. Once in the room she pushed the door tight.

Her mother was standing to the side of the couch. "I'm not going to stay," she said, "but I must talk to you. You . . . you said you would call in, but you haven't seen fit to do that, so I just had to come. I felt it my duty to warn you because I know you are deaf to what anybody else but that man says. It's about this child that he's making you adopt."

"Nothing of the sort, Mother; he's not making me adopt the child. You don't know what you're talking about."

"Oh! don't I, girl. Can you tell me of any man who's hoping to marry a woman with three children who would want to adopt another one unless there was something behind it?"

"Mother! Be careful." Her jaws were tight, her teeth moving over each other now: the sound was almost audible.

"I am careful, and careful for you. He's . . . he's a disgrace. Of course he wants you to adopt this child. Of course he wants to bring it into a family, because it's *his*. He had been carrying on with that woman for years. Oh, she was married all right and had another child, but he was never away from her house. Mrs Poller could tell you a thing or two."

She heard herself say grimly, "Mrs Poller? Who is Mrs Poller?"

"The woman, of course, he lived with before he came here."

"Oh; not Mrs Quinn this time? And so you have been to this Mrs Poller, have you, to investigate?"

"No; I did nothing of the sort. I happened to meet her in the paper shop and she was on about him. She had heard about the adoption and it was she who told me that he was never off her doorstep, supposedly because the young husband worked for him. But she had seen them both in the car together. What more proof do you want? And it was he who had to take the girl to the hospital when she was having the child. The husband was down with flu, so he said. He's a disgrace. He had been carrying on with her for years, all the time he was staying at Mrs Poller's. And God only knows how many more flyblows he's got kicking around the town. And he's duped you into. . . .'

Fiona let out a high cry as the door burst open. She saw a man who didn't look at all like Bill spring across the room and grab her mother. Her own screams were joined by those of her mother and the cries of the children in the hall.

"Bill! Bill! For God's sake! No! No!" She was tearing at his

54

hands that were gripping her mother's shoulders close to her neck, and he was shaking her like a rat as he cried, "You dirty-minded old swine! I could kill you this minute. Do you hear?"

It wasn't Fiona's efforts that loosened his hands but the realization of what he had said that slackened his grip on her mother. And he watched her fall back full length onto the couch, where she lay straddled, gasping and moaning, her eyes staring wide in terror.

After some seconds Fiona made to go towards the couch, but Bill thrust her roughly aside, crying, "Don't you touch her, she's putrid!" Then he was bending over the couch, yelling into the frightened face, "You're putrid, filthy! Do you hear? Your mind, all of you, dirty, rotten. And listen to this: I'm master in this house now whether I'm married or not, and I'm telling you I give you fifteen minutes to get out and never put your face in that door again, because I won't be responsible for what I'll do to you."

He stepped back from her but stood panting, his jawbones moving and showing white through his skin. There was no sound for a moment except the whimpering of the children. Turning slowly about, he walked towards them; then picking up Willie, whose face was awash with tears, he went towards the kitchen, Mark walking on one side of him and Katie holding onto his trouser pocket at the other.

Fiona continued to stare at her mother; she was feeling now she couldn't go towards her, she couldn't touch her, whereas she might have a few moments ago when she thought she was gasping her last. She watched her slowly pull herself into a sitting position and push her skirt down over her knees. She watched her mouth open twice before managing to say haltingly, "I'll . . . I'll have him to court for . . . for attacking me."

Fiona's own voice was trembling as she replied, "That's if he doesn't have you up for defamation of character before, together with your friends. And I'll tell you this: the mother and father of that child were like a son and daughter to him; he thought of them as his son and daughter; he had looked after the man since he was a young boy. It is a serious accusation you've made against him and it will surprise me if he doesn't go to a solicitor."

It would have surprised her if he had because he was a man

who fought his own personal battles, mostly with a laugh, as she had found out. Nevertheless, this was different: she herself had been afraid of him and he could have throttled her mother. My God! yes, he could have. But that her mother was far from being dead she now realized when she said, "You must take me home; I can't walk that distance."

"I'll not take you home, Mother; I'll order a taxi for you." And on this she went into the hall and did just that. But instead of returning to the sitting-room she went to the kitchen.

The children were sitting at the table again, and so was he, but none of them was eating. She didn't look at him but at Mark to whom she said, "Finish your tea and then go upstairs;" and he answered quietly, "Yes, Mam." She had turned about and reached the kitchen door when Willie's voice piped up, saying, "Are we not gona have the baby then?"

She turned and looked at him. They must have all been in the hall listening. She was about to answer when Bill yelled, "Yes, we're going to have the baby."

The children were startled and frightened for a moment and he, bowing his head now, said, "It's all right. It's all right. I'm . . . I'm in a paddy. But yes, we're going to have the baby." And he put out one hand to ruffle Willie's hair and the other towards Katie to take hold of her hand while his eyes rested on Mark. And he smiled at him and again he said, "You bet your life we're going to have that baby."

She closed the door and walked slowly across the hall, pausing to steel herself before entering the sitting-room.

Her mother was now sitting quite upright. Her bag was open to the side of her and she was dabbing her face. She still used powder, and she had covered her entire face with it giving her complexion a sickly pallor. And as Fiona watched her, any grain of sympathy that she might have had for her fled. She knew that she would make straight for one of her cronies and would give her a detailed description of what had happened. And so she said, "Mother, if I hear one derogatory word that you have said against Bill, I shall tell him. And I can assure you that won't be the end of it. He's a determined man and he values his good name, and it is a good name. So you'd be wise to take this as a warning." She turned her head, saying now, "There's the car."

She watched her mother rise slowly to her feet, pick up her

handbag, adjust her coat and with a steadier step than she herself had so far maintained walk past her without a glance. She stopped at the front door, but only to open it, picked up her umbrella and walked down the pathway to the waiting taxi.

8

She was wearing a slack off-white coat, a small turban type hat to match, her brown hair curling inwards onto her shoulders and picking up the tone of her tan-coloured close fitting woollen dress.

He was standing close by her side in a well cut dark grey suit. He looked very well groomed and could, at this moment, have been termed handsome.

One of the two men behind the desk, pointing to the card in Bill's hand, was saying, "Repeat after me: I do solemnly declare. . . ."

And after Bill had made his declaration, Fiona was asked to make hers; yet both seemed deaf to what had gone before and to what precisely followed after until the man smiled, then said, "I suppose you know it's customary to kiss the bride?"

As they kissed Katie giggled. Mark made a shushing sound, and Willie looked up at his new grand-dad, as he had been told to address the strange man who had arrived with a strange woman at their house yesterday, and in whom he was more interested than in his new father, because, after all, *he* was still Mr Bill, and he knew Mr Bill, whereas he had to get to know this other tall man who made him laugh.

They were now in the outer hall of the Registry Office. Fiona had been kissed by her Alcoholics Anonymous friend from London, and then embraced by her friend's boy friend, a member of the same society; there had been more hugging by her new father-in-law and by his girl friend about whose age Bill had erred, for Madge would never see sixty-five again; then hand-shaking by Barney McGuire and his wife who had acted as their two witnesses. And then it was her turn to do some embracing. First she kissed Mark who smiled at her but said nothing. With Katie it was different. "Can we stay up for the party?" said her daughter.

"Yes, for a short while."

When she came to her small son he brushed her kiss aside, saying, "I don't want to go to the party, I want to go to the hospital."

"Presently."

Bill now put his arm about her shoulders and they all went out into the bright sunshine and got into their respective cars and drove to a nearby hotel where, in a private room, a table had been set for them: no wedding cake, just an ordinary meal. Later, the present party and all Bill's men and their wives were to have a wedding dinner in the grander Palace Hotel, followed by a dance. It had been arranged like this because the family had something of import to do in the afternoon.

It was a merry meal that went on for two hours and when the party broke up, Fiona's London friends went back to their hotel, Bill's father and Madge went back to the house, while Bill and Fiona drove with the children to the hospital. Arrived there, they did not this time make their way to the ward but went straight to the superintendent's room, where a nurse was sitting on the couch holding the free hand of a little girl who was wearing a pinafore frock which enabled her plastered arm to be free.

As soon as she saw her new family she wriggled from the couch and came towards them. But her hand wasn't held out to her Uncle Bill's, as she thought of him, nor to that of her new mother, nor to Katie or to Mark; but it was to Willie she gave her hand. And it was he who grinned at her as he said, "You all ready?"

She nodded at him and smiled.

Everybody was smiling, and the superintendent took Bill to one side and briefly he told him that he understood the adoption papers would be ready in a few days when the legalities were gone into. Bill thanked him, and with the child in his arms they all went out together.

The children in the car and Fiona in her seat, he then placed the little girl on her lap, and, taking his place behind the wheel, he drove them home. But the excitement and pleasure was pierced when, all of them settled in the sitting-room and surrounding her, the child said, "My mammy coming soon?"

No one spoke for a moment, but all eyes were turned on Fiona, and she said, "Yes, soon, dear." Then came the question, "And Daddy?"

It was the first time since their first visit, to their knowledge, that the child had asked about her parents. And it was Willie who saved the day, albeit unconsciously – who was to know – by saying, "I've put your name on my horse's belly next to mine, an' you can ride him."

"Stomach, Willie."

"Its stom . . . ack." He pursed his lips and pulled a laughing face at his mother and the tension was broken. . . .

With regard to leaving the children so that they could attend their own wedding party, it had been arranged that Barney McGuire's sister-in-law would come and baby-sit. Then only this morning Barney had come early to say his sister-in-law had a stinking cold, but he'd shop around and try to find someone else for them. It was then that Mr Bailey senior said there would be no need, that he and Madge would be only too happy to stay put with the bairns. And so it had been arranged; and also that the old couple hadn't to stay up as the newly weds naturally didn't know at what time they would be able to get away. . . .

It was seven o'clock when they saw Katie and Willie and their new daughter to bed. They had put another single bed next to Katie's, and had left them happily playing with their dolls and bears.

When a short time later Fiona stood in the hall in her evening dress, a cloak around her shoulders, and Madge put her arms around her and hugged her as a mother would, she felt for a moment she'd burst out crying, because not for the first time on this, her special day, she had imagined how different she would have been feeling if she'd had a mother who could have been happy for her.

When Bailey senior jerked his head and said, "By! you're a good-lookin' piece, girl," Bill demanded of his father, "Do you think I would have picked her if she hadn't been?" Then he won her heart in yet another way by bending down to Mark and saying quietly, "You'll see to them up there, won't you? Don't stand any nonsense." And she watched her son's eyelids blink and his neck stretch as he said, "Yes, Mr Bill; I'll . . . I'll see to them."

"That's the ticket," Bill said, touching Mark on the shoulder; then turning to Fiona, he took her arm, saying, "Come on, love," and they went out together, leaving Mark standing on the step between Bill's father and Madge. And when the old man called,

"Come back sober, mind," Bill did not answer him with any quip, but, as he took his place beside her in the car, he took her hand and held it firmly as he said, "Tonight, if only for once in me life, I'll aim to join Alcoholics Anonymous."

It was two o'clock in the morning when they tiptoed up the stairs, and on the landing when she whispered, "I'll just look in on them," he hissed back, "No, you won't. There's only one person you're going to look in on tonight, or this morning. Come on."

They had taken off their shoes and outer things downstairs, and now in the bedroom they stood looking at each other. He did not make any attempt to embrace her, but he took her hands and held them tightly against his chest as he said softly, "You know, I'm speaking the truth now, but I never thought I'd make it. Honest to God, I didn't. Right up till this mornin' I thought something would happen: your mother would put the 'fluence on us in some way and I'd have a crash in the car; I felt sure that some disaster was bound to happen. I've been worried for weeks, me with me big mouth acting as if I was God's secretary. Still I never thought I'd have you. And that day of the big affair when I almost throttled your mother, I thought that in some part of your mind you might believe I really had been the gay Lothario. See, I know some big names."

For a moment he was silent; then softly he said, "You know, most of my life I've been full of just wind and wishes. Not that I haven't been about, but I'm certainly not the skunk she made me out to be. And when I've thought of what might have happened that day which could have separated us for life, and I might have done life at that for her, if some part of my mind hadn't warned me what I'd be losing if I hadn't you." Again he paused; then tracing his finger across her cheek he said, "I love you, Fiona. I can't tell you to what extent I love you, that would be impossible, but I'll show you in the years to come. I've got ideas, whopping ideas. And one day I'll put you in a big house standing in its own grounds with two or three cars on the drive and servants and. . . ."

"You'll do nothing of the sort, Bill Bailey, so get your whoppers out of your head. All I want is . . . oh, shut up!" And turning her back on him, she demanded, "Undo my zip!"

He let out a high laugh, then choked it as he pulled her round to him and whispered, "You know what? You're talking just like me; you sounded right common."

They were clinging to each other now, their bodies convulsed with their silent laughter.

After a moment she pressed herself from him and, looking into his streaming face, she said, "Remember that day you told me about your father and his girl friend, and I was surprised at him having a girl friend at his age and sarcastically I said that you must take after him, and you replied that yes, you did, and you couldn't take after a better man. And so I say to you now, Bill Bailey, if I'm talking like you and acting like you, I couldn't have a better pattern. And at this moment I know what you're wanting to say in your own inimitable way." Her voice now changed as she finished: "Stop your chit-chat, it's me weddin' night. Let's get to bed."

His mouth wide, he put his hand across it; then she was lifted off her feet and waltzed round the room. Of a sudden he stopped, put her down, turned her round and then deliberately and slowly undid the zip of her dress.

9

"Why on earth couldn't you let her wear her good coat?"

"Because, Mr Bailey, her good coat is not half as good or as thick as her school coat and, as you yourself pointed out in your own polite way, it's so cold outside that it would cut the lugs off a cuddy, not to mention its tail and other extremities. And—" She now turned from her husband and looked at her ten-year-old son and his six-year-old brother and added, "And you two stop that giggling, because if your sister doesn't put in an appearance within the next minute no one of us will see the school concert tonight; I'm not going in there once it's started."

"Oh! woman, be quiet." Bill went to the foot of the stairs and yelled, "You! Katie. Come on pronto!" At the same time the sitting-room door opened and a young woman appeared and, looking at Fiona, she said, "Will I go up and get her?"

"No, Nell; nobody's going up to get her; she knows her way downstairs. But if she's not here within the next minute we're going without her. She's been playing up of late."

"You wouldn't do that." To which Fiona answered, "Wouldn't I just!" But she smiled at her neighbour.

During the last four months, apart from having acquired a new husband, Fiona had also acquired a friend from among the family who had come to live next door. These were a Mr and Mrs Paget, a couple in their fifties. It was as though the husband had arrived to join the rest of the redundant managers in the street. And with them had also come their daughter-in-law Nell and her husband Harry, who had only last week found a job after two years unemployment. Only Nell had been employed and then part time in a store in the town. So she was very glad to do baby-sitting or anything else that came her way. And, too, she was about Fiona's own age and of similar tastes, so they got on well together. And tonight, because Mamie had a cold, Nell was once again baby-sitting.

Fiona now asked, "Is she all right?"

"Fine," Nell answered; "she's galloping with Bugs Bunny." Then their attention was drawn to the stairs, for there at the top stood the cause of the hold-up. But she was making no attempt to come down; instead she stood sniffing.

"Do you hear me, Katie? Come down this minute, or you'll go straight to bed."

As Katie now descended the stairs a chorus of sniffs rose from the hall.

"What . . . on earth . . .!"

"Phew! She smells."

"What have you been up to, child?"

"I couldn't help it, Mam. I was only going to put a drop on, and . . . and it slipped and tipped, all the way down."

Fiona now pushed Katie none too gently to one side and dashed up the stairs, but within a minute she had returned, her arm outstretched and in her hand a scent bottle with just a drain left in the bottom.

Holding it up to her husband, she said, "Look! Look at that."

And Bill looked at it; then turning his gaze down onto Katie's snivelling face, he said, "You know what I paid for that, Katie Bailey? Forty-nine quid. A bottle of Chanel she said she wanted. And where's it gone? On your school coat. And now, when she wants to smell nice, she'll have to wring it out. Aw! come on now; stop your crying. Worse things happen at sea. But by God! forty-nine pounds down the drain."

"No, down the school coat." He turned to a grinning Mark; then looked at Willie whose nose was now distorting his face as he said, "She stinks."

"I don't! I don't! I'll slap your face."

"Come on. Come on; we'll have none of that." Fiona grabbed her daughter's hand and pulled her back to the stairs and up them. And Bill, turning to where Nell had an arm tight around her waist to stop herself from laughing outright, said, "I must have been barmy, right up the pole to saddle meself with this lot. I didn't know when I was well off. A middle-of-the-road man, that's what I was, Nell, a middle-of-the-road man. And now look at me, lumbered."

"I'm sorry for you."

"Aye, I know you are." He glanced now at Mark, saying, "And you're not much help." Then looking down on Willie, he added, "As for you, you should be shut up in a home, or sent to your gran's. Aye, that's the place to send you. Aye, that's what we'll do with you, we'll send you to live with your gran. I'll have to see about it."

As he turned away to look up the stairs Mark said, quietly, "Mr Bill." Then he nodded towards his young brother, and when Bill turned it was to see Willie's face screwed up now, not against the smell of the scent, but with tears.

Going swiftly to the boy, he swung him up in his arms, saying, "Come on, Willie-wet-eye; you know I was only jokin'. I wouldn't send a dog with rabies to your granny's, unless" – he poked his face towards the wet cheek – "it was to bite her."

As he growled and pretended to bite the child's ear, Fiona, preceded by a still snivelling Katie, came down the stairs, only now Katie was dressed in her best coat.

"Ah! Ah!" Bill put Willie down on the floor and looking towards his wife, he said, "If you'd let her have her own way at first I wouldn't have lost forty-nine quid."

Without looking at him Fiona marshalled her small horde towards the door, saying, "You lost it when you bought the bottle. And please don't remind me again what you paid for it."

"Not remind you? By God! I will; every chance I get. So be prepared. Well, get moving, the lot of you. Bye! Nell."

"We won't be all that late." Fiona turned towards Nell, and Nell answered, "Oh, it doesn't matter. Go out to supper after; have a fish and chip do."

"That's the idea. That's what we'll do." Bill took up Nell's words. "A fish and chip do to get over the misery of the school concert."

"We'll do no such thing. It'll be ten o'clock before we get out of there."

"Pattisons in the town is open till half-past eleven."

"*Bill.*"

"Yes, Mrs Bailey?"

When the door closed on them Nell Paget went back into the sitting-room where Mamie was bouncing on the ouch, and, sitting down beside the child, she sighed not a little in envy of this family, of her new friend who could have three children of her own and adopt another, whereas she, who had been married thirteen years, had no hopes of ever having a baby."

10

She was brought from her first sleep by the sound of the window being opened. And in a kind of panic her hand shot out and switched on the light. Then she almost splattered, "What . . . what on earth are you doing, Bill?"

"Letting a little air in. The room stinks," he whispered hoarsely.

"You'll freeze. Get back into bed."

"Far better freeze than be suffocated with that smell. I don't know how you can stand it."

As he snuggled down beside her again, she said, "It's supposed to go on a drop at a time and not a whole bottle. I'd only used it twice. But the carpet got more of it than her coat. I'll wash it tomorrow. What time is it?" she asked now.

"Half-past one."

"Haven't you been to sleep yet?"

"No; I've got tomorrow on my mind. Four of those ten I set on are a dead weight; it would take a gaffer to watch each of them. They'll go as soon as I get in in the morning. I didn't get back into Newcastle until they had all gone, but Barney was waiting for me. There was a drizzle of rain," he said, "and there they were in the hut while our own fellas keep at it. And as Barney said, no matter how loyal our lot are they're not going to put up with shirkers like that. And there's another one I'd like to get rid of an' all and that's that Max Ringston. He's a good enough worker but I don't trust him somehow. I can't pin anything on him, but when there's stuff being lifted as I told you about afore, such as door frames, and floor boardings, he's been one of the two who've been on the lorry that day, the other being Tommy Turnbull. But I'd trust Tommy with me life. And Dave, Dave McRae. He usually takes the other lorry, but he's been in hospital, as you know, for some weeks now. And so Ringston's been doing the driving."

"Can't you have him watched?"

"It's difficult. And when he brings in the loads they always check with the lists. Barney sees to that. But it's not until they start putting the window frames or the door up they find there's some missing. And they're all locked up at night in the shed. Barney and me are the only ones who have got keys, and added to that, there's the watchman. Oh, I'm tellin' you, Mrs B, life ain't easy." He hugged her to him, then added, "Except when I've got you like this."

There was a pause while they both lay quiet; and then, his voice soft, he said, "You know, I sometimes ask meself, what kind of a life did I lead before I had you, before I came in as your lodger?"

Laughing softly now, she said, "I know what kind of a man you were, as you were forever telling me, a middle-of-the-road man; but you didn't go on to say that you draw your women in from both sides."

"Aw, that was mostly talk."

"Mostly?"

"Do you love me?"

"Yes, Bill Bailey, I love you. And I too can't imagine what my life was like before you came into this house as a lodger. And as for the children, if you were their father they couldn't love you more; in fact, I must admit that they love you as they never loved their father. And then there's Mamie. She's like one of our own now."

"Do you think she's forgotten about Susan and Dan and her brother?"

"Well, it's some weeks since she mentioned them. You remember that night at the table when of a sudden she said, 'Will my mammy soon be back from her holidays?'"

"Yes, yes, I remember that. God in heaven! I didn't know what to say. Then when Willie put in, 'When I die I'm going to have wings on my heels so I can fly upside down.' Remember? we sat there both dumb."

They now laughed and held each other tightly, and Bill repeated, "Wings on his heels so he can fly upside down. He comes out with things, that fella."

He stroked her hair back from her face now as he said softly, "You know, I was thinking the night when I saw you walk across that schoolroom after you had been talking to the teacher,

I thought you looked so young, so girlish. And you are young and you are girlish, and I wondered if you would like to go to a dance sometime, a nice dance, not a romp; you know, a dinner dance. Aye, that's it."

She giggled now and her body shook against his as she said, "Thank you, Mr Bailey. I'll think about it, but it's on two in the morning and if I'm not mistaken you've got a stiff day before you tomorrow. That's what's kept you awake. So we'll discuss taking this young girl out to a dance some other time, but now go to sleep."

"Yes, Ma. Good-night, Ma." He kissed her long and hard; then almost caused her to choke by saying, "The only thing I thank your mother for was getting pregnant by you."

"Mammy B."

"Yes, darling?"

"When will I get new teefths in?"

"Oh, they'll soon grow, dear."

"Big ones?"

"Yes. Just a nice size to fit your mouth."

"With a band on?"

"A band, dear? What do you mean, a band?"

"Like Katie's."

"Oh. No; you won't have to have a band like Katie's. That is just to keep Katie's teeth straight; your teeth will be nice and straight to begin with. Come on; we'll go and meet her and the rest of them, eh? Tie your scarf nice and tight because it's very cold outside."

She helped the child to knot the pom-pommed scarf, and pulled the woollen hat down around her ears; then lifting her up, she went out of the front door, locking it behind her, and hurried down to the car; and after strapping the child into the back seat, she drove away from the house.

Five minutes later she stopped outside the playground of the junior school. In the distance she saw Willie, but he did not rush towards her as was usual; instead, his step was slow and his head was down. She got out of the car and went to meet him.

69

"What is it? What's the matter?"

When he raised his head her mouth fell into a gape for he had the nearest thing to a black eye.

"What have you been doing?"

He walked past her, pulled open the car door and sat himself beside Mamie.

She was seated behind the wheel now, half turned in her seat, and he said, "Betty Rice hit me with a ruler."

"Oh. And what had you done to Betty Rice?"

"I . . . I punched her."

"Why did you punch her?"

"Because she took my book and wouldn't give it back." He now put his hand in his pocket, and as he handed her the envelope across the seat he said, "Teacher said to give you that."

"Oh." She did not open the envelope because she knew it would be a further explanation of what had happened; time enough to go into that when she got home.

"Is it sore?" It was Mamie asking the question of him now. And in true boyish fashion he answered, "Yes, of course it's sore. If somebody hit you with a ruler wouldn't it be sore?"

"Yes, Willie; yes, it would be sore."

Already Fiona knew that nothing Willie could do could be wrong in Mamie's eyes. She started up the car, saying, "We'll talk about this when we get home."

She knew that Mark was playing football today and as on other occasions when this happened he was always a little earlier than Katie, so he was the next one she picked up.

"Cor! What's happened to you?" were his first words when he took his seat beside his mother and looked behind him to Willie.

"I was hit by a hephelant's trunk."

Fiona bit on her lip. That was Willie. There was nothing much wrong with him except that his pride was hurt.

Then she had to check her elder son when he said, "Oh, just a hephelant's trunk?" He mimicked his brotther's inability to pronounce some words correctly, then added, "I thought he must have stood on your face."

"Mark!"

Mark laughed; then leaning towards his mother as she started up the car, he said, "What happened?"

And in an aside she answered, "A little girl got the better of him." . . .

Two blocks further on, she stopped the car again and Mark, looking out of the window, said, "She's not there; she's likely waiting inside out of the cold."

"Go and fetch her."

She watched Mark run across the schoolyard. Then less than a minute later he was running back towards her.

Opening the door, he said, "She's not there. They say she's gone."

"Gone? She can't have gone."

She got out of the car now and looked towards where three girls were standing beyond the gate. They were well wrapped up, but they were hopping up and down. She recognized one of them; she was in Katie's class. She went up to the children now and asked, "Have . . . have you seen Katie?"

The two older girls shook their heads, but the smaller one said, "Yes; she went home, Mrs Nelson."

"She went home? She walked?"

"Oh, no." The child smiled. "Her new father came for her. He came along there." She pointed. "He called her name and she ran to him and she got in the car."

Fiona stared at the child for a moment. She wanted to say, "Oh, that'll be all right, she'll be at home," but she couldn't for a great fear was assailing her. Bill had never come and taken any of them home. She heard herself say, "What . . . what did the man look like?"

"Her father? Oh, he was in his working clothes. I don't know what his face was like but she told us her new daddy built big houses."

Of a sudden she was running back to the car.

"What is it?" Mark said.

She didn't answer him but started the car noisily with her foot hard down on the accelerator pedal; and then she was speeding, not towards home, but towards the works.

Five minutes later she was swinging the car into the rough road that led to the buildings; and having brought it to a stop outside some sheds that formed the office and the men's cabin and the tool house, she jumped out and gabbled at a surprised workman: "Where's Mr Bailey?"

It was one of the new men. She didn't know him, and it was obvious that he didn't know her, for his manner was quite off-hand as he said, "You'll likely find him in the office, there."

When she thrust open the door of the hut Bill was sitting at his desk, but before she could speak he was holding her by the arms, saying, "What is it? What's the matter?"

"Where . . . where is she? Katie? Why did you? You never have. . . ."

"Stop it! Stop gabbling. What about Katie?"

"They . . . they said you came and took her from school."

His arms dropped from her and his words came in a thin whisper from his lips, "Who took her? Who said I took her?"

"Oh my God! My God!" She was holding her head. "The little girl, she said Katie's daddy had come in the car and called her and . . . and she got in."

"*Almighty God!* When? When?"

"Just a short while ago. It must have been immediately she came out of school."

He turned now and grabbed up the phone and dialled a number. His voice was a gabble in answer to someone speaking from the other end: "My . . . my daughter's been picked up. Someone . . . someone impersonating me. Yes! Yes! Yes!"

She watched him close his eyes, then say, "My name is William Bailey. I'm a contractor; I'm building the new estate just beyond the top of Brampton Hill."

"What? What?" He looked towards Fiona. "The child's school? It's the junior in Mowbray Road. No, no; I can't give you other details. I've just heard. My wife's here. Look. Get crackin' will you? For God's sake do something."

He did not thrust the phone back on its stand but laid it down as if in slow motion. Then he stood, his head bent, drawing in deep breaths for a moment before he turned to her where she was still standing holding her head in her hands. Taking her into his arms, he said, "Can . . . can you think of anything else the child said?"

She shook her head. Then looking at him, her eyes wide and staring, she said, "But . . . but it must have been someone who knew what time she would be coming out of school. It couldn't be just a passer-by, because he . . . he called her name. That . . . that was likely why she ran to him."

"Well, well. Now . . . now try not to worry; that'll narrow things down a bit. Try not to worry, I said; my God! what prattle! Try not to worry."

"Oh, Bill, Bill. If anything should happen to. . . ."

"*It won't. It won't.* It can't, not to Katie. I . . . I love them all, you know that, but . . . but Katie was somebody special, she was. Oh" – he lifted his head – "that must be the police car. Well, I can say this, they were quick off the mark; they must have got hold of one of the patrol cars."

When they went outside two policemen were getting out of the car and before they could speak Bill was relating all he knew.

In a few minutes it seemed that from every one of the part-built houses men came pouring out, so quickly had the news gone round that the boss's bairn had been picked up by some bloke.

It was Barney McGuire who said, "What can we do, boss? Every man-jack will stay on an' help look."

But it was the policeman who answered, "We'll likely need all your help later on; but the inspector will be here any minute and he'll go into things first."

Taking Fiona by the arm, Bill led her towards the car, saying, "Take the bairns home."

"I can't. I can't, Bill."

"*Listen!* Take the bairns home. Get Nell to come in and see to them. Then if I don't turn up within half an hour or so you can come back here, and by that time something should be under way. Go on now, there's a good lass. It'll be all right. It'll be all right. I swear to you, it'll be all right, else by God I'll—" He shook his head, then pressed her into the car, saying, "Steady now." And looking down at Mark, he said, "See to your mother, lad."

"Katie?"

"She'll be all right. She'll be all right." . . .

She didn't know how she had driven the car home and she sounded incoherent as she tried to tell Nell Paget what had happened. But now the three children were aware that Katie was lost and all of them started to cry, including Mark; and this upset her still further and, taking him aside, she held his face between her hands, saying, "You're the eldest, dear; you've . . . you've got to help me. See to the others and try . . . try to keep them happy. Nell will do her best, but you know them better, and I rely on you."

"But" – his lips were trembling – "but Mam, what . . . what if they can't find her?"

"They'll find her. You know nothing gets past Mr Bill; you

73

know that, don't you?" When he suddeny leant against her and put his arms around her waist she felt that she would not just give way to tears but that she would howl aloud to release this dreadful feeling inside which was being probed by the poignancy of her son's love. She kissed him now; then pressing him away from her, she said, "Go and help Nell to get the tea. I'll . . . I'll be back shortly."

But she did not immediately leave the house; she ran upstairs and into her bedroom and, throwing herself on her knees by the bed, she began to pray. She prayed as she had never done in her life before. During the years she had been forced through her mother to attend church, she had never really prayed; but now she beseeched God to keep her daughter safe and to let her be found soon. Oh yes, God, soon.

After washing her tear-streaked face she went downstairs. Bill had said if he didn't return home in half an hour . . . well, the half hour wasn't up but she couldn't remain here. She said to Nell, "Can you stay this evening?" And Nell, gripping her arm, said, "Girl, I'll stay as long as I'm needed, today, tomorrow, a week. Don't worry about them, I'll see to them. You go on. But what you could do if you are not coming straight back is phone me and let me know what's happening."

"I'll do that. Thanks, Nell."

As she ran down to the car she wondered why she should think that God provided because he had sent her someone like Nell. It was a ridiculous thought when her child had been abducted; yet she would have had to stay at home if Nell hadn't been there.

The yard was abuzz when she arrived. There were four police cars and a number of policemen and strange men standing in small groups.

In the hut she found Bill, the inspector, and a sergeant. The first thing Bill said to her was, "Do you know the name of the little girl that told you about Katie?"

"Yes, it's Rene Smith. But I don't know where she lives."

"And you don't know the names of the other two girls?" It was the inspector speaking now.

"No."

"That's all right. We can consult the headmistress. Well now." The inspector rose from a chair, and looking at Bill, he said, "We have the names of four men you dismissed. Had you any hot words or arguments with them before they left?"

"No; but they weren't very pleased."

"Anyone of them that might bear a grudge you would think?"

"Two were a bit mouthy, Ringston and a fellow called Flint. Flint had only been here a week."

The inspector now looked at the sergeant. "We'll check on the schoolgirls first, and we might get a lead. They will likely remember the colour of the car at least. I've got no hope that they would take the number, although some of them do." Looking at Fiona now, he said, "Try not to worry, Mrs Bailey. I know that's easier said than done, but I'd go home if I were you."

"I've just come from home." Her voice was terse.

"Well, I'm afraid there's little that can be done at the moment. As far as I can judge it's no use sending out search parties because if the man knew her name it points to a local job, and that narrows it down considerably.

Without further words he turned and went out, followed by the sergeant.

And now Bill, coming over to her, put his arms about her, saying, "As he said, it narrows it down, and that's a hopeful sign."

"Do ... do you think it was one of your men, one you sacked?"

"I don't know. They didn't seem that type, only lazy devils. It's more likely someone she's spoken to before; she's a chatterer. I've seen her chattering to different people in the street. The very look of her made people want to stop an' talk to her."

He turned from her now and, supporting himself by his doubled fists on the edge of his desk, he said, "Whoever it is I swear to you I'll kill him. No matter what the consequences, I'll kill him."

"*Oh, don't say that, Bill.* Don't talk like that." She pulled him round to her, then whimpered, "As long as we get her back. . . . I'm frightened Bill. That child a fortnight ago, they. . . ."

"*Be quiet!*" His voice was a bawl now. "Look, as the inspector says, you can do nothing; get yourself away home. Now go on, see to the kids, do something. It'll take your mind off it."

"Take my mind off it?"

"You know what I mean." He pushed her roughly from him, then turned and hurried out.

Dropping into a chair, she leant her elbow on his desk and lowered her head on to her hand. Why was it that things never ran smoothly? They had been so happy. She was in a new life. Yes, she was in a new life. Like the song, everything was coming up roses. But then roses had thorns, although the only thorn in her life up till an hour ago had been her mother. The thought brought her to her feet. What time was it? Close on six. If it was on the local radio, and it just might be, because there was always a reporter hanging around the police station and they got news like this very quickly, and if her mother was to hear it she would be over and her tongue lashing out as usual. And if she found only Nell there she'd take control, even after all that had happened.

When she went into the yard there were still a lot of men about. And it was Barney McGuire who came up to her and said, "I'm sorry, Mrs Bailey, I am to the heart of me. But pray God they'll find her soon. She was such a bonny bit. She romped through here the other day chatting to the men. She picked the house that she would like. And the boss was barmy about her; that was plain to see. He carried her shoulder high at one time over the puddles and she laughed her head off and. . . .'

She had to stop him. "Are . . . are you staying on, Mr McGuire?" she put in quickly.

"Yes, ma'am, as long as I'm needed."

"Well, if you hear anything will you phone me? that is if Bill isn't back."

"I'll do that. I'll do that, ma'am, pronto, the minute I hear anything. You go on home now." . . .

She went home and when she entered the house it was unusually quiet, so much so she thought that Nell had taken the children next door, until she opened the sitting-room door, and then from the couch they all rushed to her.

"You found her, Mam?"

"Is she coming home?"

"She can have my spaceman. Mam, Mam, she can have my spaceman. She wanted it and I wouldn't. . . ."

She picked up Willie from the floor and held him tightly, saying, "It's all right. It's all right. Yes, she knows she can have your spaceman, dear, and she'll soon be back to play with it."

"Mammy B."

Mamie stretched out her arms towards her from where Nell

was holding her, and she put Willie to the floor and took the child.

"Mammy B, I want Katie and Uncle Bill."

"They'll . . . they'll be back soon, dear. Have . . . have they had their tea?" she was looking at Nell, and Nell said, "Yes, but for a change nobody seemed very hungry."

Fiona now looked down on Mark, saying quietly, "Take them up to the playroom, will you, dear?"

He stared at her for a moment before turning to Willie and saying, "Come on, you. And you too." He held his hand up to Mamie, and Fiona put her on the floor, where she started to snivel a little but nevertheless took Mark's hand, and the three of them left the room together.

Fiona and Nell looked at each other, and it was Nell who spoke, saying, "It's no use asking if they've made any headway, it's too early."

Fiona didn't answer but sat down on the couch, and what she said was, "I'm sick, all my body and brain is sick, Nell. I'm thinking all the time what he could be doing to her."

"Don't." Nell sat beside her and put her arms around her shoulders. "If, as you said, the man knew her name it's someone local. It could be someone from this very street, you never know people. I'll tell you something: I was kidnapped once."

"Never!"

"Yes. It was a man three doors down. He had a wife but no children. He had just retired from a decent job too, highly respectable. He gave me a ride in his car, which he had done once or twice before. But then he had put me off at the bottom of the street; this time he kept on driving. He took me to a fair-ground; then we went to the pictures, and afterwards into a café for tea. Then when I wanted to go home and started to cry he drove round and round. It was in the summertime and he said we would sleep on the sands. Fortunately the police caught up with him. They stopped the car; his wife had tipped them off. He had done this before but had always brought the child back the same day. I don't think he intended to this time. Anyway" – Nell turned her head to the side and looked towards the window as she ended – "I wasn't upset about this man until I got home and found Dad was going round the bend. But Mam had taken it in her usual stride, and she greeted me as if I'd just been out to play in the street. I can see her now looking down on me, saying, 'You enjoyed yourself then? Causing trouble as usual.'"

"No!"

Nell now turned her head and nodded at Fiona. "Oh, yes, yes."

"How old were you?"

"Seven, nearly eight."

"Really?"

"She couldn't stand me because Dad made a fuss of me. She led me hell until I left home. Quite candidly, I ran away when I was fifteen. I went down to my aunt's in Wales, her sister, who was as different again from her, and my Dad said I could stay there. It was there I met Harry. Again she looked towards the window, saying now, "I was married when I was nineteen. Thirteen years." She said the last words with a sigh. "And the only thing I've wanted is a family, and the only thing he didn't want, and will never want, is a family."

"Oh Nell, I didn't know."

"Well—" Nell smiled at her, adding, "You can see why I'm so pleased to have a second-hand one next door."

Their hands joined for a moment and then they put their arms round each other, and both of their faces were wet when they separated. And it was Nell who now said, "I wouldn't like to be the man who's done this if Bill gets his hands on him."

"That's what I'm frightened about too. He swore that he'd kill him."

"I don't blame him."

It was at this point the phone rang and they both sprang up. Then Fiona ran through the room and into the hall and, grabbing the mouthpiece, she was about to say, "Yes?" when the voice said, "Fiona."

She closed her eyes, "Yes, Mother."

"What is this? What is this? It can't be. The local wireless, it's just said that Katie is missing. What have you been up to?"

"Mother! Mother!"

"Never mind, Mother, Mother, why didn't you pick her up from school as usual?"

Fiona held the mouthpiece well away from her and glared at it before bringing it slowly towards her again.

"I was at school, Mother, to pick her up, but she had been picked up before."

"What are you doing at home then? Why aren't you out looking?"

"Don't be silly, Mother."

"Don't take that tone with me, Fiona; I'm not going to stand it any more. Now I'm coming round."

"You're not coming round, Mother."

"You try and stop me. She is my granddaughter."

"Mother!" The line went dead. Slowly she put the mouthpiece back, then turned and, leaning her buttocks against the telephone table, she bent her head.

"Your mother?"

"Yes, Nell, Mother. You've never met her, have you? Well, you're about to. My dear, dear mother, who has always done everything for my own good. You'll hear all about it and the dreadful man I have married, and Katie's disappearance has come about just through that. You'll hear it. Oh my God! I can't stand much more, I just can't, not Mother tonight."

"Come on." Nell took her by the arm. "Come on and have a drink; that'll fortify you."

"Nothing can fortify me against my mother."

"Funny about mothers. Mine was a swine. I can say that now, a selfish swine. But there's Harry's mother and father next door, you couldn't find a more caring or nicer couple in the world. They're thoughtful, even loving. Yet Harry hasn't inherited any part of them, not that's noticeable. Although I say it, and only to you, life ain't all roses. The world owes Harry a living and Harry owes the world a grudge."

For a moment Fiona forgot her own trouble and said, "I wouldn't have thought so. He seemed so ... well, quite charming."

"Oh, yes, yes; that's the outward skin. But like all of us, he has a facade. I can only wish it was hiding a nature like his father's or his mother's. Anyway, what is it to be? Sherry? Gin and lime? A whisky?"

"Gin and lime, dear."

She didn't care for gin and lime, but she imagined it had a much more sustaining quality than sherry, and at this minute she needed sustaining.

*

79

It was only fifteen minutes later that the sitting-room door burst open and Mrs Vidler stared at her daughter sitting on the couch with another young woman . . . drinking.

Fiona was on her feet, gasping slightly. She needn't ask how her mother had got in, she had come by the back way, perhaps thinking she wouldn't be allowed in the front door.

"Well!"

"Yes, Mother, well!"

Mrs Vidler took four steps into the room and glared down on the glasses on the small table to the side of the couch; then lifted her gaze to the open drinks cabinet at the end of the room, before exclaiming in icy tones; "I can see how troubled you are that your child is missing. Disgraceful!"

"Be careful, Mother."

Nell now rose from the couch, saying quietly, "Your daughter was exhausted and distressed; she has only just sat down. . . .'

"Who are you, may I ask? And I don't need any explanation from a stranger with regard to my daughter's odd conduct, and I'll thank you to leave the room, as I wish to speak private-ly. . . .'

"I'll leave the room when Fiona says so and not until, and I'll thank you not to use that tone with me, or I'll consider it in-sulting and take the matter into my own hands. So I'll advise you to moderate not only your voice but your whole attitude."

At any other time Fiona would have almost cheered Nell's approach; it was so like Bill's would have been, only said in a more refined tone. But at the moment her emotions were very mixed, that of fear being dominant, and so, her voice low, she said quietly, "Mother, this is Mrs Paget, my neighbour. She has been of great help to me, and so I would ask you. . . ."

"Oh, and I haven't of course. That's what you are inferring, isn't it? Oh, I know you of old, oh I know you. . . ."

What happened next startled both Nell and Mrs Vidler, for Fiona, grabbing up the glass, threw it with force at the marble-framed fireplace and her scream mingled with the sound of the shattering glass: "Go! Get out! Leave me alone. Do you hear?" She took two steps towards her mother but how she would have followed up this action she never knew because Nell gripped her arms and, looking at Mrs Vidler, she cried, "You had better go, hadn't you?"

But Mrs Vidler did not immediately react except to gulp before having the last word: "She's drunk. Disgraceful!" Then she marched regally out.

Fiona, dropping onto the couch, burst into tears, and Nell, holding her, said to no one in particular, "By! I thought mine took some beating, but that one takes the cake."

It was nine o'clock. The children were in bed but only Mamie was asleep, the other two were wide awake, sitting up waiting, as she had been waiting seemingly for years. Bill had phoned her twice: first; to say the little girl who saw Katie get into the car thought the car was blue. Through her they had traced the other two girls. One said the car was black and the other said she thought it was dark green.

The second time he phoned he said the police had interviewed the men who had been sacked. Two of them hadn't cars. The third, a young fellow, owned a battered old mini with stickers plastered on it. And it was considered the children would surely have picked that one out. The other one had a grey Austin 13. His last words were, "I'll be home shortly. They say there's nothing much more thay can do tonight."

Following the second phone call, she had walked from the sitting-room to the dining-room, then into the study, back into the hall again and, finally, as she had already done numbers of times, ended up in the kitchen because there she could find something for her hands to do.

She had been alone for some time now as Nell, at her husband's suggestion, had gone home. She didn't care for Nell's husband and it wasn't because of what she had learned of him through Nell. Although his manner could be quite charming he was, she considered, a cold fish. And this evening he had seemed a little irritated that his wife should be more concerned with the loss of a neighbour's child than with his achieving the enviable job of clerk in an accountants' office, and the duties thereof.

She started to pray again with, "Oh, dear God! Oh, dear God!" only to stop abruptly as she reminded herself she had always condemned people who went to church in the last resort to beg for something. Why couldn't she just think positively, her child would be all right. But she couldn't think positively. When children were taken away, as Katie had been, they were never all right; even if they were found alive, it left a mark on them.

It was as if in panic that she rushed out of the kitchen and into the hall, there to see the front door opening. And with an audible cry she fell into Bill's arms.

"There now! There now! Stop it! Stop it! Stop it! You'll make yourself ill." He pressed her gently away, took off his hat and coat, then, once again holding her, led her into the sitting-room.

When seated, she didn't actually ask if there was any news, she just stared at him through her streaming eyes. And in answer he said, "They can do nothing until daylight. They'll be out at first light, the inspector said. And I've just come from the site. I've had to send Barney and four of the fellows home; they've been going out in relays. Tommy Turnbull and Dave McRae have never been home. So, everything that can be done has been done, at least for tonight."

He turned from her, lay back against the head of the couch and, gripping his hair with both hands as if intending to pull it out, he said, "And I made all that fuss about that damn scent. And the last thing I said to her this mornin' was, 'I'm going to keep it out of your pocket-money, miss. Forty-nine quid you've got to pay me for that bottle,' and she said, 'Well, there's still some left, it wasn't all spilt.' Oh, God Almighty!" He leant forward now and, his hands between his knees, he rocked himself and groaned, "Forty-nine quid. I'd sell me all down to the last penny and buy a scent factory if she was only up above at this minute."

It was her turn to comfort now. Putting her arms about him, she murmured, "She loved you. I . . . I can tell you she never showed the same affection for her father. She worshipped you."

"Don't say it like that" – he almost pushed her from him – "as if she was gone, dead. Oh, I'm sorry, love." He pulled her to him again. "Look" – he rose abruptly to his feet – "what I think we must do is have a bath, then get a couple of hours sleep. That's if we can. We'll put the alarm on for five. And if we've never prayed afore, we'll pray the night."

11

❧

It was on the eight o'clock news; it was on the nine o'clock news; and in an interview on the one o'clock news the inspector had said that he felt the search must now go beyond the town, for although it was being assumed the kidnapper knew the child, he must have driven her away. He also stated that a number of men had already been questioned and premises searched.

Bill had called into the house and so heard this latest news but he made no comment, except to say, "I'll be away; I'll keep in touch."

"Mr Bill."

"Yes, Mark?"

"Can . . . can I come with you? I . . . I can look."

"I'm sure you could, laddie, but there's a lot lookin'." You stay and look after your mother, eh, and these two?" He patted Willie and Mamie on the head, and the children remained silent and watched him as he walked from the room followed by Fiona.

At the door she said, "Where are you going now?"

"To the bank. It's pay-day and I'll get it over early on because some of the lads are coming out with me over towards. . . ." He didn't finish but put his hand out and patted her shoulder as he turned away, pulled on his coat and cap and went out. But he was only half-way down the drive when he turned and, almost at a run, he came back as she was closing the door and, pulling her into his arms, he said, "Look, love; I'm not being off-hand but I'm just near breakin' point. We both are, I know. I've . . . I've never felt so womanish in me life 'cos I just want to sit down and howl me bloody eyes out."

"I understand, dear, so don't worry about me, please. That's the last thing you need do."

He kissed her, then again made his way down the drive.

At the bank he drew out enough money to meet the wages and what was needed for his own requirements. But here he found he was again on the verge of breaking down because everyone was so sympathetic. Another time he would have laughed at the idea of the manager walking with him to the door and opening it for him.

When he arrived at the site Barney looked at him and he looked at Barney but said nothing; and after a moment Barney said, "You want to get away, don't you? Will I call them up?"

"Aye, do that."

He went into the hut and, sitting down at his desk, opened his big leather bag and lifted out an assortment of notes and silver. Then he drew towards him the ledger and a small stack of pay slips and envelopes.

Checking the slips against the ledger he put money into named envelopes. He came to the name, T. Callacter. After staring at it he went to the door from where he could see the men emerging from different parts of the building and, seeing Barney talking to one of them, he shouted, "Here a minute!"

Back in the hut he pointed to the name, saying, "He was cleared on Wednesday."

"Aye, boss, I thought so an' all at the time I made the slip out. It's my fault: twice he did an hour's overtime and I never booked it. I'm sorry."

"Why didn't he ask for it on Wednesday?"

"He said he didn't notice it until he got home, and that when he did he thought, Oh, to hell. But I think he's a bit tight now for cash. Anyway, he said he'd left some tools here kicking around and wanted to pick them up. But as I said, it's my fault, he's due for that."

"He didn't seem short of a penny from the place he lives in."

"Aye, it's a biggish house but it's dropping to bits. It used to be a farm. His dad ran it. But it's gone to pieces, I understand, since he died. From what I can gather he and his dad didn't get on. He used to live on his own but after the old fellow dropped down dead – and he wasn't all that old either – he came into the place. But there was no money to keep it up and as far as I can gather it was mortgaged to the hilt. I got all this from Morris. He lives quite near him. He tells me he's a queer fish and says he doesn't know if he's just gay or glad."

At another time Bill would have let out a laugh, but now he

said, "What the hell are we bothering about him for? Let them in."

The hut was a long one and Bill's desk was at one end of it. Eight men came in, stood in a line and received their pay, but with no back-chat today. Then some of them went out and so made room for the rest. The last one to reach the desk was Thomas Callacter. He was dressed, not as the others, but in a good quality black overcoat and a trilby hat, and he was carrying a small leather bag with an open top, showing a number of tools. And when Bill's gaze was drawn on them, the man said, "They're mine, Would you like to examine them?"

"I'll take your word for it."

"*Thank you.*" The words were stressed and caused Bill's jaws to stiffen. Picking up the small envelope from the table, he held it out and as the man leant forward to take it from his hand, Bill's nostrils stretched, his eyes widened, and his mouth dropped into a gape for a moment. Then his two hands springing out like an animal's claws, he gripped the lapels of the dark coat and pulled the man more than half-way across the desk and, like an animal, he sniffed at it. Then the cry that escaped his wide open mouth startled the remainder of the men who were in the hut. And they couldn't believe their eyes when they saw their boss grasp the man by the throat, then drag him round the side of the table, the while screaming, "Where is she? Where is she?" and then begin to rain blows on the man who retaliated with both fist and feet.

"Hells bells! What's up with you?"

"Give over!"

"God's sake! stop it, boss."

"Come on! Come on, boss! Let up! What's he done anyway?"

The clamouring appeals came from the men trying to separate them, for by now Bill had his fingers on the fellow's throat and they were both writhing on the ground.

The commotion had brought other men from the yard and the hut was now a mass of workmen, some holding Bill and some the man who had worked with them not so long ago.

"*It's him. It's him.*" Bill's voice was a choking scream.

"Give over, boss. Give over."

"Let me go, blast you! I tell you it's him; he's got her."

It was evident from the looks exchanged between the men

that they thought the boss had flipped, and they looked with something like pity on the man who was still struggling to breathe evenly and whose lip was bleeding and one eye almost closed. But their attention was once again drawn to their boss when he shouted to Barney, "The scent! Barney. I told you about the scent and the bairn spillin' it all over her. It stank. It stank, I tell you. And his coat, smell it! Smell his coat."

There was silence in the room except for the heavy breathing of all of them. Then Barney took three steps forward and as he went to bend his head to smell the man's coat, the fellow's foot came out and only just missed Barney's groin. But now Barney had him in his grip, not by the throat but by the lapels of his coat and he sniffed at it. Then still holding him he turned his head towards his boss, saying, "You're right. You're right, Bill; it's scenty."

"Some fellas use scent." The voice came from one of the men. And another said, "Aye; it could be deodorant."

"Leave go of me. It's all right; just leave go of me." Bill looked from one side to the other, then down at the hands that held him and slowly the men released their grip on him. And looking at them, he said, "My kid spilt a big bottle of Chanel scent over her school coat. It was saturated; the house stank. It's . . . it's an expensive scent. I had it in me nostrils, couldn't get rid of it, and it's on his coat. She was wearing her school coat when she disappeared."

One of them now looking at Callacter demanded of him, "Well, what have you got to say to that?"

And the man, who seemed to be foaming at the mouth now, said, "Big shot. Come up from the gutter. Scum. All he can do is bawl. . . ."

The arms were on Bill again, and Barney was entreating him: "Steady, Bill. Steady. Let him go on."

Callacter went on, the while rubbing his throat: "Marrying a lass young enough to be your daughter. Playing the big daddy to her kids."

"Shut your mouth or I'll shut it for you." Bert Ormesby was stepping forward now, which was surprising, for he was the churchman who neither drank nor smoked. And his threat was followed by someone else saying, "And I'll help you."

Bill now shrugged off the hand and picked up the phone without ever taking his eyes off the man. And when he got through to the station he said, "Bailey here. Is the inspector there?" And the voice answered, "No, sir, he's out."

"Well, get in touch with him and tell him we've got the man. Tell him we're at the buildings. We'll wait for him here."

"You'll never find her until she's rotten." It was a scream, and when Bill's hand sprang to a heavy steel paperweight on the table, Barney McGuire and Harry Newton, as if of one mind, each took a hold of him and almost dragged him through the press of men and into the yard. And there they talked to him and at him until ten minutes later the inspector's car, followed by two others, came into the yard.

Slowly, as if he was finding difficulty in forming the words, Bill explained to them what had happened. When he had finished the inspector said, "There's barns there, but the men went right through them."

It was when one of the sergeants said, "But he may not have left her there," that Bill turned his eyes on him and the man returned his look for a moment, then looked away.

It was half an hour later and they had searched the barns and all they had discovered were some of the window-frames and doors and floorboards that had been missing from Bill's stock. The rest had evidently been sold. Bill had not been with the police when they first went through the place or he would have recognised his own materials then.

The house was an old one, with steps, some going up, others going down leading into the different rooms and after searching it from top to bottom, the police and Bill were now standing in the yard once more. Suddenly, the inspector turned from Bill and went to the car where Callacter was being held and, bending down to him, said, "It's no good, you know we'll find her, so you might as well tell us now."

"I know nothing about it."

"I understand you've already made the statement that the child would be rotten when we came across her."

"I just said that to get one back on him. He's a big mouth, no education, nothing. He's a lout and I've always hated his kind."

87

"That's as maybe, and your opinion, but you'll help yourself if you tell us where the child is."

The man now sat back into the corner of the car and there was a sneer on his face as he again said, "I know nothing about it."

Returning to Bill, the inspector said, "I don't think we'll get any further here."

"*She's here.*"

"Well, we've searched, Mr Bailey."

"I've got a feeling that she's here; I know it somehow. I want to go through the house again."

The inspector sighed, then said, "Just as you say, Mr Bailey. Sergeant." He beckoned the sergeant towards him and he in turn beckoned a young policeman, and again they entered the house.

"Where do you want to begin, sir?"

"Upstairs somewhere, near the lumber room."

"That's at the end of the house."

"Yes, at the end of the house."

They went into the lumber room. And it was a lumber room: there were a number of broken chairs, an old sideboard, two tables that had evidently been in a fire, some large empty boxes and a pair of steps. Just as they had done before they moved everything and examined the floor boards. They next went into a back room. It had one small window, and two of its walls were obviously cavity ones, but showing no sign of having been cut into.

Then they were standing in the bathroom. This must once have been a small bedroom. The fittings were old and dirty. The inspector looked at the sergeant, raised his eyebrows and was on the point of going out when Bill glanced up towards a trap-door in the ceiling. Then he stared at it, his head back on his shoulders, his eyes fixed tight on it, and he said slowly, "That's been moved recently."

The inspector followed his gaze, saying quietly, "It's hardly big enough to get through."

"Somebody gets through; there'll be a tank cupboard up there. . . . There were steps in that lumber room."

"You'll never get through there, sir."

Bill turned and looked at the young sergeant and said, "Maybe not, but he could."

The young policeman now glanced at his superior, and the inspector said, "Bring the steps."

The steps had four rungs and a flat platform, and when the young policeman stood with knees bent on the top, Bill said, "I don't know how long it could be since the wiring's been done there but once you lift the trap up you might find a switch. Grope round and see if there is one."

"I have a torch, sir." The young man patted his pocket.

They watched him push up the trap-door; they watched his shoulders moving as his hand groped around the side of the open space; and then there was a click and the dark hole was illuminated.

The policeman looked down towards them for a moment before hoisting himself through the hole. They waited, their heads back on their shoulders as they listened to the sound of his steps overhead; then his voice came muffled, saying, "There's nothing up here except two tanks." Then again the sound of his footsteps and his voice once more: "And there's nothing in the tanks except water." ... The next words that came were faint but sounded like, "Eeh! God!" And they all had hold of the steps when his face appeared above the hole. It looked whiter than the light around it and he brought out on a stuttering gaggle, "Sh ... she ... she's here, be ... be ... behind the tank ... trussed."

As if he had been shot, Bill was now standing on the top of the steps, but when he attempted to get through the hole his shoulders stuck. And it was the sergeant who said tersely, "Take off your coats, sir."

The next instant both his overcoat and jacket were thrown to the floor; and then he was squeezing himself through the aperture.

He had to bend double to get behind the tank, and what he saw brought his mouth wide and his eyes almost lost in the contortion of his face, for there was the child. She was lying on her side: her arms were tied behind her back, her ankles were also tied with a leather belt, and in her mouth was a gag held in place by a piece of cord tied round her face. Because of the sloping roof he could not lift her up from the position he was in, and so he pulled her gently towards him; and then she was in his arms and he was staring down onto her closed eyes.

His head went to her breast, and when he felt the soft beat of

89

her heart it was as if his own had come back to life. There was no way he could untie her here and so, bent double, he passed her through the hatch into the arms of the sergeant. And seconds later he was kneeling beside her on the floor tearing the gag from her mouth while the inspector undid the strap on her legs. But when it came to freeing her arms it was the sergeant who said, "Don't try to bring them forward yet, sir, they'll be in cramp, just rub them gently."

And this is what they did, the inspector at one side, the sergeant at the other, while he held her slight body and longed to cry his relief while at the same time the desire to murder the man who had done this to a child gathered pace. . . .

When they reached the yard Bill had his jacket on, but Katie was wrapped in his overcoat. And at the car in which Callacter was sitting, he stopped just long enough to bend and looked into the man's face and growl, "I'll get you! By God! if it's the last thing I do, I'll get you."

"Come along, sir." The inspector touched his arm and drew him away, saying quietly, "He'll get his deserts, never fear."

"Aye. Ten years; time off for good behaviour and come out and do the same again. I tell you, I'll. . . ."

"Sir" – the inspector's voice was firm – "be thankful you've got her in time." And he added, "She must go straight to hospital."

"What! She'll be better at home."

"The doctor will have to ascertain if everything's all right with her, and she seems to be in an unnatural sleep. The sergeant has already got through." He motioned back with his finger. "They'll be expecting us. You understand?"

Bill let out a long deep breath, then nodded. He understood.

The sergeant had taken over the wheel of Bill's car, and he was about to take his place beside him when he turned to the inspector once again and said, "Will it be possible to inform my wife?"

"Yes, we'll do that, sir. I'll get on to the station and they'll do that straightaway. Don't worry any more. But let's get her into bed." He smiled gently, then closed the door; and they drove off.

12

After last night, Fiona naturally did not expect to see her mother again, at least for some time, but here she was and unbelievably still in fighting form, albeit quietly so.

"You've never known any luck since you got entangled with that person," she said.

What was she going to do? She couldn't tackle her; she was so tired. Oh, Katie. Katie.

But as if it were in another's voice, she was saying, "He is not that person, he is my husband, Mother. Please don't forget that. As for luck, I hadn't much luck before."

"Well, no matter how ineffectual Ray was he was a gentleman."

"Oh, that's news to me. I always understood that you saw him as a worthless, freelance journalist, who couldn't look after his wife and family and left them penniless; even the roof over our heads was your suggestion because he was so useless he wouldn't have thought about it."

"You're exaggerating as usual."

"I can tell you this much, Mother, you never have nor ever will meet a man as good as and caring as Bill and who is my kind of gentleman."

"Good and caring, you say, when your daughter. . . ."

"Mother!" Her voice was a scream now. "How could Bill help that? Don't be such a fool."

"Calm yourself, girl; we want no more hysterics like last night, and I'll overlook the fact of your speaking to me as you do because you're in a state; but, in a way, it's only to be expected that you now feel remorse for you've been so besotted with that man that your children have come to mean little to you."

She was choking: she had the greatest desire to do what Bill had done recently, go for her, grab her by the throat and shake her like a rat. But what she said now from behind her clenched teeth was, "If I've no love for my children I'm following your pattern, Mother, because you never liked children, you never wanted children, you didn't want me. The only love I ever had in my childhood was from my father. And when you were fighting your refined fights in the bedroom you told him once you had been forced to have me, but never again. So don't talk to me of loving children. You've never loved my children; in fact, you don't like them. You're incapable of loving but not incapable of jealousy; jealous that I had three, and loved them; and now you are jealous that I have Bill because, let's face it, you wanted him for yourself. And why you hate him is because he showed you up as a middle-aged or old middle-aged woman."

She shouldn't be saying this. She didn't care a scrap what her mother thought of the children; all that was consuming her at that moment was the loss of her daughter. So why was she talking like this? Why was she bothering? She was so tired, so tired. She wanted to drop down and sleep but her eyes wouldn't close; they were staring as if into her brain, looking at the pictures there that presented the different ways her daughter could have died. . . . But her mother was talking again. What was she saying? She had become deaf to her voice for the moment. She was saying: "You have become utterly vulgarised by that individual, and it's a sort of comfort to you to imagine that other people might have wanted him and are jealous of you. But let me tell you, Fiona, I would never have demeaned myself to allow a man like that even to touch me. There is such a thing as dignity and you are utterly without it. What you have said doesn't upset me, it only makes me sorry for you and pity you that you are so in need of a man that you had to take that ignorant, brash, loud-mouthed individual."

Fiona did not see her mother leave the room, for she was leaning against the mantelpiece trying to stop herself from passing out. She had never fainted in her life, but she knew she was near to it now. And as she gripped the mantelpiece, endeavouring to steady herself, she asked if there was any one in the world who had a mother like hers. Other mothers, she imagined, would be comforting their daughters, or would be upstairs in the playroom assuring the children that Katie would come back.

When the phone rang she had to pull herself from the support of the mantelpiece and her hand was trembling when she lifted the mouthpiece.

"Mrs Bailey? I . . . I have news for your. Your daughter has been found."

Her head drooped forward onto her chest, then jerked up again as she stammered, "All . . . all . . . I mean, is she . . .?"

"As far as I can gather she is all right. Your husband is with her. She has been taken to the General."

"Tha . . . thank you. Oh, thank you. Thank you." She rammed the phone down; then, as if imbued with new life, she sprang up the stairs, thrust open the playroom door where Mark was sitting looking out of the window, Willie curled up in the corner of the couch and Mamie doodling with some blocks on the low table.

"She's found! She's found! They've got her!"

They were all hanging on to her at once, all gabbling: "Oh, where? Where?"

"Is she all right, Mam?"

"Katie coming back?"

She lifted Mamie up into her arms and, hugging her, she said, "Yes, yes, she's coming back. She's coming back. Don't cry. Don't cry." She put the child down, then put her arms around the three of them now and pulled them towards the old couch. And speaking directly to Mark, she said, "You'll see to things, won't you? Nell's had to go into Newcastle, but I'll ask Mrs Paget to come in and give an eye to you."

"No need, Mam; there's no need." The boy moved his head from side to side. "I can see to things. They'll both stay up here" – he thrust his finger from one to the other – "and I'll answer the phone. And I won't open the door to anyone except I know them. So please don't worry."

Gently she touched his cheek, saying now, "No, I needn't worry when you're in charge. So I'll go now, but I'm sure I won't be long."

"And you'll bring Katie back?"

She looked down on Willie, saying, "Yes, yes, I'll bring her back."

"I'm going to give her my Ching Lang Loo book."

"Oh, she'll love that, Willie. She always liked to read your Ching Lang Loo book."

The small fair-haired boy nodded at her, then said solemnly, "And not for a lend; she can have it for keeps."

"That's very kind of you, Willie. I'll tell her." She smiled down at them, then hurried out, and into her bedroom, where she grabbed up a coat; but then, about to leave her room, she stopped at the door and, looking upwards and very like a child, she said, "Thank you."

13

ᏧᎤᏧᎤ

It was three days later and Katie was still in hospital: the doctors'
reports were that she hadn't been interfered with but that she
was still in a form of shock, so much so that as yet she hadn't
spoken a word.

The police had ascertained from their questioning of Callacter
that he had given her strong sleeping tablets, solely because she
had been kicking her heels against the tanks. And the local papers
had run headlines suggesting that he had abducted the child to
get his own back on her stepfather because he had bawled at
him about his work, and then questioned whether the man would
have let the child die up in that tank room, for he showed no
remorse. One newspaper headlined the case: "SCENT TRAIL
FATHER RECOGNISES KIDNAPPER THROUGH
PERFUME SMELL."

Now, three days having passed, the headlines had changed;
and there were no more reporters coming to the house or waiting
outside the hospital for them. The only reference to the affair
today was in a small paragraph at the bottom of the middle page
which said, "Kidnapped child still unable to speak".

Bill and Fiona were now talking with the doctor, and it was
Bill who said, "Once she's back home with her brothers and
sisters she'll have more chance of coming to."

"Yes, perhaps you're right; but she'll still need careful attention."

"Oh, she'll get that." Bill pursed his lips in confirmation, then
asked rather tentatively, "How long does this state generally
last?"

The doctor looked down at the pad on his desk; "There's no
knowing," he said.

"You mean, it could be permanent?" Fiona's voice was small.

"As I said, there's no knowing. She's had an awful shock. I

won't say another kind of shock could bring her speech back, but love and contentment which, summed up, means living in a happy atmosphere could work wonders. But there's no guarantee. Subconsciously she feels that if she talks she will create the experience again. Anyway" – he rose to his feet – "you may take her home. I'll get in touch with your local man and he'll pop in on and off for the time being to see how she's doing."

They didn't thank him but they looked at him and he at them, and he smiled.

It was the evening of the same day. Katie had been home for some hours. She had been greeted joyously by the three children; she had then been put into bed in her own room which was bright with her toys and fresh flowers. She had eaten a light meal but she had neither smiled nor spoken.

Willie, the potential actor who already had a sense of timing, had left the presentation of his rag book to a period in the evening when there seemed to be a pause. Leaving his mother and Bill and Mark and Mamie in the bedroom, he went out, and returned bearing in his hands the Ching Lang Loo book, the pages of which were made of rough-edged linen with a poem written on one side and a picture depicting it on the facing page. There were twenty-six poems in all, and the first poem carried the title.

Advancing slowly towards the bed, Willie placed the quite weighty tome on the counterpane while looking at Katie and saying, "It's for keeps, me Ching Lang Loo book."

There was silence in the room. All eyes were turned on the little girl in the bed who seemed, in a way, to have shrunk during her short absence. They watched her look down on the book, then put her hand on it and stroke its rough cover, then lift her hand and put it out towards Willie. And they watched him grab it, then take a big breath before bursting into tears and turning to fling himself against Bill's knee.

"There now. There now. She's pleased with it. Be quiet now. Be quiet."

"What?" Bill bent his head towards the mouth that was dribbling now, and what he heard was, "She . . . she didn't laugh."

"No, no; but she will." And Bill now looked up towards the bed where Mark was standing gulping in his throat and he said loudly, "Come on, Mark, do us Ching Lang Loo." And when Mark muttered, "No, you do it," Bill cried, "Oh, I can't do Ching Lang Loo like you, McGinty is my piece."

"Come on, Mark." Fiona's voice brought the boy close to the bed and, looking down on Katie, he said, "Would you like me to do Ching, Katie?"

His sister looked at him. Her eyes blinked but she didn't speak. He now glanced towards his mother, and when she nodded he picked up the book, and it was evident he had to force himself to take the pose of a small sea captain. However, he did so and went into the poem. His voice taking on a pseudo deep note, he began:

I said to Ching Lang Loo today,
What shall we do, O' mate?
He said, We'll board a windjammer
And feel the fresh sea spate.

Leav'ee it to me, captain, said Ching,
And I will take you where the waves sing
And the breakers, with rolls and tosses,
Gallup upon their pure white hosses.

We'll stand firm upon the rolling decks,
With coloured hankies round our necks;
And we'll shout: Ahoy! there. Sails away!
Full tilt, my brave lads, for Biscay Bay!

And dipping down then rising again,
We plough our way through the mighty main;
Our hair standing straight with wind and spate,
We tear along at a mighty rate.

Then far, far in the distance we spy
A ship that looks like a little fly,
Until we look through BIN . . . OCK . . . U . . . LERS. . . .
Why! She's a pirate. . . . After her! sirs,

Ahoy, there! you shipmates, east by northeast;
We are right on her heels, the nasty beast.
After her, lads, and into her hold,
For she's bound to have treasures untold.

If she has *Oranges*, and *Lemons* too,
Won't the galley cook be pleased with you,
Said my brave Chinese mate, Ching Lang Loo.

With the exception of Katie they all laughed and clapped; then they looked at the white-faced, big-eyed child staring at Mark. They watched her hold her hands out for the book, and when Mark placed it on her upturned palms, she brought it to her small chest and hugged it; then sliding down in the bed she lay back as if meaning to go to sleep. And at this Fiona made a signal for them all to say good-night, and in turn the children kissed her and hugged her. Then Bill, leading Fiona to the door, said, "See them off, then get yourself to bed; you're all in."

"Not half as much as you are."

"I'm all right. I'll arrange the bedchair by her side. We must find out how she reacts in the night, and you don't want her to wake up and find herself alone here, do you?'

"Oh, Bill.'

"Now, now, stop it. We've got her back, and by hook or by crook she'll talk. Being Katie she'll talk . . . you've got to believe this, woman." He gripped her shoulders. "We've all got to believe it."

He kissed her now and pushed her out of the room, and when he returned to the seat by the bed Katie looked at him and held out her hand, and he sat down and took it in his. . . .

At two o'clock in the morning when Fiona gently opened the door she saw them both still hand in hand fast asleep.

14

❦

It was a fortnight later. Katie was up and to outward appearance
had apparently returned to normal but as yet she hadn't spoken
a word and except for the movement of her upper lip she hadn't
really smiled, nor had she played with toys, the only thing she
seemed to want was the clouty book. And although she seemed
to read the poems for herself, each evening she would push the
book into either Mark's or Bill's hands and listen to them reading
and acting the rhymes; but their antics never elicited any laughter
from her.

During the first week too, Fiona and Bill had taken turns of
sleeping by her side in the chairbed, but she'd had no nightmares.
So now they were in bed together and Fiona was asking, "Who
do you think gave them the story about the scent and the school
concert?"

"Oh, likely one of the lads."

"It'll certainly be a good advert for Chanel . . . 'Kidnapped
Child Saved By Chanel Scent'."

"Well, they deserve it all because that was what she was saved
by. He must have held her close to him; likely she was struggling.
And that school coat, as you know, was soaked with it. She
swanked, didn't she, about going to school in a scenty coat?"
Then his mind jumping ahead, he said, "His case comes up in
three weeks time. God!" Then grinding his teeth, he said,
"They'll likely give him life, so I'll have a long time to wait to
get at him."

"Don't! Don't!" Fiona beat against his shoulder with her
clenched fist. "Don't carry that hate with you over the years.
We've got her back, so be thankful."

"Yes, we've got her back, a dumb child, whereas, before, she
lived to talk, didn't she?"

"Well, she will again."

99

He turned from her and looked up at the ceiling, then said, "I had an idea today. I don't know whether it will work. You know the Chinese restaurant in the market place?"

"There are two about there."

"Chang's House, the posh one."

"I know it, but I've never been inside."

"Well, I used to eat there often before I came under your indifferent cooking." He slanted his eyes towards her and she said, "Yes, go on: before you came under my indifferent cooking."

"Well, as I said, I have an idea."

"Well, what is the idea?"

"Oh, I'd better keep it till tomorrow night as you mightn't see eye to eye with me."

"Don't be so infuriating, Bill."

"Well, I'll tell you this: I want to buy something from him but I don't know whether I'll have enough money to do it, that's speaking metaphorically." He now took his heel and kicked her leg gently as he said, "That's another big one. Surprise you, did it? All right. All right. Well, what I mean is, I've got enough money really to buy his business, that's if I sold mine, but there are things people put value on and no money can buy them."

"Well, what is it?"

"It's a Chinaman."

"A Chinaman?"

"Yes, dear, a Chinaman. Now that's all I'm going to tell you. I'm going to sleep; I'm very tired and I don't want you to disturb me or make love to me because I've got a headache." Turning swiftly, he pulled her into his arms and all she could say was, "Oh, you! You!"

Nell had picked up Mark and Willie from school. It was a new arrangement because Fiona felt she couldn't leave Katie because Katie couldn't leave her: she followed her wherever she went, even to the toilet, which proved that the fear was still rampant in her, and she always wanted her hand to be held.

The doctor had called earlier in the day and suggested that the child be taken for psychiatric treatment. Even the word sounded ominous. What was more, she had become puzzled all day about the Chinaman that was coming. What did Bill expect her to do with a Chinaman? Did he mean her to take him on as a kind of daily help? Likely it was a Chinese boy or young man he meant. She had nothing against Chinamen, they were always so very polite, but she didn't know how she was going to go on with one in the house even for a few hours a day. She wished he was home, and that she knew what he was up to; whatever it was, he was thinking of Katie. . . .

Bill was a little late in arriving home. It was close on six o'clock. Nell had just taken the children up to the playroom and she herself was on the point of leaving the kitchen when the back door opened, and there he was by himself, no Chinaman, except he was carrying a very long box. It was all of four foot.

"What's that?"

"Wait and see. Here, hold it." He put it into her arms, and she was surprised it wasn't as heavy as it looked. He pulled off his hat and coat, then took the box from her, saying, "Come on. Where are they, in the sitting-room?"

"No, in the playroom, with Nell."

"Good." He bounded up the stairs before her, burst open the door, crying, "Abaft there! shipmates." Mamie, jumping down from Nell's knee, ran to him, crying, "Uncle Bill. A present for me?"

"No, not for you, dear, not for you." He wagged his finger at her. "And not for you." He pointed to Willie. Then to Mark, "And not for you either. This is for who?"

The three children now looked towards the sofa, and one after the other they cried, "Katie!"

"Yes, this is special for Katie. Stand aside everybody." He thrust out his arm, and it accidentially pushed Nell back against the chair and she, joining in the chorus, said, "Yes, sir. Yes, sir. As you say, sir." And the children laughed.

Before whipping the paper from the long box he glanced at Fiona who was staring at him; then he looked fully at Katie and said quietly, "Who do you think I've got for you, Katie, eh? Who do you think I've got in here?" He patted the box.

She was sitting forward on the edge of the couch now; her eyes were wide but she said no word, nor did she smile.

Slowly now Bill lifted the lid and exposed a long colourful object. Then in standing upright he slowly drew it forth and there emerged a beautifully clothed Chinese figure, held upright by strings attached to wooden rods that Bill was now slowly manipulating. The figure was that of a Chinese boy with a long pigtail and dressed in a blue satin gown with an orange sash and black calf shoes. When the arms were lifted it looked as if the gown had wings. But what had been added to the figure's head was a pirate's scarf. They all stood spellbound as Bill awkwardly, yet definitely, moved the legs and so walked the Chinese pirate towards Katie. And as he did so he almost let go of the strings for the muscles of her face were moving upwards into a smile. And when he made the Chinaman bow to her she thrust out her arms and grabbed the puppet to her, and her mouth going into a gape and her small breast heaving, she brought out the words: "Ching . . . Lang . . . Loo."

The room was in an uproar; they were all crying now both verbally and tearfully.

"Ching Lang Loo. Yes, Katie, it's Ching Lang Loo." Bill was sitting on the couch beside her, holding both her and the puppet tightly in his arms.

"Mine?" The word was whispered as she looked up at him.

"Yes, love, yours, all yours."

Her mouth now opened and shut three times; then she swallowed before she said, "Mr Bill."

"Aw, lass. Aw hinny."

Bill knew there was something about to happen to him and that he must do something quick to prevent it, and so, pulling her upwards, he shouted to Nell, "Put her on a chair Nell, and get her to work him." Then thrusting the puppet into Nell's hand, he hurried from the room, and Fiona after him and into their bedroom. And there, dropping on to the dressing-table stool, he covered his face with his hands and let the tears flow, and as she held him, her tears joined his; and after a while he turned his head from her, saying, "Bloody fool I am."

"And the best bloody fool in the world. And that's their sign, isn't it? It used to hang in the window sometimes, and someone worked it, and everybody used to stand and watch it. It's a beautiful thing. How on earth did you manage to persuade him to let you buy it?"

"I didn't."

"You didn't?" She moved away from him in a sort of horror, then said, "You didn't?"

"No, no, woman, I didn't." His voice sounded more like himself now. "Pinched the damn thing? No! of course not. But he wouldn't take a penny for it; he said he can get another one made quite easily. And what's more, he's invited us all to dinner. That'll save a bit." He grinned at her before again wiping his eyes and blowing his nose.

Smiling at him now through her own tears, she said, "What gave you the idea?" And to this he answered thoughtfully, "I don't know. I just don't know. The same thing I suppose that made me look up to the trap-door into that tank room. Funny that. D'you think I could be physic, or psychic?"

Her smile was soft as she said, "No, I don't think you could be physic or psychic, Mr Bill Bailey, only overflowing with love."

15

"I'd never thought I'd miss him so much."

"Well, it was your idea."

"Aye, I know it was. But you were for it, weren't you?"

"Yes; yes, of course, Bill, I was. And it's early days; we'll get used to it. And don't forget there's another three upstairs."

"Aye well; they're missin' him an' all, the kingpin's gone."

"Oh, Katie's taken over I think. She had a row with Willie in the car, so that's healthy."

"D'you think they're settling down in the new school?"

"Yes, I do. And it's different altogether; there's more personal attention. Yet they did very well at Beecham Road."

"Aye. But Beecham Road is a good mile and a half away whereas this place is practically on the doorstep, and no matter what time you turn up there's a teacher there with them."

"Bill."

"Yes, love?"

"This is going to cost a packet, not just this year but every year, three of them to pay for. Mamie's will come out of her trust, but. . . ."

"Look, woman; we've been into this. But, mind you—" he laughed now and pushed her in the shoulder as he said, "a thousand quid a term! When he said that I let out so much surprised air me trousers nearly dropped down."

She was laughing as she said, "Yes; and by the look on your face I was expecting them to. But I warned you before I went. Then there are the others. . . ."

"Well, they're two for the price of one really."

"Yes; but they are just day pupils; you've got to take that into consideration. And I told you what it would be. . . ."

"Look! who's grumbling, woman? Not me. I want to do it. And I'll go on doin' it. But I'm saying what these blokes and blokesses charge. And what about Katie's and Willie's Miss Widdle! Did you ever hear of a name like that? It asks to be called wet pants, doesn't it? And a private school at that, kids calling their headmistress, wet pants. I wonder if she knows."

"Very likely; they've got to be broad-minded."

"How long will it be before half-term?"

Fiona burst out laughing. "He's only been gone three days. It'll be some time in November."

"And we're still in September."

Fiona's voice now changed and she said softly, 'Look, if you think we've made a mistake we can always bring him nearer home; he can go into Newcastle as a weekly boarder and be home at the week-ends."

"No, no; we've made no mistake. What was good enough for Sir Charles Kingdom's sons is good enough for mine." They fell against each other and laughed. "That's what made me want to send Mark there, 'cos the elder one, Sir Percy went and Norman, the one that's in America on the films now, he was there an' all. And the old boy's a nice fella, no side."

"You know something, Bill Bailey?"

"What, Mrs Bailey?"

"You're a snob at bottom."

"Is that what I am? Oh, I'm so pleased; it's much better than being a brash ignorant slob. Of course slob and snob don't seem very far removed, do they? Oh! Who's that now?"

The phone bell was ringing, and Fiona went out into the hall and picked it up and heard Nell's voice saying, "Fiona?"

"Yes, Nell."

"Can . . . can I come round?"

"Nell, what a question to ask, of course you may come round."

"Well, you know how I feel about coming round at night when. . . ."

"Don't be silly. Get yourself round here. What's the matter anyway?"

"I'll tell you in a minute."

As she re-entered the room she said, "That was Nell. She asked if she could come round. She sounds as if there's something wrong."

"She asked if she could come round? Why? She doesn't usually ask."

"Well, if you were given to noticing anything, Mr Bailey, but the requirements of your stomach and how quick you can get upstairs and act the goat with that lot you would have noticed that she never comes in at night unless it is to baby-sit; she wants us to have time to ourselves."

"Oh that's thoughtful of her. But with regard to music lessons, they ain't actin' the goat."

"Music lessons I agree aren't acting the goat, but to my mind tin whistles don't come into that category."

"Well, it won't be tin whistles any longer, I've ordered flutes, three different sizes."

"You haven't! Oh, my God! Anyway, I wonder what's happened to bring Nell round."

"Well the quicker you let her in the quicker you'll find out. The back door's locked I suppose?"

"Yes, of course." Fiona now hurried from the room and through the hall and into the kitchen, and she was just opening the door when Nell appeared.

It was evident that she had been crying. But she didn't immediately say anything, only sat down at the kitchen table, joined her hands together and sat looking at them for a moment. And then she said, "Bill's in of course?"

"Yes. Yes, he's in the sitting-room. Come on in there, it's warmer."

"No, no."

"What's wrong?" Fiona drew a chair up close to her. "Had a row?"

"Huh!" Nell now jerked her head back and laughed, but it was a bitter sad laugh and, looking at Fiona, she said, "Do you know what it is to feel like dirt, of no consequence? No, you wouldn't, dear, no. You've had your mother to put up with but she's never rejected you, quite the reverse."

"What are you talking about? What's happened? Something to do with Harry?"

"Yes, something to do with Harry. He's gone."

"*Gone!* You mean, left you?"

"Just that. He's gone, he's left me. And he didn't even tell me to my face, he told his mother. She and Dad are in a state. After all, he's their son. But as Dad's just said, he's known for a long time he's bred something rotten. He hasn't been five minutes in that new job and he was supposed to be doing overtime. But Dad saw them out together and tackled him. . . ."

"He's gone off with someone then?"

"Yes, yes, Fiona, he's gone off with someone."

"Oh. Oh, I'm sorry."

"I'm sorry too." Nell put her hand out and gripped Fiona's. "I . . . I don't know where I am at the moment."

"But . . . but as you say, dear, he hasn't been five minutes in the job, he couldn't have known. . . ."

Nell was nodding her head now. "Oh, he was only five minutes in the job but he's known her, as far as I can gather, for some time, and she got him the job. I'm stupid and mental, besides being blind. But then I've told myself it's happening all the time, why should I be an exception to a man walking out on me? And that's another thing. When I get meself sorted out I know that I'll see it as just hurt pride because I haven't lost love; love flew out of our window many years ago. But he was there and I saw to his needs and life had become a pattern you get used to. . . ."

The kitchen door opened and Bill put his head round, saying, "Is there any room for a good-looking, interesting and successful man in his prime in here?"

"Stop fooling, Bill." Fiona's voice was flat.

"Trouble?" He came to the table and looked down at Nell, but Nell turned her head away and looked towards the window while Fiona said quietly, "It's Harry. He's walked out."

"No!"

Fiona and he now exchanged glances, and when she made a little motion with her head he said, "Bloody fool." Then taking Nell by the arm, he pulled her up from the chair saying, "Come on. What you need is a drink. And I repeat, he is a bloody fool, 'cos he doesn't know a good thing when he's on it. But I'll say this an' all: he wasn't worth you, not your little finger from what I can judge, and I'm no mean hand at that, at least where blokes are concerned. So come on, let's all get drunk,"

Nell resisted being pulled towards the door, saying now, "Thanks, Bill, but I must go back home; they're upset, upset for me. They're nice people, Bill. I can never understand why he was so different. I . . . I love them both, and . . . and she's been a mother to me. You understand?"

"Yes, lass. Yes, we understand. And the morrow night . . .

look, bring them in for a meal. How about it?" He now looked at Fiona, and she said, "Yes, that would be nice."

When the door closed on Nell they looked at each other; then they walked slowly side by side into the sitting-room again and, going straight to the drinks cabinet, he poured himself out a drink, saying, "You want one?"

"No thanks."

She watched him sip at his whisky before coming and sitting down beside her and saying abruptly, "How's she fixed?"

"You mean financially?"

"Aye, I mean financially. Can't you understand my language yet?"

"It's difficult at times, Mr Bailey." She pursed her lips. "But to answer your question in your own jargon, most of the time she's on the rocks. She hasn't said so much plainly, but I know she hasn't bought a new thing since she came here, and the fact that she doesn't like talking about clothes told me a lot."

"Well, we'll have to see to things, won't we? You could take her on in place of Mrs Thingumajig. I don't like her anyway. Twice I've come up with her and she's smelt of beer. Funny, but I don't like women who smell of beer or spirits. Now what d'you think of that?"

"I think you're a very odd man, Mr Bailey. But I don't know whether Nell would want to be a mother's help."

"She likes being here with the kids doesn't she, baby sitting? Anyway, you can tap her, see what she says. I'll make it worth her while."

"I know you will." Her voice was soft and she leant against him.

When the phone rang again she said, "What now?" then added, "No; stay where you are; you're an elderly man who needs his rest."

He gave her a not too gentle slap across the buttocks as she passed him and she was still holding the offending part when she picked up the phone.

"Hello, Mam."

"Oh, Mark. Mark." She turned her head to the side and actually yelled, "Bill! it's Mark. Where are you? I didn't think you'd be allowed to phone, I mean so early. Are you all right? Nothing the matter?"

There was a short silence before his voice came again, not very steady, saying, "I'm missing you all."

Her own voice dropped now. "Yes, yes, of course you are. And we are missing you, terribly, but. . . ."

The phone was snatched from her, and Bill, his voice hearty, now said, "Hello! there, boy."

"Hello, Mr Bill."

"How's things?"

"Oh, all right."

"You settling in?"

There was another pause before Mark's voice came: "Yes; yes, I am."

"I didn't think you'd be allowed to phone."

"Mr Leonard gave me leave. He's . . . he's my housemaster."

"That was nice of him. Well, stick it out, boy. Have you eaten all your tuck? Would you like another box?"

"We . . . we are only allowed one a month, you know."

"Oh, yes, yes, I forgot. Anyway, boy, here's your mam."

"Hello, darling. Oh, you'll never guess who are pouring down the stairs? Can you have a word with them?"

"My . . . my time is nearly up; I'll just say hello."

Bill had grabbed Mamie up in his arms; Willie and Katie had their hands on top of their mother's holding the phone and they both yelled together, "Hello, Mark. Hello, Mark."

His voice came back, saying, "Hello, Katie. Hello, Willie. Hello, Mamie. I've got to go now. Mam, Mr Bill. Be seeing you."

"Yes, darling."

She heard the click; then turning and looking at Bill, she swallowed deeply before saying, "Wasn't that nice? He must be a very understanding man, Mr Leonard. I . . . I didn't think they were allowed to phone, except under special emergencies. You don't think he's sort of pining?"

"No, no, no." He put Mamie down on the floor. Then, looking from one to the other of the children, he said, "Wasn't that fine, hearing him?"

It was Katie who answered first, saying, "It didn't sound like him." Then Willie, always to the point, muttered, "'Tisn't the same as him being here. Why can't he come home every night like us?" He looked from Bill to his mother, and it was for her to answer, "It's a different school, dear; they learn different things."

"We learn different things." Willie stared up at her. Then turning his gaze on Bill, he added, "He could learn different things here and save a lot of money and we could go on a holiday."

With this statement of fact he walked towards the stairs; and as usual Mamie followed him, but she was snivelling now. And after a moment spent looking to the side as if considering the matter, Katie said, "Anyway, it was nice hearing him." And then she too went upstairs.

In the sitting-room, Bill took another sip from his glass of whisky; then running his hand through his hair, he said, "The verdict of the family spoken by the now male head of the upstairs apartments." Then flopping down into the corner of the couch, he looked up at her, saying, "He could be right. What d'you think? Have I persuaded you into something that you really didn't want to do?"

"Oh, no, no. You're doing for him what I would never have been able to do and what his own father would never have done even if he had had the money. He was against private schools, in fact, schools of all kinds. I think he'd had a rough time himself. No, no"; and she moved her head from side to side as she said this; then, sitting down beside him, she took his hand in hers, saying quietly, "Anything you do for them, Bill, I know it's for the best."

After a moment he said on a laugh, "That Willie's a character, isn't he? He had thought it all out, even to the holiday. That's a point: we've never had a holiday; what with one thing and another. And when I come to think about it, Mrs B, you've never mentioned it."

"Well now, if I had, what would you have said? I know exactly what your answer would have been: What! Go on a holiday with that so and so Brown breathing down my neck? He's out to get me that fellow. It's a good job I've got old Kingdom-come on my side. That's exactly what you would have said, now isn't it?"

"No, Mrs Bailey, not exactly. You've missed out a number of adjectives such as" – he raised his hand now, palm upwards, almost blotting out her face – "I'll use the alternatives, budg-erigar Brown and blue pencil neck."

"Oh" – she thrust his hand away – "that's what I wanted to have out with you."

"Oh my God! What now?" He turned away and put a hand to his forehead, then sighed deeply as she said, "This is serious. You know what Master Willie came out with in the car coming home?"

"No. Tell me; I can stand it." He thumped his forehead.

"He was addressing his sister and called her a budgerigar bitch, and I nearly went into the back of the bus because it was a full-mouthed yelled retort."

"He didn't!" He was laughing at her.

"Bill, I'm serious." Her voice was a plea now. "It's a very nice school, as you know, and just imagine if he comes out with something like that.'

"Well, you can't blame me for the bitch, I never use that word. I know a lot of them but I never use it on them; with one exception, and you know who that is. As regards the other, who's going to translate budgerigar into bugger? Aw, come on, don't look so worried. Just think of poor old Nell next door. Now she has something to worry about."

"Yes, yes, you're right. It must be a terrible feeling that, to be rejected, just left without a word. . . . If you ever walked out on me, Bill. . . ."

Her shoulders were suddenly gripped and his face came within an inch of hers as he said, "Don't joke along those lines, Fiona; nothing could make me ever walk out on you. Nothing. Nothing. Do you hear? But I can tell you something and I mean this, as I meant what I've just said, if you ever decided to walk out on me you wouldn't last long, 'cos I'd shoot you, by God! I would, and the bugger you went with. And with him I'd aim for the place where it hurts most."

"Oh, Bill. Bill." She fell against him, her body shaking with laughter, and as she did so part of her mind was thanking God once again for bringing this man into the narrow household life she had led for years.

16

❧❧

The weeks sped by. Nell had gladly accepted the position of mother's help. Her husband had asked for a divorce and she had willingly conceded.

She and Fiona spent long coffee breaks talking about the past, the present, and the future. They had become very close during these weeks and Nell had expressed openly how grateful she was for the friendship and wondered what she would have done if they hadn't come to live next door. She had definitely become as one of the family, and the children were fond of her, as was Bill. But, as he stated bluntly, she was a tactful piece for she knew when to make herself scarce, which was in the evenings when he was at home and most of the week-end, except on a Saturday night when he would take Fiona out to dinner and she would baby-sit.

But now it was November 9th and the night when Mark was coming home for his first leave from school.

On Monday they'd had a little bonfire in the garden when they'd eaten baked potatoes and sausages on sticks. Mr and Mrs Paget and, of course, Nell had come in from next door, and such was the success of the evening that before it was half over Katie and Willie, agreeing for once, said they were keeping some of their fireworks back so they could have a repeat performance on Saturday night. And now the two of them, together with Mamie, were bursting with excitement because Mark would be home and they'd have some fun.

They had left the children at home in Nell's care as usual, and were now speeding towards the school. It was forty minutes run from Fellburn and situated in its own extensive grounds in which were a covered swimming pool and two Rugby pitches. The house itself was an imposing structure, though not as large as great country houses were apt to be and apparently not large enough to provide all the classrooms necessary, for to the left were three fabricated buildings which were used as classrooms. It was close on four o'clock when they arrived and the facade was lit up. The forecourt was busy with boys getting into cars and parents calling goodbye to other parents.

As they entered the hallway a senior boy stepped forward and, smiling at them, said, "Good-evening." And to this Bill answered, "Mr and Mrs Bailey."

"Oh, yes, yes." And the boy, nodding towards another standing some way back, said, "Take Mr and Mrs Bailey to Mr Leonard."

They followed the boy across the hall, along a corridor, up a flight of stairs, and along another corridor, at the end of which he tapped on a door, and when he was told to enter he stood aside to allow Fiona and Bill to pass him.

"How do you do?" Mr Leonard sounded very hearty. He shook hands with both of them; then addressing Fiona, he said, "I know you are dying to see your boy."

"Yes. Yes, I am . . . we all are. We've missed him so much."

"How's he been doing?"

Mr Leonard looked at Bill. "Oh, very, very well. He took a bit of time to settle in. It's all strange, you know, coming away from a good home into a madhouse composed only of boys" – he laughed heartily – "but as I said, he's settling in. He hasn't been very well this last week. Matron kept him in bed."

"He's not . . .?" Fiona began, and Bill put in, "He's ill? What's the matter with him? Why weren't we told?"

"Oh, it's nothing serious, just a cold. Anyway I'm sure you'd like to see him." He pressed a bell on his desk and was about to say something when Fiona asked, "How do you find his work?"

"Oh, well, varied, like most of them you know." He again laughed. "But he's very good on the maths and science side. He leans towards them, these subjects. History, art . . . well he's improving in that quarter."

"What about sport?"

The housemaster now looked at Bill, saying, "Well, truthfully he doesn't take too well to rugger. I think soccer was his favourite game. He's good at running, too. He came second in the last cross-country. Oh, he'll do nicely, never fear. And as for his character and disposition, I'm sure he must take after his parents."

His smile encompassed his face, but Bill's eyes narrowed as he stared at the man and said flatly, "I'm not his father."

"Oh. Yes, of course. Ah!" The exclamation came as the door opened; and there he was, a pale-faced boy who seemed to have grown inches during the last few weeks. He hesitated somewhat before approaching them; and then he seemed to have difficulty in saying, "Oh! Mam." He kept an arm's length from her but took her hands; then looking at Bill, he said simply, "Mr Bill."

"Hello, there." Bill put his hand on Mark's shouder, saying with forced heartiness, "By! you have sprouted. What have you been up to?" He checked himself from adding, "Standing in manure?" but said instead, "The gang won't recognise you. We left them, yelling their heads off; they can't wait to see you."

Bill watched the boy gulp in his throat, then smile a little as he said, "I can't wait to see them. It seems years."

"Well, now, if that's the case don't let's waste time." And Bill turned to the housemaster, saying, "We'll be off then."

"Yes, yes." Mr Leonard came and, bending his long length towards Mark, said, "Will you be all right, old chap?"

And Mark, looking into his face, said, "Yes, sir."

"That's it then, away with you."

There was more handshaking; and then they were outside on the drive, and Bill, turning to Fiona, said in an undertone, "Sit in the back with him."

This she did, and they'd hardly got out of the gate when Mark suddenly leant his head against Fiona's breast and put his arms around her waist; and she held him tightly to her, but neither of them spoke, nor did Bill who could see what was taking place through the mirror. . . .

It wasn't until they were home and Mark had been swamped with hugs and kisses from Katie and Mamie and none too gentle punches of affection from Willie, and the four of them had got through a fancy tea set out by Nell and were now up in the playroom that Bill, looking from Fiona to Nell, said quietly, "What d'you two think? I know what I think, everything in the garden isn't lovely at Swandale."

"He looks peaky."

"Yes, Nell, he looks peaky. Well, what about you?" Bill turned to Fiona, and she put the tray down on the draining board before turning towards them and saying, "I feel the same way as you do: he's changed, he's not chirpy any more. He used to cap everything you said; in fact, he was quite witty at times."

"Aye, yes, he was. But not any more seemingly; you've got to ask him a question before he speaks."

Nell walked over to the sink and, pushing Fiona gently with the back of her hand, said, "Leave those, I'll see to them. The both of you go up and have a game with them; that might loosen his tongue. Get him to read the Ching Lang Loo book again; he was really funny when he read and acted those rhymes."

"Aye, perhaps there's something in that." And Bill held out his hand to Fiona, saying, "Come on, woman." Then as he made for the door he looked back at Nell, saying, "Life never runs smoothly, does it?" And the answer was, "I wouldn't know, would I?"

Outside in the hall, Fiona said, "What a thing to say to Nell."

"Aye." Bill wrinkled His nose. "I suppose it was tactless. But she understands me by now."

They played games for two hours on that Friday night. On the Saturday morning they all went into Newcastle, shopping. In the afternoon they saw a Disney film and when they came out they had tea in a posh restaurant where, yet again, Katie remarked aloud, "On white table-cloths."

Later that evening they played more games, and after a great deal of coaxing Mark was persuaded to read something from Katie's Ching Lang Loo book while Katie manipulated the doll. But what they all noticed was, he just read it, he didn't act it:

> "McGinty is the gardener
>   And he sometimes swears;
>
>   Pongo is the poodle
>   With only half his hairs;
>   Father is the parson
>   Reading from a book,

Says I'll take some saving
  By
    Hook
      Or
        By
          Crook.

And there's also my chinese doll Ching Lang Loo
Who wants to be in
And says, 'How do you do?' "

They all clapped and laughed, with the exception of Willie who stated flatly, "You didn't do it properly. You didn't act them, not any of them."

But when Mark came back with a shadow of his old self, saying, "What do you want, blood?" Willie joined in the laughter.

By arrangement Fiona managed to get Katie, Willie, and Mamie to bed, and so left Mark with Bill. And Bill, diplomacy not being his strong point, came straight out with, "What's up with you, lad? Something wrong at that school?"

"No, no."

"Aw. come on. You're not yourself; somebody been gettin' at you?"

"Well—" Mark wagged his head now and in an off-hand manner said, "Everybody gets someone at them when they first go to school . . . any school. It's a recognised thing."

"What is a recognised thing?"

"Well . . . well, bullying."

"A lot of it there?"

"It . . . it goes on."

"Have you been bullied?"

"I've . . . I've had me share."

"And . . . and you found it bad, you couldn't stand up to it? Is that it?"

"*No, no; it isn't.* I did stand up to it, I did."

"All right, all right, boy, don't shout."

"I'm sorry, Mr Bill."

"Don't be sorry, lad. Have you made any friends?"

"Yes. Yes, two. Like me, new starters, Arthur Ryan and Hugo Fuller."

"Fuller? Hugo Fuller? Is that the Fuller who has the good tailor shop in the town?"

"Yes; that's his father."

"Oh, you're in good company. I might get a suit cheap." Bill grinned and Mark smiled, but a small tight smile.

There was silence between them for a moment before Bill asked quietly, "Is there anything you'd like to tell me, lad, on the side like, that you don't want your mother to know?"

There was another silence before Mark replied, "No. Nothing. I'll get used to it. I . . . I was homesick at first . . . very. I . . . I missed you all."

"And we missed you, lad. Well, if there's nothing seriously wrong, come on and get yourself to bed." He put his arm round the boy's shoulders and led him to the door and onto the landing, and there, pointing along it, he said, "Listen to them! Those two are separated by a wall and they are still going at it. Sometimes I wish Katie's tongue hadn't been loosened so much. Good-night, lad."

"Good-night, Mr Bill."

It was some three hours later. They had been in bed for more than half an hour. They had talked and loved, and now, their arms about each other, they were approaching sleep when both of them became aware of the door being opened and the small voice hissing, "Mam!"

Fiona was sitting stiffly up now, having switched on the side light, and, blinking at Katie and Willie approaching the bed, she muttered, "What on earth!"

"What's the matter?" Bill's voice was thick and gruff. "Got a pain? Why are you both up at this time?"

It was Katie who answered in a whisper. "Willie came into me. I was asleep. He woke me; he said Mark was crying."

"Crying?" Fiona swung her legs out of the bed and grabbed at her dressing gown, but Bill's hand stopped her from rising: "Wait a minute. Wait a minute," he said; then he was leaning across the bed, his face close to Willie, asking now, "Why . . . why was he crying?"

Willie not only wagged his head but his whole body as he said, "He'd punch me if I told you and Mam."

"Tell." Katie now dug her brother in the side with her thumb. "They've got to know."

"Well come on, spill it." Bill was now out of the bed and sitting on the edge holding Willie's hand, and Willie, looking up at him, said with a quivering lip, "It's his bum ... bottom." With the last translation he cast a glance up at his mother. And it was she who said, "What's wrong with his bottom?"

"It's all burnt ... and his leg."

"What!"

The word was so loud that Fiona said, 'Shh! Keep your voice down, Bill."

Bill now said, "Go on. What d'you mean, burnt?"

"Well, I was going into the bathroom and he was standing with his pyjamas down looking at his bottom in the glass, and it was all down one side ... burnt. And he said I hadn't to tell you, or else. They put a lighted firework down it, his trousers, on Guy Fawkes night."

"My God! God in heaven!" Bill was now on his feet and making for the door. He hadn't bothered to put on a dressing gown. And Fiona, following him, said, "What are you going to do?"

"What d'you think I'm going to do? I'm getting to the bottom of this."

"He'll hammer me."

Bill now turned towards Willie and in a more gentle voice, he said, "No, he won't, Willie. Don't you worry; you were right to go to Katie; and Katie was right to come to us. Now Katie" – he pointed at her – "you go back to bed. We'll tell you all about it in the morning. That's a good lass. And you, Willie, come on and get into bed an' all and under the clothes and pretend you're asleep."

"I can never pretend I'm asleep, Mr Bill." This was a whispered comment, and Bill, bending down on him, hissed, "There's always a first time. Now go on in ahead. Don't let him hear you."

He now stood looking towards Fiona who was pressing Katie before her into the bedroom; and when she returned he said to her, "It's no use hanging on till the mornin' to get to the bottom of this, his defences will be up again, so come on."

One thing was immediately evident as they stood by Mark's bed, and that was he, unlike his brother, could feign being asleep.

"Mark." Fiona's voice was soft. "Come along, you're not asleep, sit up. Now don't worry. Come along, sit up. We know all about it. I'm going to put the light on."

"No, don't, Mam. No, don't."

Fiona switched the light on to reveal the tear-stained face of her son. And it was Bill who said, "Turn over."

"No, Mr Bill."

With one movement Bill stripped the clothes down the bed; then gently he lifted the boy up and turned him onto his face. But when he went to pull down Mark's pyjamas he found them fastened, and he motioned to Fiona, saying, "Untie them."

Fiona now put her arms around her son's waist, untied the cord of his pyjamas and gently pulled them over his buttocks. Then both she and Bill stood staring down in disbelief at what they were seeing, for there, on his left buttock, was evidence of a bad burn about four inches long and three inches wide, and, like drips from a candle, smaller ones linked up half-way down his thigh.

A muttered blasphemy from Bill broke the silence; but such were Fiona's feelings at the moment that she made no comment on it; instead, throwing herself on the bed, she laid her head on the pillow near that of her son. And when his arms came around her neck she held him close to her; but she was unable to speak any words of comfort: her throat was full, her whole body was full of rage and indignation. And it was Bill who voiced her exact thoughts when he said, "That flaming lot saying he had a cold! It could have turned septic. It could, even yet. By God Almighty! They'll pay for this. You'll see if they don't."

On the last words, Mark loosened his grip on his mother and swung round, only to wince as his raw buttock touched the bed. And now, looking up at Bill, he pleaded, "Don't . . . don't do anything, Mr Bill, 'cos . . . 'cos the masters and the matron and all them, they . . . they are all right, they were good. It was only him and. . . ."

When he stopped and hung his head, Bill sat down on the edge of the bed and, taking the boy's hand, he said, "Who's him? Come on, you might as well tell me because I'll go to that school and I'll get to the bottom of this. By God! I will."

"I . . . I can't, Mr Bill, 'cos . . . cos when I go back. . . ."

"Listen to me, boy: you're not going back."

"No? I . . . I won't have to go back?"

"No, not to that place. By God! no. So come on, spill the beans."

Both Fiona and Bill watched the boy now lean back against the bedhead and look up towards the ceiling and slowly let out a long breath. Then his eyes once more on a level with Bill's, he said, "He's the dorm captain. He's the biggest and ... and a year older than the others. There are seven of us in the dorm but ... but he made me fag from the beginning."

"What d'you mean, fag?"

"Well, I had to clean his shoes and make his bed."

"*You what?* I thought all that was finished with."

"They all have to do it, fags. But ... but he kept picking on me. And ... and he took most of the tuck-box. ..." He now looked at Fiona.

"Never!"

"Yes, Mam. You see, they get the pick of the tuck-boxes in each dorm, the captains. But he took the best bits, the big cake, and the shortbread. ..."

Bill rose from the bed and walked towards the door, then back again, saying, "I can't believe this. I just can't believe this."

"It's the rule, and ... and it doesn't matter."

Bill was now bending over Mark, saying, "Didn't you stand up to him?"

"Oh, yes, yes, Mr Bill, I did ... I did. One time when he called you ... I mean, me names."

Bill lowered himself down to the edge of the bed again and he brought his chin tight into his chest as he said, "He called me names? Why did he call me names?"

"That was ... what I mean, is. ..."

Bill now held up his hand, "What you mean is, that was a slip of the tongue. But slips of the tongue nearly always speak the truth. Now what name did he call me?"

"Well" – Mark bit on his lip – "it ... it wasn't really what he called you, he called me Brickie Bailey."

There was a short silence before Bill said, "He said I was a brickie then?"

Mark didn't answer and Bill said, "Did you tell him I wasn't a brickie? Anyway, how did he know I had anything to do with buildings? Did you tell him?"

"No. He ... he told me his father knows you."

"His father knows me? What's his name?"

"Brown. Roland Brown."

Bill's mouth went into a gape. He looked at Fiona, and she returned the look and nodded knowingly, and Bill said, "Now there's light upon the subject. When did all this happen?" He was addressing Mark again. And the boy said, "Last Sunday after his father brought him back. He came with some friends and they took him out for the day. I saw them when they first came. I was passing through the hall, and I'd met Mr Brown before, you know when we were on the site, and he looked at me but he didn't speak. And it was when Roland came back that he called me Brickie Bailey and said things about. . . ." His voice trailed off, and Bill said, "I've a good idea who he said things about, laddie. And you stood up to him?"

"Yes . . . yes, I hit out at him; but it wasn't hard enough to knock him down, yet he tripped over something. It was really Arthur's foot, he had stuck it out, and everybody laughed, even Roland Brown's pal Roger Stewart. And then it was on the Monday night they caught me, and they pushed the lighted firework down my . . . my trousers. I . . . I couldn't get it out and I . . . I screamed. The doctor came on the Tuesday and they kept me in bed."

It was Fiona who asked now, "But why didn't you tell us this before?"

"Well, because the head said you would only be worried and Mr Leonard said the same, and Matron said that nothing like that had ever happened before, well not as bad, in the way of pranks, and it would get the school a bad name. She's very nice, the matron."

"Get the school a bad name. Don't tell your parents because it'll worry them. The shifty lot of buggers."

"Bill!"

"Oh, to hell!" He waved his hand back at her. "That's how I feel, an' that'll be nothin' to the language I'll use on Monday mornin' when I confront that lot. But it's all right." He turned swiftly to Mark and, thrusting his arm out and pointing his finger at him, he said, "You'll never darken that door again, I'll promise you that, laddie. Nor will you go to any bloody boarding school. There are good schools in Newcastle, and you can come home at night. But that'll be after Monday. Here, get yourself up and come across into the bathroom, I want to see that in better light."

In the better light they were even more shocked at the sight of the scars. When Bill said, "Have you any ointment that you can put on?" Fiona answered, "No, better not; just let the air get at it as much as possible. And it's drying."

"Well, we'll see tomorrow morning. I'll get on to Davey Hall."

"It'll be Sunday tomorrow."

"I know it'll be Sunday, Mrs B" – he nodded towards her – "but Davey will come out on a Sunday, or in the middle of the night if he's needed, you know that. He's not a nine to fiver. So come on, let's all get back to bed because I want some sleep afore the morrow; I've got a lot of thinkin' to do." He put his arm around Mark's shoulder and walked him out of the bathroom. And at his bedroom door, he said, "Go on now, you don't need any tucking in. You'll sleep now, won't you?"

"Yes, Mr Bill." The boy really smiled for the first time since he had come home. Then turning swiftly to his mother, he put his arms about her and kissed her before running from them and into his bedroom.

Doctor Hall said, "Fireworks! They want banning altogether, as does the one who did that." He jerked his head upwards towards the ceiling. "It's healing all right, but it's still nasty. He must have gone through it having to sit on that side and not let on. You think he would have gone back and not said anything?"

"More than likely. You know something? I can't wait until the morrow mornin'."

"I understand how you feel; but if I were you I'd have a photograph taken of it."

"That's an idea. I've got a good camera and I'm not a bad hand at snaps. Yes, that is an idea."

As Fiona entered the room carrying a tray of coffee and as Bill went to take it from her, the doctor rose to his feet, saying, "How's that pain? Any more twinges?" But before she had time to reply, Bill, looking from one to the other, demanded, "What pain?" And when neither of them answered he said, "Come on.

Come on." And he banged the tray down on the table, spilling the coffee here and there as he said, "Come on. What's this about a pain? You've never told me."

"It's nothing. It wasn't worth mentioning. Grumbling appendix." She looked towards the doctor, as, too, did Bill as he demanded, "It it?"

"Yes, it could be; or, on the other hand. . . ."

"Yes, on the other hand, what d'you mean?"

"Look, Bill, stop it!" Fiona's voice was sharp. "This happened long before you came on the scene. I was in hospital for a few days because I had a pain in my side and they could find nothing wrong."

"But that must be over eighteen months ago if it was afore my time. Has this been a recent visit?"

He was now looking at the doctor, who, obviously slightly embarrassed now, was about to speak when Fiona said, "Yes, yes. I popped in the other morning just to see if everything was all right."

"Because you had a pain, woman, that I knew nothin' about? Eeh! My God! This house." He turned from them. "You talk about a secret society: first the son and then the mother."

"Don't be silly, Bill. The trouble is I've got a grumbling appendix and will have to have it out sometime."

"Aye, when it gets perforated I suppose."

And now turning to the doctor, he said, "And you'll let her hang on until then, wont' you?"

"Yes, yes, that's what I'll do Bill." As he took the cup of coffee from Fiona he smiled at her, adding now, "But don't you have me up in the middle of the night; I've been out three times in the past week and I'm going to report to the union that any more and I go on strike."

"You can be funny but I don't see it that way."

"Bill!"

"Oh, shut up! woman. He knows me. And I'll tell you something you didn't know, his father was a brickie an' all."

"No, he wasn't" – the doctor's voice was indignant – "he was a carpenter."

"Not much difference when you're on the job. Anyway, the brickies earn more money."

And so the chipping went on until Bill closed the door on the doctor; but then he almost bounced back into the sitting-room, saying, "That's a nice thing to do, to keep it from me, making a bloomin' fool of me. What am I supposed to be? Your husband or still the lodger?"

"Oh, Bill, please, don't go on." She slumped into the corner of the couch. And he, dropping down beside her, demanded. "Well, woman, don't you understand how I feel?"

"Yes, Bill." Her voice was quiet and patient. "It's because I understand how you feel that I didn't worry you with a trivial thing like a pain in the side. You see. Listen." She smacked his cheek with her finger-tips. "Listen to me. They don't know if it's a grumbling appendix, it could be a little twist in the bowel, diverticulitis.'

"*What?*"

'Diverticulitis, it's a weakness in the bowel, it's nothing. Hundreds, thousands of people have it."

"Well, you could have told me about the diver . . . tickle . . . itis, or what have you."

"Look; forget about it. And tell me, what do you intend to to tomorrow?"

And he told her what he intended to do, which caused her to plead, "On Bill, please be careful."

"Well, d'you want me to pass it over?"

"No, but I know you when you get going, so please keep your temper. Promise me."

"I promise you," he said.

At seven o'clock that evening the phone rang. Bill happened to be passing through the hall and he picked up the receiver and heard a pleasant voice ask, "May I speak with Mr Bailey?"

"Bailey here."

"Oh. Good-evening, Mr Bailey. Leonard speaking. I'm calling from Swandale. Is anything wrong? Mark hasn't returned."

"No, he hasn't returned and he's not returning." And with that he banged down the phone.

Later, he asked Mark if he was in the same form as the Brown fellow. And Mark said he was.

"And where would you likely be on a Monday morning?" Bill had gone on.

"In room two in the annexe."

"About what time?" Bill asked.

"The first lesson after hall."

"And what time would that be?"

"Nine o'clock until half-past; then we go to the labs."

17

Bill arrived at the school almost on the point of nine.

As he entered the main doors it seemed that he was about to be engulfed in a wave of boys when an adult voice called an order to the unruly group; and so he made for the man, saying abruptly, "The headmaster, is he out yet?"

The man stared at him for a moment; then apparently realizing who he was, he turned his head towards the far end of the hall and pointed, saying, "He . . . he has just gone into his study. If you can wait a moment, I . . . I will announce you."

"You needn't bother, I'll announce meself."

He had been in the headmaster's study before when he had been smiled on and given a cup of tea. This time he knocked hard on the door once before thrusting it open and entering the room, to see two men, one seated behind the big desk, the other standing at his side, both their faces showing a mixture of surprise and indignation.

Bill was the first to speak. Walking towards them, he said, "Have no need to introduce meself, have I? And you know why I'm here."

The headmaster, Mr Rowlandson, said quietly, "Take a seat, Mr Bailey."

"I've no time for sittin', thank you; I've just come to do two things: to tell you something, and to ask you something. And the first is, I think you should be damned well ashamed of yourself to allow the things to go on that do go on in this school."

"This is a well-run school, sir!" It was the deputy headmaster, Mr Atkins, speaking now. And as Bill turned his steely gaze on the man, the headmaster made a motion with his hand for his second-in-command to hold his peace. But he endorsed the statement by saying, "We have never had any complaints about the way the school is, Mr Bailey."

"Then there's something radically wrong with the parents of the lads, that's all I can say. Now, first of all, you must have known that my boy had been badly burnt and, too, worried enough to get a doctor to him. And I'll have something to say to him an' all, for he should have informed us. But perhaps he wanted to and he left it to you. And then what do you do? You get my lad to keep his mouth shut."

"I did no such thing, sir! You should be careful what you're saying."

"I know what I'm sayin': Play up and play the game, it's all in good fun, or words to that effect. You translated it into telling him that he wouldn't want to upset his parents, didn't you? And so it would be better if he kept his mouth shut."

"What happened to your son was merely the outcome of a prank. He was party to it: they were playing with fireworks." It was the second master again. And now Bill bawled at him, "They were not playing with fireworks, at least my son wasn't. The bully boy Brown doesn't play with anybody; he punches them into submission. Makes them clean his boots, make his bed, as my son's done since he came into this damn place. And what is more, he steals their food, not only my boy's, but from every tuck-box that goes into that dorm he takes the lion's share. And don't tell me you don't know these things go on."

A quick glance was exchanged between the headmaster and his deputy. And it was the headmaster who said, "Well, we look on fagging as a form of discipline which helps the boys to be of service to others."

"Aw, come off it." Bill flung his arm wide. "It's degradin' to make one kid clean another one's boots. It'll have one of two effects: make him feel damned inferior as he grows up or turn him into a bully an' all to get his own back."

"No, sir, you are wrong. We have proof from all the old boys who return here that such training makes them into men, fine men."

Bill looked at the assistant head, then glanced at his watch before saying, "I haven't much time, I have things to do. Will you be good enough to bring my son's clothes down? I've a list of them here." And he thrust the piece of paper across the table to the headmaster, and he, handing it to his deputy, said, "See to that, Mr Atkins."

As the man made towards the door Bill again looked at his

watch and said, "I'm in a hurry." And at this the deputy head cast a disdainful glance back at him before going out. And now Bill addressed the headmaster once again: "The second thing is, what has happened to Master Brown?"

"What do you mean, sir, what has happened to Master Brown?"

"Has he been expelled? That's what I mean."

"Expelled? Certainly not! As I have informed you, it was the outcome of a prank. Unfortunate, very unfortunate. No one realized that more than I did, but we did everything for your . . . your son. He's had the best of care."

"Best of care." Bill's voice was grim; and now he went on, "And what punishment did you mete out to a boy who got his cronys to hold my son to the floor, then thrust a lighted firework, and not a small one, down his pants, then roll him onto his back so that he was sitting on it?"

The headmaster's eyelids were blinking rapidly and his words were slightly hesitant as he said, "Well . . . well, that is not the version that I heard. I understood they were all larking about."

"They were not larking on. That Brown scum of a boy had been taunting my son by deriding me. Now I ask you again, what happened to Master Brown for his bit of fun?"

"He . . . he was given lines."

"*Lines?*"

"It is a punishment that boys don't like. They would rather have anything than their spare time taken up with lines and being kept from the playing fields to work at them."

"Really!" The sarcasm in the word was not lost on the headmaster and he came back, saying now, 'You are not conversant with the rules that govern a prep school like this, Mr Bailey. We spend our lives in aiming to turn out decent, honest citizens with a cultural background. . . .'

"And no thought of making money out of the cultural background, eh?"

The headmaster's face became suffused with colour, and his jaws tightened before he said grimly, "One has to live. And there's nothing in this business compared to that made by developers."

"I'll take your word for that. But when we've hit on money, I paid you a year in advance, I'll want two terms back."

"We don't do things like. . . ."

"Well, if you don't do things like that, sir, the Newcastle papers are going to sing, and they'll be accompanied by a photograph of my son's backside, and leg, and a report from my doctor."

"You cannot blackmail me, Mr Bailey."

At this point the door opened and Mr Atkins dropped a case none too gently onto the edge of the headmaster's desk, then threw onto the floor, almost at Bill's feet, a tennis racquet and a cricket bat with a pair of boots attached to it by the laces.

Bill lifted the lid of the case, flicked through the vests and pants, pyjamas and shirts, then, looking at the second master, he said, "Where's the burnt pants and vest? Done away with them, I suppose. Aw well, it doesn't matter." He banged the lid closed, locked the case; then gathering up the racquet, the bat, and boots, he looked at the headmaster and said, "If I don't hear from you within a week you'll be hearin' from me." Then he inclined his head from one to the other and went hastily out.

On the drive he threw the things into the back of the car, then hurried along by the side of the school to where the annexe was situated. It was now three minutes to the half hour. The three classrooms were merely prefab buildings; number two had a half-glass door. He looked through the door and saw a young master talking to a class of about twelve boys. Then pushing the door open, he entered the room to find all eyes turned in his direction.

His voice was level and even pleasant as, looking at the young man, he said, "We've met before, haven't we?' And at this the young fellow hesitated, then said, "Oh, yes, yes, Mr Bailey."

"This was my son's class, wasn't it?"

"Yes, yes, Mr Bailey, it is. I . . . I hope he's all right."

"Yes. At least he will be; he's suffering from shock at present." He smiled as he said the words and nodded his head. Then he looked at the sea of faces staring at him. It would seem that each boy in that class knew who he was and why he was here. Bill was still smiling quietly as he said, "You have Brown here?"

The young fellow hesitated just for a fraction, then turned his head and looked in the direction of a boy sitting in the end seat of the front row. His head seemed to be on a level with the rest of the class; his face was longish and thin; but he had a breadth of shoulder. After having glanced at the visitor he was now looking down towards his desk. Bill said, "Ask Master Brown to come out."

"Mr Bailey" – the young man's voice was just above a whisper – "please."

"What is your name? I've forgotten."

"Howard, sir."

"Well now, Mr Howard" – Bill put his hand out and laid it gently on the young man's shoulder – "will you oblige me by going to the back of your class?"

It seemed for a moment that the petrified class came alive, for a slight titter passed over it.

"Please, Mr Bailey, I . . . I wouldn't do anything that. . . . Let me dismiss the. . . ." But Bill was leaning forward and whispering in the young man's ear, "You wouldn't like me to use force, would you? It wouldn't be seemly. Perhaps though you could just resist a bit so the boys can verify that you put up a stand, eh?"

The poor young fellow stood gaping at this man who wasn't any taller than himself but emanated such strength that he found it formidable. And now he muttered, "Yes, yes, it would be." So, at this Bill's bark almost bounced the boys in their seats and it certainly shook the young teacher as he made play of pushing Bill, only to find himself turned around and thrust none too gently up the aisle between the desks. Then Bill, looking into the startled face of a small boy sitting in the front seat, said quite gently, "Would you like to get up, sonny, and go and join the master?"

Before he had finished speaking the child had scrambled out of his desk and dashed up the aisle. And now looking towards the boy who was staring at him wide-eyed, Bill raised his finger and beckoned him. And when the boy made no effort to get up, he said, "Come here, Brown."

"I'll not. I'll not. If you touch me I . . . I'll tell my father."

What happened next brought a gasp from the whole class when they saw bully Brown lifted almost by the collar of his shirt and plumped in front of the desk that the boy had vacated moments earlier.

"Take your pants down."

"I . . . I'll . . . I'll . . . I'll not. You'll get wrong. My fa . . . father knows you, you'll . . . you'll get."

As if Bill had been used to stripping boys of pants every day of his life, Brown's pants came down, his underpants with them. He was twisted round and pushed over the desk, so exposing two very white buttocks.

He was yelling at the top of his voice now as Bill, thrusting a hand into the inside pocket of his overcoat, brought out a ruler and began to lay it across the screaming boy's bare pelt. When he had counted six he looked over the startled faces, shouting now, "Who's Arthur Ryan?"

When a wavering hand came up, he said, "Would you like a go, Arthur, for all you've had to put up with off this bully?"

Arthur's hand came down but he didn't move.

"Who's Hugo Fuller?"

A boy who had crouched away from the proximity of Brown's flailing arms, stuttered, "M . . . m . . . me, sir."

"Well, I'll give him one for you, Hugo. And here's another for Arthur."

By now there was a commotion outside the door; and when it burst open the deputy headmaster rushed in, only to come to a dead stop at the sight before him.

Bill pulled up the wailing Brown onto his feet and, thrusting him towards the master, he said, "I didn't burn him as I should have done. I thought of it, mind. But there, he's all yours. Now get on the phone and tell his father what's happened. If you don't he will. And let this be a lesson to you, sir, to know what goes on in your school under your bloody nose . . ."

The boys outside had to make a pathway to let him pass, and when he reached the end of it he turned and, raising his arm and wagging his finger from one startled face to the other, he said, "Brown is a bully. He's got his deserts and you all know why. Now, should anyone bully you in the future, stand up to him. And if you're afraid write home to your parents and tell them. It isn't cissy. D'you hear me?"

Mouths opened here and there but no one answered.

A few minutes later as he was turning his car in the drive he had another audience of boys. And when two hands, held at cheek level, made waving motions to him, he waved back at them and gave them the "V" sign.

He now drove straight to the works, and there, seeking out Barney McGuire, he gave him a brief picture of what had happened; and he finished, "So there you are, Barney, he'll be out for blood. And you know what that means, he'll never be off the site."

"Aye, you're right there, boss. We can look out for squalls."

"Aye, so that being the case, tell our lot to hang on for five minutes or so the night; I'll put them in the picture so they'll keep on their toes. I'm going down home now but I won't be more than half an hour." . . .

A short while later he thrust open the kitchen door to see Fiona and Nell sitting at the table having coffee while Mamie sat on the rug in front of the stove stuffing dolls' garments into a miniature washing machine, and at the sight of him the child jumped up, crying, "Uncle Bill!" But when she ran to him he did not lift her up, or make some facetious remark about hard working housewives; instead, he pointed to the coffee jug and said, "Any of that left?"

They had both risen from the table and Fiona, looking hard at him, said, "Yes, yes;" then added, "What happened?"

He gave a short laugh before answering, "Well, you know our marching song, 'There Is A Happy Land'?"

Before she had time to make any comment the small voice piped up, "Far, far away, where all the piggies run three times a day." And seeing that she had the attention of all the elders, Mamie went on gleefully, "Oh, you should see them run when they see Bill Bailey come, three smacks across their—" she now put her hand over her mouth and whispered "bum" and finished on a laugh, "three times a day."

Bill now playfully smacked her bottom, saying, "And that's what you're going to get, my lady, three times a day."

"You didn't! I mean?"

He looked at Fiona, nodded his head, then said, "Yes; eight of the best."

"Oh, Bill."

"Good for you."

At this Fiona turned on Nell, saying, " 'Tisn't good for him, Nell," and she, holding out her hand to Mamie, said, "Come and help me tidy up." And as she led the child to the door she said to no one in particular, "Cannons to right of 'em? Cannons to left of 'em, into the valley of death rode the six hundred." Then as she closed the door they heard, as if from far away, her voice ending, "And they were all called Bill."

A grin on his face, Bill nodded towards the door, saying,

"I've noticed Nell always gives you something to look forward to."

"It's no time for joking, Bill."

"I'm not joking, lass." He went to her and put his arm around her and she said, "Couldn't you have let it go with a talk to the head?"

"Oh. I knew what that would mean afore I met him. And you know what punishment young Brown had? He was given *some lines*. But there's one good thing I've done if nothing else, I've put the wind up the rest of the bullies in the school, and there's bound to be more than one. And you know something?" He grinned again. "Two little nippers gave me a wave on the quiet as I was coming out. Huh!" His head went back now and he laughed. "I must have appeared like Superman to those bairns. Oh, and that poor young teacher. Anyway, we worked out an alibi, him and me."

"What do you mean?"

"Oh, I'll tell you all about it the night but I must get back. Where's Mark?"

"He's up in the playroom; he's reading."

"We must go into Newcastle and see about a school."

"I've already been looking into that."

"Well, I'd better get back, as Nell says, into the valley of death. And that's what it'll be if dear papa has his own way. But what Mr Brown doesn't know is, I'm covered with battle scars."

"But what can he do really?"

"Oh, he can make life a bit hot for us. He can find complaints about the workmanship, an' with some of the new squad I've taken on that won't be too hard for him. Anyway, I'm goin' to spread them out among our own fellows. Some of them are all right, quite good, in fact, but there's always some and some. And then there's the schedule; we're getting behind time: it takes no account of rainy spells when the brickies and tilers can't get at it, the job. But Hey! ho! I must be off."

"Do the others come around like Brown does?"

"No, Old Kingdom Come's been once on the site. Ramshaw and Pilby, they've been two or three times but couldn't be more pleased with things. And the architect, you know, is Pilby's brother-in-law. Anyway, love, I must tell you . . . you still make rotten coffee." He drained the cup.

"Bill."

"Yes, love?"

She put her hand up and stroked his cheek as she said, "Promise me you won't do anything more? I mean, when Brown comes. You won't lose your temper and . . . and . . .?"

"Hit him?"

"Something like that."

"Don't worry. I'll try me best not to."

She smiled at him as he said, "Remember what Katie says when Willie gets at her. 'Sticks an' stones will break me bones but callin' will not hurt me.' Oh, that saying, like lots of others, is daft when taken to pieces, for I'd rather have a black eye than turn me back on the fellow who said me mother didn't know who me father was or words to that effect. And that, Mrs B, actually happened when I was on the buildings. He was an oldish bloke, oldish to me anyway, he was in his thirties then, but before he gave me a black eye I split his lip an' told him his trouble was he had never had the chance to turn a young lass into a woman. Think that one out, love."

"You're an awful man, Bill Bailey."

"I know that. Goodbye love." As he went out of the door he turned and grinned at her, saying, "If the police ring up, you'll know I'm in clink."

He was half-way down the path when her voice halted him. "Be careful, for my sake." He made a face at her, then went on.

Mr Brown did not put in an appearance but his wife did. Bill happened to be at the far end of the estate when one of the men came hurrying up to him, saying in an undertone, "Mrs Brown's in the cabin, boss."

"You mean, Mister."

"No, boss, Missis."

"Mrs Brown?"

"Aye."

He straightened his collar, pushed his tie up into a knot, tugged his coat straight, pulled his tweed cap to a slight angle; then, as a somewhat deflated man but one ready for battle, he made his way to the cabin.

Mrs Brown, he saw immediately, was one of the unusually tall women that seemed to be bred these days. She looked like a Miss World type: she was plainly but expensively dressed; she wasn't good-looking by his standards, he would have called her arresting, but when she spoke her voice stamped her class.

"Mr Bailey? I'm Mrs Brown."

"How d'you do? Won't you sit down."

"Thank you." She sat down at the other side of his desk, crossed her legs, then leant her right forearm along the edge of the desk and, looking straight at him, she said, "You will of course know why I'm here."

For answer he gave a small huh of a laugh and said, "I'm trying to guess, but candidly I was expecting your husband."

"He happens to be in London and won't be back until tomorrow evening. My son phoned me from school, as did the headmaster. I understand from both of them that you thrashed the boy."

"Yes, yes I did, ma'am, I thrashed him. But do you know why?"

"As a result of a prank I've been informed. But I felt there was more in it than that to warrant your action."

Bill stared at her for a moment, then leant to the side, pulled open a drawer and took out three snaps and, laying them on the table, he twisted them around, then pushed them towards her, saying, "That's the result of your son's prank on mine. I brought them to show your husband. These were taken by an instamatic, but there'll be some clearer ones later on which I took with a proper camera. My boy was held down by your son's crony and your son pushed a lighted firework down his trousers. Would you call that a prank, Mrs Brown? And this happened because my son stood up to him. I think he objected to cleaning his boots, making his bed, havin' to give him the best part of his tuck box. But the final thing that broke him was to hear me slandered. So he retaliated."

He watched her now pick up one snap after another and stare at it, and then, when she looked at him without speaking, he said, "I could, of course, have made a case of it, which would have hurt a good many people, so I decided on the old Jewish maxim, an eye for an eye, a backside in this case. What is your opinion, Mrs Brown?"

She didn't speak for some seconds, and when she did, she

said, "In your place I would have come to a similar decision. But I must tell you that my husband won't see it in the same way, and I hope that after what I am now going to say, you will do me the kindness to forget that I've said it. It is simply this: my husband should have followed your example years ago. Had he done so, this incident would never have happened."

She rose to her feet; he too, and, moving round the table, he held out his hand to her, and she placed hers in it. And they stared at each other before he said, "Thank you, Mrs Brown."

He now escorted her to her car, and as he held the door open for her she again looked at him and said, "Of course, you understand, my husband will make more of this, although I shall indeed put the facts to him as you have given them to me."

"I understand, Mrs Brown . . . perfectly."

She turned her head away now and looked towards the buildings, saying, "I like your houses, Mr Bailey; they have individuality, they're not merely boxes. It's going to be a fine estate."

He had to check his tongue from saying, "I wish you'd tell that to your husband." He smiled at her, inclined his head towards her, then closed the car door on her after she had taken her seat behind the wheel.

He remained standing where he was until she had turned the car around, and as she passed him she glanced at him and smiled, and he smiled back.

When he opened the back door at his usual time there were no cries from the children, and the kitchen table was clear of food. Taking off his outer things, he went quickly into the hall, there to meet Fiona coming out of the dining-room.

"What's up?"

"What d'you mean, what's up?" she said.

"Where's everybody?"

"Oh, that. They've had their meal; they're all upstairs. I . . . thought we'd have ours in the dining-room tonight. I lit the fire."

"Celebrating something?"

"No; but I thought you'd be coming in, well, full of steam and you'd want a little quiet. But" – she gave a slight shrug to her shoulders – "you appear normal. What happened?"

"He never turned up . . . but his wife did."

"His wife?"

"Look, Mrs B, my stomach's yellin' out for substance. Get it on the table and then I'll tell you all. By the way, what is it?"

"Roast lamb et cetera."

"Good."

As she made to move away he checked her, saying, "Here, woman."

"Yes?"

"You haven't kissed me."

"You didn't proffer your face, Mr Bailey, so now you can wait."

"You'll pay for it later." He laughed as he turned from her. . . .

They had been seated at the table for some minutes when Fiona said somewhat impatiently, "Well, tell me what happened. why did she come? And what is she like?"

"To answer the first part, she came to apologize. As regards the . . . what is she like?" He now placed his knife and fork slowly down each side of his plate and, looking along the length of the table, he said dreamily, "Smashing."

"Don't be silly." She gave a laugh. "Was she as bad as that?"

"No." He picked up the knife and fork again, put a piece of lamb in his mouth, chewed on it, then said, "That"s what she was, smashing. No kiddin'."

"Really?" The word came out on a high note then she added, "You were definitely impressed?"

"I'll say. Who wouldn't be? Five foot nine, I'd say, a figure like, you know . . . pounds, shillings, and pence, and clothed to match."

He glanced at her. She was looking down at her plate while she chewed slowly. And when he said, "She was your type," she looked up at him, saying, "I am not placated."

"Well, you should be" – he again put down his knife and fork and, reaching out, caught her wrist – "because every inch of her put me in mind of you. And I'm going to tell you something more: I know you took a step down when you married me, but by God! that one took a big jump when she got hooked up with

Brown, because he's a slob at bottom and his veneer doesn't cover it. How in the name of God that woman married him will always beat me."

"She did impress you, didn't she?"

"Jealous? Go on . . . say you're jealous. Oh, I'd love you to be jealous."

"Don't be silly. And that lamb is congealing. Anyway, let's get to the point: why did she come in place of him?"

Again he took up a mouthful of food and chewed on it before he said, "Well, it's like this. The bold boy's in London on business. He's got his fingers into numbers of pies that one, money talks. But to keep to the point. Her son had phoned her, and the head had phoned her . . . all about the prank the dear child had played. Well, she didn't call her son a dear child. Believe it or not, in a way, she actually thanked me for what I'd done, and off the cuff of course and mustn't be repeated, words to the effect that she was glad I did it and that her husband should have done the same a long time ago."

"She didn't."

"She did though." His voice had a serious note to it now. "I couldn't believe it. Yet all the time she was talking I couldn't help thinking, how in the name of God had she got linked up with that fellow 'cos she's county and he, you could say, came from the same backyard as me, except" – he wagged his head now – "he hasn't got my charisma. But seriously love. . . . By the way, you've never seen Brown, have you?"

"No, I haven't."

"Well, you'd have to see them together and listen to them to get the full value of my meanin'."

"I'd like to meet him, I'd likely find him very interesting."

"Aw, there we go again." He was grinning now and flapping his hand out towards her. "Don't worry, my dear, I'm not goin' to walk out on you."

"*Bill!*" The movement she made thrusting her chair back from the table startled him somewhat. "Don't say things like that, even in fun. Remember Nell."

"Oh, honey" – he was out of his seat bending over her – "you should know by now it's just me and me tactlessness; I must be funny or die. I'm sorry, love."

He kissed her; then, pushing her roughly by the shoulder, he said, "Anyway, it's your own fault; you should have been working on me an' smoothing off me corners."

"I'm no magician."

He laughed now as he said, "Aw, hitting below the belt. And you know what? You sound just like your mother there." He sat down again, saying now, "Had any word from your dear mama lately?"

"Yes, I had a letter from her. She's thinking of moving."

"Good. How far? Australia?"

"No, only a quarter of a mile nearer here."

"Aw! no."

"It's a smaller house, a bungalow. I can understand her doing that because, as she said, what does she want with nine rooms now and on her own."

"Poor sod."

"Bill!"

"Well, there's nobody else to hear me except you, and you should be used to it by now, and that's what she is, at least the latter word. Now tell me some nice news. What have the bairns been up to?"

Some seconds passed before she said, "There was a bit of a to-do with Mamie today. It started in the car. I couldn't understand it at first. Apparently Japan had come up in one of Willie's lessons, and you know how he goes on when he's excited about anything. And he happened to say 'I'm going on my holidays to Japan, Mam; I'm going to save up.' And that's as far as he got because Mamie turned on him and hit out at him and shouted, 'You're not going on holiday. You're not! You're not!' In fact, I had to stop the car and bring her into the front seat. And when we came in I couldn't pacify her for a time and she kept begging me not to let Willie go on holiday. Then it dawned on me."

"What dawned on you?"

"The word holiday."

"Oh. Aye, aye." He nodded at her. "You've always said Susie and Dan and the lad were on holiday. Well, we'll have to do something to change the meaning of that word for her, won't we?"

"I don't know how; it will be engrained in her mind, and the word is bound to come up among them, it's only natural."

"How is she now?"

"Oh, she's all right. I made Willie tell her that he's not going on holiday. I explained to him as simply as I could why. She adores Willie. And there's another thing. I was on the phone to the headmaster of The Royal Grammar School. He said to bring Mark down tomorrow. He'll have to go through a test of some kind, for the prep department."

"Well that'll be nothing to him. He"s got a head on his shoulders."

"He may have, Bill, but inside he's afraid of another new start. Yet he's relieved that wherever he's going it's as a day pupil. But to get back to the Brown business. Do you think he'll turn up?"

"Oh, yes, yes, he'll turn up all right. But I'll be ready for him, more so than ever I was now I know his home situation."

"Yes, of course, now that you know his home situation."

"Drop that tone, Mrs B, now I'm tellin' you, else I'll skelp your lug for you. Eeh!" He closed his eyes and rocked his head on his shoulders. "Will I ever get to know women?"

She rose from the table, smiling at him now and saying, "Oh, I shouldn't worry; your practice is bound to pay off, just keep at it. . . . Do you want rice pudding or apple tart?"

It was Wednesday morning when Brown came into the yard. Although he was on Bill's mind his entry into the office touched on surprise because the door was thrust open and there he was.

Bill remained in his seat as he said, "People usually knock; this is my office."

"Yes, yes; and you'd better cling on to it, Bailey, for it mightn't be yours much longer." He was now at the other side of the desk, his hands flat on it, and leaning towards Bill, and he growled out, "Who the hell do you think you are, daring to lay a hand on my son!"

As he had done two days earlier, Bill opened the drawer and took out three snaps and, as again he had done on that day, he laid them flat on the table, saying, "Look at those. That's the result of your son's venom."

Brown hardly glanced at the snaps before scattering them across the table with a sweep of his hand, saying, "It was just a prank."

"A prank that frightened the headmaster and his staff into

coercing my boy to keep quiet about it. There were two options open to me: to let the newspapers deal with it, or take matters into my own hands. And which would you have preferred, *Mr Brown?* You'd rather have your son skinned alive, wouldn't you, than let the newspapers get hold of it?"

"There was nothing for the newspapers to get hold of. They would see it as something petty. They would have seen it as another way of blowing your big mouth off. Anyway, I'm warnin' you, you'll have to keep your nose clean in future else you'll find yourself suffering the same medicine as you doled out to my son. But it'll be more lasting because you'll be plumb on your arse outside."

"Well, I can promise you this, Brown, that, if I go, I swear to God I won't go alone. Keep me nose clean, you say. Well, here's some advice to you. Keep your fingers out of little men's pockets. You're on the council – aren't you? – and as far as I understand it's not only frowned upon but illegal to extract your pound of flesh by ten per cent in pushin' jobs here and there."

Of a sudden Bill had the satisfaction of seeing the man's face become suffused with colour. He watched his mouth open and shut twice before he managed to say, "You'd better be careful what you're insinuating."

"I insinuate nothing that I can't prove. You sent me a letter two years ago, and if you remember I refused your offer of help because" – now his voice became a growl – "I've worked too hard all me bloody life to get where I am today to give back-handers to swines like you. Now get out of this office. And If I see you round this yard again before it's finished, I'll put it before the next meetin' why I object to your presence here. And I'll make plain to them some things that'll not only surprise them, but you an' all. Now get!"

"You'll regret this day. Oh, you'll regret this day."

After the door had banged on the man Bill slumped in his seat. He knew only too well that he might regret this day because anything he brought up against the man he'd have to prove; and fellows like Brown were wily, they never put anything in writing, except in that one letter he'd sent to him. And a clever lawyer would read it as suggestion helpfully put. For there was no talk of a rake-off as such in it.

Yes he might regret, not only this day, but this whole week.

18

He had gone out at half-past seven to the works. He returned home at half-past nine, had a bath, got into a smart suit, came down and had his breakfast; then he was ready to go.

In the hall Fiona helped him on with his overcoat and her hands had a nervous tremor to them as she patted the lapels, saying as she did so, "I like you in this. It's very smart."

"Damn good right to be, two hundred and forty quid."

"Well, you shouldn't go beyond your station and have your things made."

"Well, don't forget, Mrs B, I had it made before I met you an' was saddled with your crew. As far as I can see there'll be no more hand-made things; it'll be off the peg or nothin' at all."

"Poor soul."

Dropping her bantering tone, she now said, "How long do you think it will take?"

"God knows. It might go on till tomorrow. You can never tell with juries; there's nearly always one . . . budgerigar decides to be awkward."

"You've fixed the television?"

"I've fixed the television, so don't worry. I've changed it over to the video channel and if she puts it on she'll get nothing but a loud noise and a snowy screen. But anyway I hope to be back before the six o'clock news."

"It isn't the six o'clock I'm worried about; it probably won't be mentioned on there, but it'll likely be reported on the Tyne Tees news or Mike Neville's programme. It's nearly sure to be one or the other, and just imagine if she saw his face on the screen, for they are more than likely to show a picture of him."

"She won't, so stop worrying about that. The only thing that's worrying me at the moment is his sentence. If he gets off lightly by God! I don't think I'll be answerable for me actions."

"Please, Bill." She had her hands on his shoulders now. "Don't cause a scene, please, whatever happens. Try not to look at him."

"What! That's askin' too much. I'll look at him all right, love. In fact, I won't take me eyes off him. I have one regret, that I won't be able to put me hands on him. I had a word with Sergeant Cranbrooke first thing on the phone from the office. He didn't say anything outright but there seemed to be a hint in his words that there'll be more revealed than Katie's case. Well now, I must be off. Oh, by the way, when you're giving me orders I'll give you one. Tear up the *Journal* or put it in the dustbin, there's no picture of him but there's that report, and you know she goes through the headlines of both papers, not only the front but the back. She said she had the first clue in the *Telegraph* crossword the other day. She hadn't, but I let her think she had. Anyway, love, I'll be back as soon as possible." He kissed her and they clung together for a moment; then she watched him walk down the drive to the car.

After closing the door she stood with her back to it for a moment. She was alone in the house: Nell had gone to the dentist's – she was having three teeth out – she had been suffering from toothache for some time now.

She started to walk towards the sitting-room but stopped when half-way across the hall, telling herself, no, she mustn't sit down; she must keep busy in order to keep this awful feeling at bay, for her mind would keep jumping back into those hours when Katie was lost. . . .

An hour later she was wishing it was time to pick up Mamie from the nursery school; she was wishing Nell was here; she was wishing one of the children were here. She wanted someone to talk to. She even wished her mother would ring; and having wished this, she knew she was in a bad way. She cleaned the odd bits of silver and brass, she turned out the china cabinet and wine cabinet.

At twelve o'clock she picked up Mamie from the nursery school, made her a light lunch, then found herself talking to the child as if she was Katie or Mark.

At one o'clock when the phone rang she was only a few feet from the table and, grabbing it up, she shouted, "Hello!"

"Hello, love." Bill's voice was quiet.

She drew in a long breath before saying, "How are things?"

"Oh, complicated, at least from my point of view. You know, it's the first time I've been in a court, and don't say, isn't that amazing! But the procedure and the waffling is nobody's business. I've seen it on the television but it's different altogether when you're in the middle of it."

"Is ... is he there?"

"Oh, yes, he's there. My God, Fiona, that fellow looks evil. I sense it coming from him. You hear a lot of chatter about good and evil, but in the main it's only words. . . . Anyway, I'm going to have a bite. I'll give you all the gen when I get back."

"Do you think it will be finished today?"

"It could be, it seems all cut and dried. It all depends on the jury. But these blokes, the defence lawyers, the prosecution fellows, my God, how they talk. It's just as if they were on telly in a play. I'll believe all I see and hear on the telly after this. Anyway love, be seeing you. You all right?"

"Yes; yes, Bill, I'm all right. Just waiting for you coming back."

"I won't be long, at least I hope not. 'Bye."

" 'Bye." . . .

It was half-past one when Nell put in an appearance. Her face looked a sorry sight.

"Oh! Nell, what's happened to you? What did they do?"

Through her swollen lips Nell muttered, "Used a street drill on a molar, and there was an abscess on two of them. God! never again."

"Have you just got back? You've been a long time."

"I ... I must have passed out. Came to on a couch somewhere."

"Come and lie down and I'll get you a drink."

"Thanks. All the same, I think I'd better go to bed and sleep it off. I ... I haven't been in home yet. How are you feeling?"

"Oh, I'm all right, Nell. Don't worry about me. Do as you say, get yourself to bed. Will I come with you?"

"No, no. But ... but I feel I've let you down; this is the day you want company."

"Don't worry about that. Everything's going fine. Bill's just phoned. It shouldn't be long before he's back."

"Good. I'll away then." . . .

She was alone again. Mamie was having her afternoon nap.

When the phone rang she ran out of the kitchen, across the hall and grabbed it up.

"Fiona?"

. . . "Yes, Mother."

"I didn't expect to find you at home."

"Well, why did you phone?"

"Well, naturally to find out. The case is on, isn't it? I would have thought you would have been there defending your daughter."

"Mother, my daughter doesn't want any defending."

"Well, you know what I mean."

"No, I don't, Mother. As usual I don't."

"Then all I can say is, girl, that you are going dim. As I see it, the presence of the mother of the child would have emphasized the wickedness of the man. And you are her only relative."

"Bill is there, Mother."

"Bill? What is he? Katie is not his child. The word 'step' can never bear any relationship, in whatever way you look at it."

"What you forget, Mother, is that the man was one of Bill's workmen."

"I forget nothing, girl, nothing at all. But I can tell you what I'm thinking at this moment, and that is you have become a most unnatural mother. And what is more. . . ."

The phone was banged onto its stand. What kind of a woman was she? She was asking the question of the mirror above the telephone table. And now she actually spoke to her reflection. Her hand out towards herself, she asked, "Can you understand her? There are mentally defective people who would act with more sense than she does. Has she always been like this?"

She was nodding at herself now, saying, "Yes, yes; more or less. Yes, she has."

Her hand now dropped to her side and she gritted her teeth against the pain there. Then looking in the mirror again, she said, "Oh, don't you start. Please, please, not today."

She told herself to go and have a drink, only once again to tell herself she certainly wasn't going to start that in the middle of the day and that it would likely do her more harm than good. "Go and have a bath," she said to herself now, "and tidy yourself up."

As if obeying an order from a mature and elderly individual, she went towards the stairs, and as she mounted them she repeated to herself, "Hurry up, Bill. Hurry up." . . .

Two hours later she picked Katie up from school. She hugged her tight – it was as if she had just got her back again – then having settled her in the front passenger seat and herself behind the wheel, she turned her head and looked at Willie, who was ensconced with Mamie in the back of the car. And he said, "I should be sitting in the front; I'm a boy."

"Oh, what a surprise! He's a boy, Mam."

Katie was looking at her mother, her face wide with laughter, and Fiona, joining into her mood, said, "Is he? I never noticed."

This brought forth a bawl from the back seat as her son exclaimed, "Oh, you! our Mam," and was followed by Mamie, his faithful champion, saying, "He is a boy," only to be bawled down by her hero yelling, "Shut up! you."

"Willie!" Fiona's voice was stern. "We'll have no more of that talk. Tell Mamie you're sorry."

"Not."

"I don't mind Willie not being sorry, Mammy B, 'cos I love him."

No one capped this in any way; and almost complete silence reigned until, scrambling from the car, Willie rushed towards the house, exclaiming, "I want to see Bugs Bunny."

"Get your things off first." Fiona's voice was steadying. "Then you'll have your tea and there'll be plenty of time to see Bugs Bunny."

Willie and Mamie followed Fiona into the kitchen; but Katie did not. Fiona knew she had made straight for the sitting-room and the television and she waited for the cry of despair, and it wasn't long in coming.

She came rushing into the kitchen. "Mam! there's something wrong with the television. It's making a funny sound and there's no picture."

"Oh, dear me. I suppose the tube's gone now."

"Oh no! Mam; I wanted to see. . . ."

"I want to see Bugs Bunny."

"And Henry's Cat." This pipe came from Mamie. And now Fiona cried at all of them, "If the television is out of order, it's out of order, and Bugs Bunny and Henry's Cat and what have you are out of order, so stop it! Come and sit down and have your tea."

When Katie's mouth opened wide Fiona thrust a finger at her, saying, "Not another word. Not one more word. Sit!"

The three of them looked at her, then looked at each other, then sat down at the table. It wasn't often their mother's voice sounded like that but when it did they knew it was time to shut up . . . or else.

It was just on five when Bill returned. When he kissed her lightly on the cheek she didn't put her arms about him but stood looking at him. His face looked grey and drawn. She asked quietly, "Was it bad?"

'It wasn't good, neither for me nor him."

"What did he get?"

"Ten years."

She let out a long slow breath. "That's good."

"He should have had life, not less than twenty by what came out after."

"What came out after?"

"Let's have a cup of tea; I'm frozen." He had taken off his outer things and now he made towards the stove and stood with the back of his hands against his buttocks, and he went on talking while she made a fresh pot of tea.

"The paraphenalia, the way they put the questions. You know, at one time I thought that his counsel was trying to get him off. In a way I suppose he was. He put him over as a sort of deprived child. His mother had done a bunk or something like that when he was twelve. He had been in Borstal for two years and after that he did two robberies and stole from his father, for which he did six months in jail; then only three years ago he was up for indecent exposure. My God! you never know who you're employing, do you? But this didn't come out until after the jury had found him guilty and it was up to the judge to pass sentence. And you know he might have got life at that only he denied flatly having said that she'd be rotten when she was found, even when Barney, Bert and meself were up on the stand and we all said the same thing."

He stood shaking his head now. "By! that's a funny feeling

being up there. You know I've always prided meself that it would take a lot to put the fear of God into me but there I was and I was tellin' the truth, but his counsel kept comin' at me, twisting me words. I was in a rage, he said. Didn't I try to throttle the defendant all because I smelt the scent on his coat?

"I had told meself to keep calm 'cos I knew these fellows try to bamboozle you, but there I was bawling at him. Huh!" He gave a short laugh now. "You know what I said? Don't be a bloody ass, wasn't the child found in his house, trussed up behind the tank? Oh" – he laughed again – "didn't that judge go for me. But towards the end he softened and said, 'We are well aware of your feelings on this account, Mr Bailey, but please remember where you are.'

"By God! I was glad the child hadn't to put in an appearance. I've got to thank the doctors for that. And that came out an' all about her losing her power of speech. There was only one light moment in the proceedings and you'll never guess who caused it."

She handed him the cup of tea and he drained the cup before he said, "Bert."

"Bert caused light relief?"

"Aye, in his own way. The fella got at him, the defence counsel. Did he think he had heard aright? Was he not being loyal to his employer? At this there was objection from our bloke and a warning from the judge to the interrogator to mind what he was saying. And then Bert caused a rumbling belly laugh in the court by stretching himself to his full height, all of five foot eight, and in tones that outdid the counsel with their dignity, he said, 'Sir, I am a Sunday school teacher.'

"After the judge had knocked his mallet on the bench he looked at Bert and said, 'I would discount the fact that religious work of any kind would have an effect on your hearing.'

"There was another burst of laughter and another banging of the mallet and what d'you think came next? Bert looked at the judge straight in the eye and said, 'My Lord, I neither drink nor smoke nor lie.' And what he was gona say next I'll never know because some bright spark from the back of the court put in a loud whisper, 'Or go with women.' Eeh! it was like an explosion. Another time I would have bellowed me head off with them but I wanted to shout at the lot of them to shut up, that this was no laughing matter.

"Anyway, everything went flat after that. The policemen were on the stand. The young one told how he found her, and the sergeant told what had been said when seated in the car outside the house. I thought it would never end. The jury were out for an hour and a quarter. That gave me the jitters. I thought they would see that he was proved guilty beyond a doubt. But as I've said before, there's always one or two stubborn buggers who just want to be different. But it was after they came back and they said that their verdict was guilty that the judge got under way, and didn't he lay into him. He said in a way he was a lucky man he wasn't facing a murder charge and that even in his early youth he'd had a grudge against society and had taken it out on innocent people, in the last case an innocent child. After he brought out the fact that the psychiatric treatment he'd had had proved that he was normal inasmuch as he knew what he was doing and wasn't mental, he sentenced him to the ten years."

Bill now moved from the stove and, sitting down at the table, he put his elbows on it and rested his head in his hands as he said, quietly, "I wonder if in ten years time I'll be over this feeling because every minute in that court all I wanted to do was to climb over those benches and into that dock and get me hands on him, because let's face it, love" – he looked up at her where she was standing to his side – "it was firmly in his mind to leave her there until she died and that could have been a day or two the way she was trussed. You didn't see it. He meant to do her in all right."

She was putting her arms around him when the kitchen door opened, and there stood Katie. She walked slowly towards the table and stood at the other end and, after looking from one to the other, she said, "I . . . I heard my name on the radio, Mam. That man, he's been put in prison for ten years, so I won't see him again, will I? I'll be old then."

They exchanged a quick glance in which they said they hadn't thought about the radio, because none of them bothered with it.

They seemed to spring round the table together and then she was engulfed in their arms. And it was Bill, his voice shaking, who said, "That's right love, now you can forget all about him cos you'll never see him again, ever, not even when you're old. Now I'll go and mend your television, eh?"

"Can you?"

"Can I?" He pulled back from her. "Did you ever know anything that I couldn't do?"

"No, Mr Bill."

"Well, come on then an' watch my magic. That fella Daniels isn't a patch on me where magic is concerned." And as Fiona followed them, she thought, And how right you are, Mr Bill.

19

Fiona stood in the hall dressed for outdoors and she looked at Nell, who was holding out a scarf towards her, and said, 'I hate scarves, Nell. One never looks dressed in a scarf.'

"All right, go on, feel dressed and get a cold on top of all the other things."

"What other things?"

"Well, that pain; it isn't indigestion nor constipation, nor. . . ."

"It's the appendix, Nell."

"Well, if you think it's only the appendix, it's only the appendix. But if you think it's only the appendix why are you worrying yourself sick, and keeping it from Bill? What if he should phone up?"

"Just say I've gone out shopping."

"Shopping! on a morning like this, rain, wind, hail, the lot?"

"My appointment's for quarter to ten; I'll be back by eleven or so. Anyway, there's no reason why he should phone. Stop fussing."

"Somebody's got to fuss. I can't understand how he hasn't noticed when you're doubled up with pain."

"Because it's only happened at rare times, thankfully when he hasn't been there."

"What if he wants to keep you in?"

"Nell, I'm only going to the surgery. Where do you think he's going to keep me? In the back room? Stop it; you're worse than Bill. Here, give me the scarf. All right, I'll put it on. But the trouble isn't in my neck it's in my tummy."

"Your trouble's in your head, doing the brave little woman stunt, and it won't work. When he finds out there'll be an explosion, if I know anything."

"Goodbye."

"And the same to you."

*

Fiona hadn't come back by eleven o'clock; but just after, the phone rang, and when Nell picked it up she heard Fiona's voice "Nell."

"Yes? Yes? Where are you?"

"I'm just outside the surgery. Look. Now, listen and don't go off the deep end, but Doctor wants me to slip along to the hospital and have a test. If I go straightaway now his colleague can fit me in, if not I'd likely have to wait another week or two. He thinks I should take the opportunity.... Are you there?"

"Yes, I'm here, Fiona. Which hospital are you going to?"

"The General."

"I could wrap Mamie up and come along."

"Oh for goodness sake!"

"All right but somebody should be there to drive you back. You'll likely feel wobbly after a test if it's one of the barium kind. I've had it. Half your stomach seems to drop out."

"That was in 1066, they have different ways now. Look, haven't any more change; I've got to go."

"I knew this would happen. You should have seen to it before now. And Christmas coming on."

By now Nell was talking to herself. She put the phone down, then stood looking at it, after which she bit twice on her lip and said half aloud, "He'll go mad. Oh, I hope he doesn't phone." . . .

It was just after one o'clock when he did phone.

"Does a Mrs B live there?"

"It's me, Bill, Nell."

"Oh, hello there, Nell. Where's the little woman?"

". . . She's popped out, Bill."

"Popped out? Where?"

"She . . . she wanted something from the shops."

There was a pause now before Bill said, "It isn't the weather for a dog to be let loose today. What's she popped out for?"

". . . I'm . . . not quite sure, Bill."

"*Nell.*"

"Yes, Bill?"

"What's the matter?"

"Nothing . . . nothing, Bill."

"Are you tellin' me the truth?"

When she made no reply his voice barked, "Are you there?"

"Yes, Bill, I'm here, and . . . and I'm not telling you the truth."

"What's up?" His voice had dropped to almost a whisper now.

"She'll likely kill me for telling you, as you will her for keeping it from you, but she's had that pain again and never let on. She went to the doctor's and expected to be back about eleven, but he's sent her for tests."

"Where?"

"The General."

She actually pulled her head back when she heard the receiver banged down, then turned sharply as a small voice said, "Mammy B's a long time."

"She'll soon be home."

"I . . . I want Mammy B."

"Now don't you start." She held out her hand to the child. "Come on and let's get the sails trimmed because there's going to be a squall if I know anything."

The squall started in the hospital reception area. It was surprising to the spectators and certainly amusing when the tough-looking individual pushed open the main door, then stopped when he saw his wife standing at the desk talking to someone at the other side. There was another man and two women waiting in the hall, and two young men in white coats going one way while a nurse went the other when Bill almost bounced up to the counter and in what he imagined to be an undertone but was clear to everyone hissed, "What the hell are you up to, woman?"

"Oh!" It was evident that Fiona was startled, but she smiled and said, "It's you."

"Of course it's me. We see each other at times you know. What you doin' here?"

As she took the card from the wide-eyed nurse across the counter, she facetiously replied, "Performing an operation."

"Well, here's someone that'll perform another one when I get you home."

The two young men had stopped and were now approaching the counter. They didn't look at Bill but at Fiona and one of them asked quietly, "Are you all right?"

She smiled broadly at him now, saying, "Yes, thank you. This is my husband." And she made quite an elegant motion towards Bill. "As you can gather he's a very mild person. Takes things in his stride." She looked at Bill now and asked quietly, "Shall we go and continue this in private?" and before he had time to make any response she turned to the two young doctors and, still smiling, she said, "It's very nice to be cared for."

They both grinned at her now, but Bill, glaring at them, said, "I wouldn't make any rejoinder to that if I were you; I'm in a mood for wipin' grins off people's faces." And with that he took her arm none too gently and marched her out of the door.

But once outside her manner changed and, endeavouring to free herself from his grip, she said, "You are the one for making scenes, aren't you?"

"And you are the one for gettin' people stirred up. What the hell's all this about anyway? Frightening the liver out of me. Why couldn't you phone me and put me in the picture? With one thing and another I'm about right for Sedgefield."

Quietly now, she said, "And that's why I didn't want to worry you more than is absolutely necessary."

"You've gone a funny way about it."

"In my opinion it was the best way."

He was leading her towards his car now and she said, 'I'm quite fit enough to drive.

"Well, if you are or you aren't, you're not goin' to. Get in."

"Bill."

"Get in."

"But what about my car?"

"I'll send a couple of chaps along." . . .

Few words were exchanged on the journey home, but once inside the door Fiona, looking at Nell, said, "I told you." And Nell replied, "Well you try fobbing him off next time."

Then both she and Bill turned quickly to Fiona, saying, "What is it?"

"Nothing. Nothing." She stood drawing in deep breaths for a moment. "I just feel a bit muzzy, that's all."

His voice soft now, Bill said, "Come on." He put his arm around her and led her into the sitting-room and, looking at Nell, said, "A strong cup of tea, lass."

When she sat on the couch he lifted her legs up, pushed a cushion behind her head, then, kneeling by the side of the couch, he took her hands and said, "Got a pain?"

"No, no; nothing like that, only a bit queasy inside."

"What did they do? Why did you go to hospital?"

"I" – she drew in a long breath – "I never intended to go to hospital. I . . . I just went to Doctor Hall because I had a twinge in the side this morning, and I explained it to him, and when I said I'd had really nothing to eat since we had our meal last night, he phoned up the hospital and spoke to a colleague of his; and it should happen that this Doctor Amble could fit me in about twelve. No waiting, I was lucky I hadn't had that breakfast." She smiled at him now, saying, "It's good to have friends at court; it's amazing the strings that can be pulled. And by the way, he asked after Mark and how he was liking his new school. He's got a son there, in Mark's department. Not for much longer, he's going on to the upper school. By the way, what did you phone up about? Trouble?"

"No; I just wanted to tell you I was going into Newcastle to a meeting and that if it was over early enough I'd pick up Mark and we'd do a bit of shopping."

"Oh, I'm sorry . . . I mean, about the meeting."

"It's all right. It's all right." He stroked her hair back from her forehead. "I phoned them up. I asked for Ramshaw. He hadn't arrived yet they said, but old Kingdom Come came on. And when I told him that my wife—" he stressed the word, then tapped her cheek as he said, "has been taken into hospital, he was not concerned. 'Don't worry old fellow,' he said; 'everything will be all right. Don't worry.' Don't worry. He must have been joking. But he's a fine old bloke, and at the present moment I need the support of fine old blokes, if never before, for although I haven't seen much of Brown I've got the feeling that there's something in the wind. One thing I'm sure, he's not goin' to let up on me; he's the kind of fellow who keeps his promises. Oh, but why worry, lass; all that is secondary. What I should be doing, woman, now, instead of sympathising with you, is to be giving you a good going over with both hands and tongue, for Nell had me scared silly."

"Nell should never have told you. It's ridiculous."

"What is? That you're bad enough for a doctor to send you straightaway for a barium? Anyway, when will you know the result?"

"Not for a few days."

"Well now" – his voice sank low – "promise me you'll never keep anything from me again. Promise me. Good, bad, or indifferent, whatever the news, you'll tell me?"

"I promise"

He stared at her; then he asked quietly, "What does he think it is . . .?"

"An appendix of course."

"Well, if it's an appendix why don't they take you in and whip it out?"

"They don't do that these days, especially for a niggling little pain that I've got. And as I've said before, it mightn't be an appendix; it might be a twist in the bowel or. . . . Oh, it doesn't matter. Anyway, here's the informer with the tea."

As Nell put the tray on the table near the couch, Fiona said, "I'll have a word with you later, Mrs Paget."

"Very well, Mrs Bailey, ma'am. In the meantime sit up and drink this tea and stop pretending you're poorly." She now looked at Bill, saying, "She's only after sympathy. I know her kind; my mother used to be the same. Oh, by the way." She wagged her finger down at Fiona. "Speaking of the devil, she phoned."

"Mother?"

"Yes, Mother."

"You didn't tell her?"

"That you'd gone to hospital? No, no. They've got enough trouble in the hospital without her going there, I should imagine."

"What was she after?" It was Bill asking the question.

And, turning to him, she said, "She demanded that her daughter be put on the line. I said that her daughter was out, and that no, I didn't know when she'd be back; she was with Mr Bailey." She inclined her head towards Bill, then said, "I thought she had gone, there was such a long pause, and then she said, 'Tell my daughter I'm moving next Friday and I need help.'"

"Well now." He turned quickly to the couch and, stabbing his finger at Fiona, he said, "No go Friday, you understand? No matter how you're feelin', because if you don't promise me to stay put, I'll go along there an' raise hell. And you wouldn't like that, would you, Mrs B?"

"I have no intention of going to help her. And please don't bawl any more, Bill; I feel . . . well" – she shrugged her shoulders – "you know, a bit weary."

And with this she put down the cup on the side table and lay back, and Nell and Bill exchanged a startled glance because this wasn't like Fiona. Each in their own way could not have been more worried at the moment if she had voiced her inner thoughts and said, "I'm frightened. I couldn't bear that. I'd rather die."

20

❧❧

It was four days later and only a week to go until Christmas when the doctor's secretary phoned Fiona and asked if she would care to come to the surgery.

When at ten o'clock, she faced him across the desk and, looking at him, asked, "Well?" he said quietly, "I would like you to see Mr Morgan. I've made an appointment for the day after tomorrow. You remember him? He saw you about three years ago when you were in for tests."

"Yes. Yes." She moved her head twice; then gulped in her throat where the words were sticking and which would have asked, "What did the X-ray show?" She knew that he would know what they had shown but that he wasn't going to tell her unless she asked. And she couldn't ask; she must put it off a little longer, for Christmas was near, and there were the children, and the tree, and Bill. Oh, yes, and Bill.

Her mind started to gabble now: It was fortunate she had Nell. It was funny how things happened. Nell had to come on the scene when she was most needed. And Nell was so good, and the children loved her, and ... and. . . ."

"Now don't worry." Doctor Hall's hand had come across the desk and was gripping her twitching fingers. "There's nothing definite, nothing to worry about as yet."

As yet. As yet. As yet. The words were going away like an echo in her mind. She stood up, telling herself that she must get out in the air.

He walked to the door with her, where he again said, "Now don't worry. Enjoy Christmas with the children. It's their time, isn't it?"

"Then I won't have to go in?"

"No, no; I shouldn't think so. No, no." He patted her shoulder. "Anyway, I'll pop in in a day or two. Now do as I tell you and don't worry."

She was out in the air and she gasped at it. She had read somewhere, or someone had told her, that if you took ten slow, slow breaths and counted each one as they came, it settled your nerves amazingly.

She was sitting behind the wheel of the car when she finished the tenth, and yes, it seemed to work, she did feel calmer. . . .

Nell seemed to have been waiting at the door for her, it opened so quickly, but she didn't ask any questions as she helped her off with her coat, but said, "The coffee's brewing. And listen to them." She thumbed towards the stairs. "They are so excited; they won't last out until Christmas. They'll burn themselves up before then. I'm glad Mark breaks up soon; he'll help keep them in order."

She led the way towards the kitchen, and not until she had poured out the coffee did she ask quietly, "Well, what did he say?"

"Nothing that I can go on. I've got to see Mr Morgan the day after tomorrow. The only thing he implied was that whatever it is there's no rush, and not to worry."

"Well, that's a relief. Now drink that and get on the phone to that fellow of yours, because if not you'll have him round here at dinner time. And there's only so much my nerves will stand." She smiled now, then added somewhat sadly, "You're lucky you know, Fiona; he's one in a thousand or more."

"Yes, I know. . . . Oh yes, I know, Nell."

"I had a letter from Harry this morning."

"You did? Does he want to come back?"

"Want to come back? He wants the divorce getting through as quickly as possible! If it wasn't that he never wanted children I would have imagined that she's pregnant."

"He'll have to support you."

"I hate that idea. I want nothing from him now; but his dad says he's got to pay. Funny you know, but they're both more bitter than I am, and he's their son. Anyway, enough about me. Drink up, then get on the phone." . . .

It was as if Bill too had been waiting at the other end of the line for before she even got his name out he said, "Well, love, what did he say?"

"Oh" – she made her voice light – "not to worry. I've got to go and see Mr Morgan the day after tomorrow. But there's nothing to worry about, no hurry."

"Is that straight?"

"Exactly his words, to which he added that Christmas is near and it was a time for children, and I must enjoy myself. I don't know whether he was classing me with the children or not."

"Oh, lass, you've taken a load off my shoulders. Now I'll be able to carry the tree back on me own."

"You've got a tree?"

"Aye. Bert, the one who hasn't any truck with either wine women, or baccy – By! they are pullin' his leg, but he's takin' it – he's a good fella in all ways is Bert, he tells me he's picked one up from the forestry. It's all of ten feet high and he's got it along at his place. He says it's practically the length of his garden. So you'd better get cracking and make room for it."

"Where do you think I'm going to put a ten foot tree?"

"In the dining-room of course, in the bay window. I'll have to get a tub for it though. Anyway, I'll see about all that when I get back. And, oh love, you've got no idea how relieved I feel . . . I love you, Mrs Bailey."

"Gert ya."

"Gert ya."

She put the phone down, turned her back to the hall table, bowed her head and closed her eyes.

By the following night the tree not only was installed in its butter tub, but also had coloured fairy lights entwined from the top branches.

Bill was standing on top of a pair of steps and the children were arguing among themselves which glass bauble would be suitable for which branch. Willie, holding a white glass swan, handed it up to Bill, saying, "Put this on the top, Mr Bill," only to be shouted down by Katie, crying, "Don't be silly! The fairy goes on the top."

"Needn't."

"She does, doesn't she, Mam?"

"Well, yes, she usually does. But Willie's swan, I think

would look better on that branch sticking out there." She pointed. "See, Bill? What do you say to that one for Willie's swan?"

"Aye, yes, I think it would show better there. Hand it here, fella."

When the swan was resting precariously on the swaying branch, Fiona stepped back, apparently in admiration, saying, "Oh, it looks lovely with the pink light shining on it."

"Swans are not pink."

"Katie!" There was a warning in the name, and Katie, giving herself a shake, said, "Well, he's always contrary."

"*Oh! Oh!* Look who's talking." Mark now laughed, and Katie rounded on him, saying, "Don't you start on me, our Mark."

Then a voice boomed over them all, crying, "An' don't any-body start on anybody! And if you want my opinion, everybody is a little tired, so I think we've all had enough for tonight. Look at the time, it's nine o'clock. It's past my bedtime. So come on, scram Sam! the lot of you."

Bill stepped down onto the floor and amid oohs and aahs and protestations he bundled them all into the hall, where Willie exclaimed loudly, "I want something to eat, I'm hungry." And Bill, looking at Mark, said, "Captain, would you mind taking this crew into the kitchen and feedin' them milk and two biscuits each. No more! Two's the limit because we don't want anybody being sick in the night. Do we now? Do we?"

"Will do, sir." Mark saluted smartly, and with this he mar-shalled the small gang of protestors kitchenwards. Then as Bill, laughing now, went to follow Fiona into the sitting-room, the phone rang and they both stopped and Fiona whispered, "That'll likely be Mother."

"Let me deal with her."

"No, no."

"I say, yes."

He went and lifted up the phone while keeping his eyes on Fiona. But the voice he heard wasn't that of Mrs Vidler, but that of his nightwatchman, Arthur Taggart, who said, "This is Taggart. That you, boss?"

"Yes, yes, Arthur. What is it?"

There was quite a long pause before the voice said, "Got bad news, boss. The . . . the show house, it's . . . it's been wrecked. It's . . . it's a mess. But I got him, at least Dandy did, as he was coming out of the window. He had taken the pane out, professionally like with brown paper."

Bill was no longer looking at Fiona but staring into the phone, saying, "Who? Who were they?"

"No they, boss, just one."

"A man?"

"No, no, it's a lad. I've got him. He's in the tool-shed. Dandy's standing guard. He's petrified now. There's another thing, boss. You . . . you know who he is?"

"I know who he is? What d'you mean?" He was yelling now.

"Well, I know who he is an' all. You see, I told you I worked there for a time afore you set me on. I did odd jobs for him, but never liked him."

"My God! No! The Brown lad?"

"No other, boss. I . . . I was gona call the polis straightaway, but thought, what'll I do? Will I ring 'em, boss?"

Bill held the phone some distance away from him and didn't answer for a moment until the nightwatchman's voice came again, saying, 'You there, boss?"

"Yes. Yes, I'm here, but I'll be with you in a few minutes. And no, don't phone the polis, I'll see to it meself."

He put the phone down, then turned and looked at Fiona who was standing close by his side now, and without any preamble he said, "That Brown bastard has wrecked the show house."

"Oh no!"

He moved from her. Going swiftly to the wardrobe in the hall, he took down his coat and cap, saying as he did so, "Now get yourself to bed; I don't know how long I'll be."

"Oh! Bill, what next?" She put out her hands and buttoned the top button of his great coat, while he repeated her words, "Aye, what next? But I've been expectin' something – I didn't know what – yet, I never thought it would come from the lad."

"If . . . if you've got to stay very long will you phone me?"

"Yes, yes, I'll do that, but don't stay up. Now promise me? Go straight to bed, and don't tell them I'm out." He thumbed towards the kitchen.

"But they'll hear the car."

"I'll run her out quietly into the road." He kissed her hurriedly, then went out. . . .

In less than ten minutes he was on the site. The light was on in the men's cabin and also in the tool-shed. Arthur Taggart met him in the yard.

"Has he said anything?"

"No, nothing. He would have defied me if I'd been on me own. He used his feet on me when I caught hold of him. But he's scared stiff of the dog. D'you want to see him first?"

"No; let's look at the damage."

The show house had been just that, a show house. He had been proud of it and proud of Fiona's choice of furnishings and colours. The sitting-room had been done in tones of mushroom, shell pink, and grey; the dining-room had been furnished with very good reproduction furniture. Now, as he stepped onto the pain-smeared carpet and looked at the ripped upholstery of the couch and chairs and the paint-smeared walls, the blazing anger died in him, and he felt the oddest feeling, such as a woman might have felt, for he had the inclination to cry.

The sight that met him in the kitchen was even worse, for the fittings had been ripped from the wall, levered off as Arthur Taggart pointed out.

Then, leading to the upstairs rooms, the banisters had been daubed with red and green paint, and the landing walls and carpets sprayed with what looked like tar.

When Bill picked up the silk bed cover that had been torn in two he looked at Arthur Taggart and said, "It must have taken him some time to do all this. Where were you?"

"On me rounds, boss. I do it every hour, honest to God! An' I don't only go round the blocks, I go in and out of the houses; except of course, the six that are already occupied at yon end. And Mr Rice in the end one, he could tell you; he said the other night he timed his watch by me."

"Aye, and somebody else has timed their watch by you, Arthur. He couldn't do this kind of damage without a torch. But he knew what time you'd be round here again. Did you change your routine the night?"

"No . . . well, not exactly. And I don't keep to it strictly. You know what I mean? I might go to the east side and end up with the west, or vice versa some nights. But it was as I came round the bottom end that Dandy's head went up and he started to sniff, and I always know what that means. And I let him off, and he caught him getting out of the pantry window. It's amazing how he got through, it can't be eighteen inches. But apparently he knew where it was. Have you seen him round, boss?"

"No; he hasn't been round to my knowledge. But then there's Sunday and I'm very rarely here then, one or the other take over. . . . Well" – he ground his teeth together – "let's go and see him."

The tool-shed was lit by a single electric bulb but it showed up vividly the boy in the paint-smeared overalls crouching among the tools, with the dog lying, paws and head forward, staring at him.

Bill did not go near him nor did he make any comment, but the boy, spluttering, said, "T . . . t . . . take th . . . th . . . that dog . . . awa . . . away."

"Not frightened of a dog are are you, a brave lad like you?" This came from Arthur Taggart. And the boy, now looking towards Bill, said, "I . . . I want my father."

Still Bill did not speak, until, turning and going out of the door, he muttered, "You'll get your father. Oh, you'll get your father." And Arthur, after commanding the dog: "Stay! Dandy," followed him.

Bill now unlocked his office door and, going straight to the directory, he found the number he was looking for and dialled it.

A woman's voice, said, "This is Mr Brown's residence. Who's speaking?"

Bill said, "Tell Mr Brown to come to the phone."

"I'm . . . I'm sorry, Mr Brown isn't in."

"Listen to me, missis, you go and tell your boss that his son is in dire trouble."

"*What!*"

"You heard."

"Yes, yes, I heard. But . . . but I tell you, Mr Brown isn't in. He isn't here. They've both gone out to dinner."

"*Where?*"

There was a pause before the answer came. "The Gosforth Park Hotel."

Bill banged down the phone, thumbed quickly through the directory, and once more lifted the receiver.

"Gosforth Park Hotel. Can I help you?"

"Yes, you can. Have you a Mr and Mrs Brown dining with you?"

"I . . . I can enquire, sir."

"Thank you. Do that." He drummed on the desk as he waited, looking now and again at Arthur Taggart. Then the voice came to him, saying, "Yes, Mr and Mrs Brown have had dinner. They're in the lounge. I think they're on the point of leaving."

"Well, will you be kind enough to tell him to come to the phone? It's very, very important,"

"I'll . . . I'll do that, sir."

Again there was a long wait, longer this time; then the recognised voice, "Yes? Who is it?"

"This happens to be Bill Bailey here. I just want to tell you that your son has completely wrecked my show house. And. . . ."

"What are you saying? What are you talking about? Now look here!"

"If you'll shut that mouth of yours for a moment you'll hear what I'm talking about. Your son was caught leaving the show house through a back window, and evidence is all over him. He under guard now. I thought I'd put you in the picture before the police take him."

"My God! You've set this up."

"Yes, of course, I've set this up. I hired him to come and smash the place up. Don't be such a bloody fool, man. Well, there you have it." He was about to put the phone down when the voice yelled at him, "Wait! Wait! Are the police there?"

"Not yet."

"You haven't rung them?"

"No; but I intend to when I put this phone down."

"Bailey. Look. Give me fifteen minutes. I'll be there."

Bill stared into the mouthpiece of the phone; then slowly he replaced it, and when a minute later he hadn't picked it up again to phone the police, Arthur Taggart said, "A patrol car passes round here about this time, you could get them if you phoned the station."

He looked up at the man, then said, "I'll hold me hand, Arthur; the police come they'll yank him straight off. I want our Mr Brown to see his son exactly where he is now with the evidence all over him. You know what he said? He said I'd fixed it."

"No! He must be bloody mad."

Bill now picked up the phone again and rang Fiona.

"Listen, love," he said, "I'm likely to be here for sometin yet. Brown's on his way."

"Is it bad?"

"Couldn't be worse if a fire had hit it."

"And you've got him?"

"Oh, yes, we've got him. And I've got Brown an' all. I God! I have. And I mean to turn the screw. . . . Are you bed?"

"No, no, of course not."

"Well, do what you're told, d'you hear? because I could like be another couple of hours if the police come in on it."

"Haven't you called the police yet?"

"No, not yet."

"I suppose you have a reason."

"Yes, I have a reason. Now get to bed, dear. 'Bye."

"Are you going to bring him in here?" said Arthur Tagga now.

"No; no, he's goin' to stay where he is cringing like the your swab he is, and so his dear papa can see him." Then he adde "You've got a good dog there, Arthur."

"The best. Within seconds he had torn the pants off him."

"He tore his pants?"

"Yes, overalls, pants, the lot, they're stripped down th back."

"Huh! That's funny. Poetic justice that." He didn't go on explain about the poetic justice, but after a moment he sai "Put the main lights on outside, Arthur, so the great man ca see where he's going and not run into the mixer. Not that I mind that happening." . . .

It was fifteen minutes later when Brown drove his car into th yard. Bill was standing in his office doorway and he kept h surprise hidden when, not only Brown came towards him, b his wife also.

"What's this? Now what are you up to?"

He ignored the man for a moment and, looking at the ta woman with the pale face, he said, "Good-evening, M Brown."

Her reply was hesitant, but when it came it sounded col "Good-evening, Mr Bailey."

"Cut the pleasantries for God's sake! Where's my boy?"

Bill now motioned the nightwatchman towards him, sayir

"First things first. Lead the way to the show house, Arthur."

A minute or so later they were all standing in the vandalised house. And it was evident that even Brown was shocked. As for his wife, she turned a painful look on Bill and shook her head, but she said nothing. But what he said was, "Mind where you step, Mrs Brown . . . the carpet has been freshly painted."

When, after going round the ground floor, Mrs Brown went to mount the stairs, her husband said, "You needn't go up there."

She turned and looked at him, but still she did not speak; then slowly she mounted the stairs.

When they were all outside once more, Brown, blustering now, said, "I don't believe it. I just don't believe it. Anyway, who was with him? He couldn't have done this on his own. Who are the others?"

"There were no others, sir," Arthur Taggart replied.

"How do you know?"

"It's my job to know, and that of my dog."

"Dog?"

"Yes, sir, my dog got him backing out of the window." He pointed along the side of the house. "He had done the job thoroughly, prepared for it, worked it out like: brown paper pasted on the window to kill the noise of broken glass. . . ."

"Where is he?" Brown was now looking at Bill.

Bill made no reply, but walked away and the others followed.

When he opened the door of the tool-shed they all filed in, but the only immediate response to the crouching boy was a gasp from his mother. But even now she didn't speak. It was the boy who spoke, saying, "Dad, that dog, they . . . they set the dog on me, Dad."

When, making to step forward, Brown dislodged some shovels, the dog turned its head in his direction and bared its teeth and growled. And at this Arthur Taggart commanded, "Up boy! Here!" And the dog, slowly rising, backed two steps then turned towards its master and stood by his side.

"Dad. Dad."

"Get up!" The boy struggled to his feet, then leant against the partition, his hands behind him holding up his torn clothes. Then turning his head away from his father's furious gaze, he whimpered, "Mother. Mother." Then added, "I . . . I didn't do it. I was just passing, and I saw."

"Shut your mouth, you idiot!"

The boy, now seeming to lose all fear for a moment, straight ened up and cried, "Well, you were always on about him: wha you were going to do, and you never did it. And they wer laughing at me at school, and . . . and giving me a nickname and. . . ."

When the blow struck his head the boy reeled to the side an almost fell into the tools. And now Mrs Brown did speak: "Tha has come too late," she said.

They were all looking at the tall indignant figure who ha now turned to Bill, saying, "Is there any place where we ma talk, Mr Bailey?"

"Yes; come into the office."

Brown did not even wait for his wife or son to precede hir into the office but marched ahead.

Inside, Bill offered Mrs Brown a chair, but she refused it wit a small shake of her head while she kept her eyes fixed on he son, who was now gripping to his side a length of his tor trousers and overall in his trembling rubber-gloved hand.

"Have you notified the police?" Brown's voice was a growl

Bill answered calmly, "Not as yet. I thought it would be wise fc you to be here when they came, for anything he says then could b taken down and used in evidence against him. That's how th procedure goes, isn't it?" He glanced at the boy as he spoke.

"Well, as far as I can see, it's a . . . well it's a private matte. I'll make good the damage, so we can let it rest there."

"*Oh! no. Oh! no.* Not this time."

"What do you mean, not this time?"

"I let it rest there when he burnt my son. And it's poeti justice, don't you think, that the dog should have got him in th same place, only his teeth didn't go far enough, not like a flamin firework. So there's no way you're goin' to settle his lates escapade in your own way. I've had enough of you and you undercover tactics from the beginning, only they've increase over the last weeks. You couldn't come yourself so you ser your stooge. And you've trained him well. So. . . ."

"Mr Bailey."

He looked at Mrs Brown.

"I'm sure you won't be troubled any further with m husband's tactics, undercover or otherwise."

"No? What guarantee have you for saying that Mrs Brown?

His voice was quiet but held a firm enquiry.

"Oh, I suppose you haven't heard, but he is resigning from the Finance Board."

The start that Brown gave as he turned towards his wife was almost like a shout of denial. But he didn't speak, only glared at her; and she didn't turn towards him but kept her eyes fixed on Bill as she went on, "We are moving to London shortly, where, as I think you know, my husband has a number of interests. Isn't that so, James?"

It looked for a moment as if her husband was going to choke, but still he said nothing, and she went on, "And my son is going to a school in Scotland. It's near where my uncle lives; it is rather remote but there's a lot of outdoor life and I'm sure the training will prove good for his future."

Her son was looking at her opened-mouthed now. And it was he who spoke, saying one word, "Mother."

"Yes?"

"I ... I promise you, I won't do ... do anything ever ... ever again."

"I know you won't, dear."

Bill felt a strange chill going through him as he looked at this tall elegant woman, for in this moment she was emanating power, a cold, even ruthless power. But how had she come by it? Evidently she had some hold over Brown, and it was great enough to have turned the man's colour to a sickly grey and caused the boy to bow his head.

She was looking at him again, saying now, "So do you think, Mr Bailey, under the circumstances, you could overlook this final insult? And I can give you my word and I have never yet been known to break it." Did she send a sidelong glance towards her husband? Perhaps it was a trick of the light, because she went on, "So I can assure you that you or yours will never again be subjected to abuse in any form from my family."

He did not answer her right away but stared at her as if fascinated. He had been attracted to her the last time she had stood in this office. Oh yes, he had. He loved Fiona and would never love anyone else like he loved her, but that didn't stop him from admiring another woman. And he had admired this one, and he still admired her; but his admiration was now tinged with something that he couldn't put a name to. But whatever it was he didn't like it, and he was damned glad she wasn't his wife. Well, of course, he told himself, she wouldn't be for he'd have never got hitched to her. But how had she come to be Brown's wife? Yes, that was the question that would always puzzle him: Why had she taken a fellow like Brown, a woman like her? And ten or twelve years ago she must have been an absolute stunner, she still was. But. . . .

He heard himself say, "Well—" Then he made himself pause and looked from Brown to his son. The boy was staring at him, but Brown was half-turned away as if he was looking towards the door. Then he went on. "If as you say, your plans are all set to move, and your husband is leaving the firm, and your son is going to be taught how to behave, and the wilds of Scotland will likely prove more effective in the long run than Borstal. . . ."

Brown's voice cut in on him like the crack of a gun as he swung round, crying, "There'd be no Borstal. He wouldn't get Borstal for that."

"Wouldn't he? Well, shall we try?" His hand went to the phone.

"James!" Almost like a fierce but whipped cur Brown swung round again towards the door, and in this moment Bill had it in his heart to be sorry for the man, for as he saw it, it wasn't right that any man, particularly a husband, should be made to look small by a woman. And he asked himself again: How on earth had this marriage come about? And to what did she owe the power that she definitely possessed?

His voice was curt when he next spoke, "As I said, I'll take your word for it, Mrs Brown. . . . And you will make good the damage?"

"Yes, of course, Mr Bailey. Thank you."

As she now walked to the door that Arthur Taggart was holding open for her, the boy scampered after her, whimpering "Mother. Mother." But it was as if she hadn't heard him.

Brown did not immediately follow them; he remained staring at Bill. And what he said now could have been enigmatic, but Bill got its meaning: his words were, "I intend to live a long time."

21

It had been quite a morning. All the men were up in arms about the vandalism, and to those he termed his Board he gave as much explanation as he thought necessary. And to a man, they said he had been daft; this was a chance to get his own back on Brown. Why hadn't he taken it? And to this he had replied, they had made a deal and Brown wouldn't be troubling them in future. That's as far as he had gone. He couldn't have said Mrs Brown had taken things into her own hands which, the more he thought about it, the more he realised were frightfully strong. And more than once during the morning when his thoughts returned to the matter he would again ask himself how she had managed to get linked up with Brown.

However, around twelve o'clock, the mystery was solved for him.

It was at this time that a chauffeur-driven Rolls came into the yard and out of it stepped Sir Charles Kingdom. The old man greeted Bill heartily, saying, "You are getting on with this lot, aren't you? What are you going to do when it's finished?"

Laughingly Bill replied, "Keep hoping that you will get me another site, sir."

"Well! well! You can always hope, you know. Can we talk somewhere?"

"You don't want to see round, sir?"

"No, no; I don't want to see round."

Bill did him the courtesy of seating him in his own chair and was surprised when the old man said, "Nasty business last night." And further when pursing his lips, he said, "You are surprised I know all about it? I knew all about it by breakfast time; Eva phoned me."

Bill's lips repeated the words but no sound came from them

and Sir Charles now said, "What you don't know is, I'm her godfather."

"Really, sir?"

'Yes, really. Wasted life, utterly wasted life. God Almighty! the things women do. You've met her twice. She told me she first saw you after you lathered the boy. You did a damn fine job there I'd say. Has it ever made you ponder, having seen her, why she got linked up with Brown?"

"To be honest, sir, it's made me ponder up till this very minute."

"And you're not the only one. But up home in Scotland" – he thumbed over his shoulders as if Scotland lay just beyond the yard – "if the truth isn't known it's pretty well guessed at. Do you know, she had every fellow in the county at her feet when she was nineteen? She had been sent to a sort of modern finishing school in Paris, and she comes back into that house, that mausoleum of a house. Her father was my second cousin, you know. Damned hypocrite if ever there was one. Supported the church, could pick his ministers; he was lousy rich, mostly inherited; but he had fingers in all kinds of pies, too, the main one a distillery. Yes, yes, a distillery, and him reading the lesson every Sunday like Michael the Archangel. And she was just as bad, his wife, Liza. Well, as I was saying, young Eva comes back to that atmosphere after seeing life abroad, and she hated it. She told me so herself. 'How am I going to get out of this, Uncle Charles?' she said, 'Marry,' I said. And I can see her now ticking off on her fingers the fellows she knew, half of them belonging to the church and half of the other given up to horse ridin' and whorin'. But that still left two or three decent chaps. But she wasn't attracted by them. . . . Aren't women fools, Bailey?"

"Well—" Bill hesitated, then added, "There are exceptions, sir."

"Few and far between. Well anyway, as I was saying, more to pass the time than anything she used to go round the works. And Brown at that time was undermanager, risen up from the bottles, he had, ambitious fellow. He was a man at this time, too, eleven years older than her, and he made it his business to speak to her every time he saw her. And she chatted to him. He was different, you see, from the usual men she met. And then came the night of the staff party. By the way she had only one brother, just one, Ian, a bit hot-headed but a decent enough chap, and he was very protective of her. Anyway, the wine flowed and Eva went missing. Ian looked for her and found her, but too late. She was in the old summer-house in the wood, and so was Brown. . . . And apparently the deed was done. My! my! yes." The old man paused and sighed heavily before going on.

"Lord above! When Liza knew, that was her mother, she nearly went insane. And you know how her father took it? He had a damned heart attack. There were great consultations. My mother was present, we lived just down the valley. She and Liza had been girlhood friends. It was proposed that the child be taken away. But apparently Eva wasn't for this. She dug her heels in. It was pointed out to her, I understand, that no man in the county would take her on, ever. And to this she had replied defiantly, that Brown would. So that's how it came about. Brown was quietly upgraded; he became manager of one of old George's many pies he had in England. And you won't believe it, it was sort of arranged by the family that before that happened Eva and Brown should do a kind of eloping act. It made everything more normal like, as they said. And that's what did happen."

The old man now took out a small snuffbox, retrieved a pinch, placed it in the hollow between his first finger and thumb, sniffed at it twice, then dabbed at his nose with a large blue silk handkerchief, before saying, "Brown thought he was clever, but he didn't know what he was taking on. Eva is a formidable woman, not only in her character, but because she holds the purse strings. I'll give her father his due, the old man never altered his will. And so when he died she got a good slice of the takings. But the old fellow had made one stipulation and that was the money must always remain in her name. And not only did she get a big dollop of cash, but she got a biscuit factory, and a share in a big healthy removal business. Oh, she's a very, very wealthy woman is Eva. But now what I'm going to say after all that is going to surprise you, Bailey, and it's just this . . . I'm sorry for Brown. Can you believe that?"

Bill was some time in answering because he was reliving the scene that had taken place in this office last night. But when he spoke he said. "Yes, in a way, but only in a way."

"Oh, I can see it from your point of view. And the man's a vindictive stinker, I know. But my God, he must have had something to put up with because Eva is like an icicle. And really he's still only a manager: although he seems to play about with money, everything has to be O.K.'ed by her. She has her hands tightly on the reins and sees to the business side of most things. Can you believe that?'

"Yes, yes, I can believe it."

"But on the other hand, just think, Bailey, if she had married a decent bloke, somebody she loved, you would have seen a woman with a heart today."

Bill now said quietly, "She's a courageous woman. She must have had that courage when she was young; why didn't she just go and have the child?"

"Simply because, I suppose, she had been brought up in luxury, and she hadn't a penny of her own and they would certainly not have given her a farthing, at least at that time, so she could see no other option."

"Is her mother still alive?"

"Oh yes; and her brother too of course. That's where she's sending the boy. He's got an estate up in the hills and the school that the boy will go to is quite near. And if between them they don't make him into some sort of a man I'll be surprised, because it's Brown's fault the boy is as he is, Brown's tried to get his own back on Eva by toadying for the boy's affection, giving him all he wanted on the quiet. But truth to tell, Eva's got no love for the lad. . . . How's your life? How do you find your wife?"

"My home life is very good, sir. I have an excellent wife."

"You took her on with three children, I understand; and adopted another?"

"Yes, I did."

"You like children?"

"Yes, I'm very fond of children, sir."

"Why don't you have some of your own then?"

"Give me time, sir. I promised her to make the family up to ten."

"Ha! Ha!" The old man laughed loudly. "What does she say about that?"

"She's quite willin'."

"You're a lucky man then."

"Yes, I'm a lucky man, sir."

"By the way" – the old man pulled himself up from the chair – "don't go spreading round what I've told you. And I can add this, I love that girl but I'm not proud of her actions last night, to bring him low in front of you and a watchman. She could have done it in another way."

"Why doesn't she divorce him?"

"Why does a cat play with a mouse? She hasn't said much about the private side of her marriage, you understand, but from the little I gather he must have given her a rough time at first. But don't forget she was a nineteen-year-old old and he was thirty, and brute strength can prevail for a time at any rate. Anyway, he soon had to find his pleasures elsewhere. He had his women on the side, a permanent one I understand."

"And she puts up with that?" Bill's nostrils had widened.

"Apparently. Do you read history at all? All wicked women are subtle. Well now, I must be away. I hate Christmas, always have done. My two sons and my daughter bring their squads and my son's daughter even brings hers. Can you believe that? I'm a great-grandfather."

Bill smiled tolerantly at the old man, saying kindly now, "I don't believe you don't enjoy Christmas, sir."

"You can take it from me I don't." He now punched Bill on the shoulder. "I went missing last Christmas Day. There was a hue and cry all over the house. I heard them. There's a closet in the attic. Well, it's a kind of little room. I used to hide in it when I was a boy and so did my sons and grandsons, but they didn't remember it until they became desperate. And I heard Geoffrey saying, 'He couldn't be in there, not all this time.' But I was, with a bottle of good port and a box of cigars. But the latter was a pleasure I had to forego because they would have smelt them. Anyway, the children enjoyed finding me. They laughed their heads off, but their parents weren't amused." He went out chuckling.

The chauffeur held the car door open for him and had already started the engine when the old man's window began to slide down and, pushing his wrinkled face out towards Bill, he said, "I've got a good wife, too." He made a deep obeisance with his head. "Very understanding. Always has been, in all ways." And now a mischievous grin on his face, he ended, "Never gave me any need to go hunting, never, except the fox. Understand?"

The window was sliding up again and Bill was left standing, the laughter in him making his eyes moist as he watched the car backing into the road.

There went a character. Wait until he got home and told Fiona.

At three o'clock, a maid showed Fiona into a room that could have been a study or a sitting-room. She took in the overall comfort as Mr Morgan led her to a seat. Then he discussed the weather loudly as he went around a teak desk and, after seating himself, he drew a file towards him which he opened, read a little, then looking at her and smiling, said, "Ah, well now . . . how are you feeling?"

"Not on top of the world. . . . Naturally, I'm worried."

"Of course, of course. Well now, we had the plates back and as you may have already gathered they show trouble with the appendix. But lower down it has revealed a . . . er . . . rather dark mass. Now, that's what we've got to think about, isn't it?"

She was unable to answer. Deep in the pit of her stomach there was a feeling that told her she could be sick at any minute. There flashed through her mind the picture of the children before she left the house and Mamie crying as she said, "You going on a holiday, Mammy B?"

It was Mamie's kind of holiday that was in her mind now, and had been for days because of the answer to the dreaded question that could lead her to that holiday.

She hadn't meant to ask. She had told herself she wouldn't ask. But she heard a small voice say, "Could it be cancer?"

"Yes, yes, it could; but of course we won't know exactly until we get inside, will we?"

My God! Just like that, straight out. He had said, "Yes, yes, it could." Why couldn't he have lied? Or put it in a different way? But to say? "Yes, yes, it could." What was she going to say to Bill who was waiting outside. She was sweating. There was a buzzing in her ears. She could hear his voice. It was as if he was standing behind her, saying, "You're going to be all right, Mrs B."

She was hearing Mr Morgan clearly once more; "We're right on the holidays and one or two more days won't make all that difference, because I know you would like to be with your children for Christmas, but if you would care to go in sooner I could get Mr Rice to see to it, although I would rather do it myself. However, it's up to you."

"Oh. Oh, I'll wait. Yes, please. But when will that be?"

"Well now; I don't think we should leave it too long." He drew an appointment book towards him and, after flicking the pages, he again said, "Well now." This seemed to be a pet phrase of his. "Well now, let's see. How about Friday. You will come in, of course, the previous day. It's the Nuffield, isn't it? Shall I make arrangements for that day, Thursday the twenty-seventh?"

"Yes, please."

"Well then, that's it."

He rose from behind the desk. She too rose, and as he led her to the door he held out his hand and shook hers warmly, saying, "Enjoy your Christmas.". . . .

The car was across the road from the house. Bill was walking up and down on the pavement.

On seeing her, he dodged between two cars and caught her arm; but not until they were seated in the car did he ask, "How did you get on then?"

She did not look at him but through the windscreen to where a line of bare poplar trees were all bending in the wind. "I'm to go in on the twenty-seventh."

"Operation?" His voice seemed to come from high in his head, and now she looked at him and said, "Yes, dear, operation the following day."

"What is it?"

She told herself she was speaking the truth when she said, "He doesn't rightly know, apart from the appendix."

"But they took an X-ray."

"Yes" – she made herself smile – "but X-rays don't exactly talk, they just indicate."

"Well, hell's flames! what did they indicate?"

She screwed up her eyes and turned her head away as she muttered, "Oh, Bill, don't shout. Don't go on."

"Oh! love." His arms were about her. "I'm nearly out of me mind thinkin' the worst. Are you sure he said he didn't know?"

"Yes, yes, dear, I'm sure. They'll know more when they take the appendix out."

"So there is more to know?"

"Yes, I suppose so. But he says, not to worry."

"Oh, that's the set phrase." He clapped his hands on the wheel now. "You would think they were talking to bairns, that lot. Not to worry. They say to all and sundry, not to worry. Why can't they think up some kind of machine they can attach to us that stops us from worrying."

"Let's get home, Bill." Her voice was quiet now. And when he started up the car, she said, "Bill." And his name was an appeal.

"Yes, love?"

"You mustn't let on to the children."

"No, you're right there. But, on the other hand, I think you should tell Mark, because he's got a head on his shoulders, that boy. He doesn't think of himself as a child any more, not on a level with the others."

"Perhaps you're right, but we'll just say it's for the appendix."

"Well, let's hope to God it is . . . just the appendix. . . ."

On entering the house, they were assailed by a loud chorus from the kitchen of "Good King Wenceslas".

They looked at each other and smiled and Bill, as he helped her off with her coat, said, " 'Bill Bailey' on the tin whistle sounded better. Leave them to it; come on and rest."

"No; let's go and see them."

There was a great rush from the table, and Nell's voice, rising above the hubbub, cried, "Manners! Manners!" to which both Katie and Willie chorused, "Pianos, piecrusts and perambulators."

"Finish your tea, all of you!"

"We've finished, Mam." It was another chorus.

"You feeling all right, Mam?" It was a quiet enquiry from Mark. And looking at him lovingly, she said, "Yes, dear, I'm feeling all right."

"We've been singing Good King Whens at last looked out."

"You keep saying it all wrong." Katie now gave Willie a none too gentle push. "It's Good King *Wenceslas*. That's his name, not When's at last looked out. That's daft."

"It doesn't matter if he looked out first, last or in between, it sounds all right to me," Bill said diplomatically now. Then looking at Nell, he asked, "Any tea going?"

"I've set yours in the sitting-room."

"Oh, hotel service now. We're going up in the world, Mrs B, aren't we?" Bill jerked his head at Fiona, and she, looking towards Nell, said, "That's nice. Thanks, dear." Then bringing her attention back to her family again, she added, "Help Nell clear, then upstairs with you. You've all got your Christmas presents to do, haven't you?"

"You coming up Mammy B to tie my bows?"

Before Fiona could make any response to the child, Katie, bending towards Mamie, said, "I've told you it's just like tying your shoe-laces, only you're doing it with ribbon."

"I'll be up as soon as I have a cup of tea." Fiona stroked the head that was pressed against her side. And as she did so she looked towards Mark, and he, getting the message, took the child's hand, saying, "Come on, you. Don't think you're going to get out of your job, you've got to carry the plates."

Bill now marshalled Fiona firmly from the kitchen, across the hall and into the sitting-room, where, drawn up near the couch, was a table set for two, and on it small plates of mince pies, bread and butter, scones, and jam.

Fiona stood for a moment looking down on it, then said quietly, "What would I do without Nell?"

Bill made no reply to this but, pulling her down beside him on the couch, he took her face between his hands, saying softly, "What would I do without you? God! woman, what would I do without you? Remember that, will you? There's a lot to be said for will power and right thinkin'. They're gettin' on to the track of that these days, right thinkin'. You can almost cure anything with right thinkin'."

As the door opened and Nell entered with the tea-tray, he sat back on the couch and, reverting to his old style, he said, "You've taken your time."

"My duty is to tend the first-class customers first," she retorted. "And if you're not comfortable in this hotel you know where you can go."

"I'll report you to the authorities, madam, for insolence."

"Do it, fella. Anyway, in the meantime get your tea, and you know what I hope it does to you."

Fiona's head was resting against the back of the couch; her eyes were closed. She knew what these two were aiming to do with their jocular abuse. She said quietly, "Will you pop in before you go home, Nell? because if I understand rightly from previous arrangements, this gentleman is going out to do some late night shopping."

"I can put that off until tomorrow."

"I don't want you to put it off until tomorrow." She sat up now and put her hand out towards the teapot as she ended, "Don't forget what you promised the squad tomorrow; the pantomime's on at the Royal."

"Nell can take them."

"Nell can't." Nell's voice was vibrant. "I live next door, you know; you'll soon have me lodging here. And I've got shopping to do, too. So stick to your plans, William Bailey, and I'll stick to mine." Her voice dropping now, she said softly, "I'll be in shortly, Fiona, when he's out of the way."

As she handed a cup of tea to Bill, Fiona said, "I repeat I'm lucky, if only for the fact that she can give you back as much as you send." . . .

It was some time later, after Bill had left the house to do his shopping and the children were upstairs tying up their Christmas presents when Nell came into the sitting-room and, sitting down on the couch and without any preamble, she said, "What did he say?" And for answer, Fiona clasped her hands tightly in her lap and bent her body forward, muttering as she did so, "Oh, Nell."

There was silence between them for a moment; then Nell said, "You asked him straight out?"

"Yes, yes, I did."

"And he confirmed it?"

Fiona now drew in a long breath and lay back against the head of the couch as she said, "Not particularly. He said it could be, but he wouldn't know exactly until they got inside." Then swinging round, she caught hold of Nell's hands and, gripping them tightly, she shook them, saying, "I couldn't bear it, Nell. I'm a rank coward, I suppose, but the thought of a colostomy and having, well, that thing at the side, I just. . . ."

"Stop it! Be quiet! You're jumping to conclusions. But if it did come to that, they're doing wonders with that kind of operation now. There's that young woman who works on the television in Newcastle . . . She's in the make-up section. She goes around talking about it now. She had that very same thing done and within six months she had another operation and everything was put back normal again. She's marvellous, better than she's ever been."

"That may be so; she's an exception; but I don't think I could go through with it, the very thought of it, in fact, I'm sure I couldn't. And . . . and I can tell you I've given it a lot of thought of late because I've known all along what the trouble was; I didn't have to wait to hear him say that's what it could be. Yet when he did I felt like passing out. But, Nell; now listen to me." She again shook the hands that were in hers. "I want to talk to you seriously. This is about the only chance I'll have before Thursday, and . . . and please don't interrupt. Let me have my say. Well, it's like this. As I see it you're on your own; your divorce will be through at any time. You'll be free to do what you like, so I'm going to ask you to take my place here and look after the children and. . . ."

"*Shut up!*" Nell's hands were dragged roughly from hers. "Take your place here, you said. I could never hope to take your place, even with the kids. And what about him? Look. You've got to think of him more than you have them. That fella adores you. He'll go barmy if anything should happen to you. Well, it's not going to happen to you. If it's what you think, you're going to go through with it. *Take your place indeed!*"

"I asked you to hear me out."

"I'm not hearing you any further on that line."

"Nell. Nell, please listen to me. It will ease my mind if I knew you would stay on here and see to them."

"You don't have to ask that. Don't be so silly. You know I'll see to them. But there's not going to be any necessity to take over from you. Now, you listen to me. You make up your mind, no matter what it is, you're coming through it. My heavens! There's people had the operation twenty years ago and they're still going strong. And I'll tell you something you didn't know. There's Mam." She jerked her head backwards. "She had her breast off twelve years ago. She looks as if she's got a big bust, but one's a good falsie. So, come on, lass." Her voice suddenly dropped and, moving towards Fiona again, she put her arms around her and, her voice thick now, she said, "You mean a lot to me. I've never had a friend like you in my life. You've saved me from despair over these past months, made me feel I was a human being again because when he walked out, as I told you, I felt less than nothing. His mam and dad were wonderful to me, they still are, but they didn't give me the boost that you did: letting me be with the kids, making me feel wanted and appreciated. Yes, that's the word, appreciated. All my married life I never felt appreciated. So you see, I'm thinking of meself, 'cos I couldn't go on without you either."

"Oh, Nell, I'm lucky to have you. And you know something? That's the third time I've said that in the last few hours."

They kissed and hung together for a moment; then Nell, getting abruptly to her feet, said, "Upstairs with you and into bed. I'll see that Bailey gang leaves you alone, until they come to say goodnight anyway."

Fiona made no protest, she just smiled at this staunch friend and went out.

Nell now went into the kitchen and busied herself at top speed: setting the table for the breakfast, putting out a tray with glasses on for the late milk drinks, and a biscuit tin by its side. Then stopping suddenly, she put her hand tightly across her eyes, and as the tears welled through her fingers, she flopped down onto a chair, and resting her arms on the table, she buried her head in them and gave way to the pent up emotions inside her.

It was like this that Bill saw her when he opened the kitchen door. Startled, she rose to her feet, and he, taking her by the shoulders, said, "What is it? What's happened?"

"N . . . nothing, Bill. Nothing."

"It's Fiona, isn't it? You know something that I don't. Come on, come on, out with it." He shook her.

"No, no, it isn't . . . not that, Bill."

"Don't lie to me, Nell. I know she's been keeping something back."

"It . . . it . . . it isn't that. It's . . . it's about Harry, and . . . and the divorce."

"Well, you knew what he wanted, and that's what you want an' all, isn't it?"

"Yes, yes." She sniffed loudly and licked at the tears raining over her lips, then said, "I . . . I got a letter from him, but . . . but he didn't say anything except he wanted it got through quickly. And then . . . then Mam was out this afternoon and met someone who knew the girl. She's going to have a baby."

"Ah, Nell. And the dirty bugger wouldn't give you one. Ah, lass."

His right arm slipped around her shoulder, and she fell against him for a moment. And as he patted her, he said, "There, there, lass. You know what they say, there's better fish in the sea. And there'll come along someone later on. Look at me. What I. . . ."

His voice halted abruptly as the kitchen door was thrust open and his head jerked to the side to see two figures standing stiffly staring at him. It was the expression on their faces that made him almost push Nell from him. Yet he still held her shoulder as he turned her around, looked towards Katie and Willie, who were about to scamper away, and he yelled at them, "Stop! Stay!" as if they were dogs. And they did just that, they stopped and they stayed. He beckoned them now with his finger, saying, "Come here."

Slowly they both came towards him, their eyes wide; and now pressing Nell into a chair, he brought them to her knees, saying, "You two stay with Nell. She's very upset about something. Now, comfort her. I'll be back in a minute."

And with that he almost ran from the room and into the sitting-room and, seeing that Fiona wasn't there, he took the stairs two at a time and burst into the bedroom.

Fiona had just got into bed and she looked startled as he came towards her, his hand out pointing but seemingly unable to speak for a moment. And then he said, "In two seconds there'll be your daughter and younger son diving into this room to tell you that they've seen Nell and me necking in the kitchen."

"*What?*"

"Just what I said."

"Well, would you mind explaining?"

He dropped down on the edge of the bed, drew his fingers across his brow as if wiping the sweat from it, then said, "I came in the kitchen and I found Nell howling her eyes out, and I got her off the chair and I put me hand on her shoulder, just like this" – he demonstrated – "and said, 'What's it all about?' In fact I thought she was keeping something back from me about you, you know. And I gave her a little shake like this" – he demonstrated again – "and she said it wasn't about you, but she'd had a letter this morning from that swine of hers. And he didn't say anything about fathering a baby apparently. But her mam was out this afternoon and met somebody who seemed to know that the girl is expecting. And that cut her up."

"*She didn't tell me that.* I knew about the letter but not about. . . ."

"Well, now you know. She likely thought you had enough on

your plate. Anyway, the state she was in she would have moved a brick wall and so I put me arm around her shoulders and she bent her head against me for a minute." He tried to demonstrate again, but she pressed him off. Her eyes were blinking, her lips were tight, as he went on, "Then the kitchen door was thrust open and there were the two of them goggle-eyed, struck dumb, and I could see that imp of Satan dashing up here and saying just that: 'Mr Bill and Nell were necking in the kitchen, Mam.' She's well advanced your daughter. That says nothing for your son."

"Oh, Bill. Oh, Bill." She was holding her side now and her body was shaking with laughter. "Oh, Bill. Oh, Bill. If . . . if you could see your face: a . . . a jury would hang you; there's guilt written all over it."

"Guilt be damned. And look, stop laughin' like that; you'll hurt yourself."

"Hurt meself? Oh, it's the best medicine I've had for days." The bed almost shook, and when her laughter became audible she put her hand over her mouth, and he put his arms around her, saying, "Give over now. Give over."

Her eyes were wet, but when real tears began to take the place of the moisture her laugher subsided, and, dropping her head onto Bill's shoulders, she said, "Oh, Bill. Bill."

"Don't lass, don't. For God's sake, don't cry; it'll break me down."

When there came a tap on the bedroom door she quickly dried her face, and Bill, standing up, called, "Come in." And in came Katie and Willie and, after passing Bill, they went to the bed. And it was Katie who spoke first, saying, "I cried an' all, Mam, 'cos Nell's husband's not coming back."

"I'll marry her."

Bill half turned from the bed for a moment; then swinging round, he sat on the edge of it and, looking at Willie, he said, "You would? You'd marry Nell?"

"Yes. Yes, I told her, when I'm ten, perhaps eleven. She said she'll wait. Didn't she, Katie?"

Katie nodded, saying, "Yes, you did; but I've told you, you can't get married at eleven or twelve, you've got to be four-teen."

"Never you mind, lad." Bill patted Willie's shoulder. "She'll wait and she'll appreciate what you've done, 'cos as you know she was in a very upset state, wasn't she?" They both looked at him and nodded, and, Katie staring at him fully in the face, said, "Some men can have two wives, or more. It was on the television. A man had five and a lot of children."

Bill's eyes widened, so did his mouth, but apparently he could find no comment to make on this statement. It was Fiona who said, "But that's in another country, dear, and it's because of the religion."

They looked at her in silence for a moment; then as they both turned from the bed Willie said, "God had five hundred."

"It wasn't God, silly, it was Solomon, the king."

"It wasn't, it was God."

The door closed on them, and Bill, shaking his head, muttered, "Those two could do a turn on their own."

Fiona now said, "By the way, you are back quickly; you couldn't have got much shopping done."

"Oh, I got all I needed tonight, and it's a beast outside, enough to cut the nose off you."

"Bill."

"Yes, love?"

"Will you have a talk with Mark, explain things to him?"

"Tonight?"

"Yes. You can take him down to help with the rest of the streamers."

"What'll I say?"

"Well, just explain I've got to go into hospital the day after Boxing Day, and you're depending on him to see to the others over the holidays; and that I'll be back home again long before he goes to school."

He stared at her, but made no further comment. Then getting up abruptly from the bed, he went out. And she lay back and closed her eyes and thought, I can't bear it.

22

❧

Two things happened on Christmas Eve, both unusual in their own way. The first began with a call from Mrs Vidler. Fiona picked up the phone to hear the voice say, "That you, Fiona?"

. . . "Yes, Mother."

"Thank you for your help yesterday; it's left me in a nice pickle."

"I told you I was unable to come round. I haven't been well. I'm going into hospital on Thursday."

"Not well? What's the matter with you?"

"It's the old tummy trouble. . . . Are you settled in?"

"Settled in, you say. I am stranded here with boxes and furniture all around me, and the furniture men refuse to come. They started their holidays last night, I've been informed, but the removal was booked for this morning. I've had to sell off half my things because they wouldn't go into the bungalow. They took them on Thursday to the auction rooms and were to come back on Friday, but they didn't arrive. And then their manager man said they would be here this morning, of all days in the year! And now he says they started their holiday on Saturday and the firm is closed until the New Year. Did you ever know anything like it? What am I to do?"

"I don't know, Mother."

Fiona turned her head from one side to the other in rejection as the thought passed through her mind to ask her to come here until she was settled, when a loud, "No?" brought her to the phone again. "Well, what can I do, Mother? I can't make the company come and move you."

"No, but . . . but" – there was a pause – "that man's firm."

"Which man's firm?"

"You know who I'm talking about, girl! He's got lorries and men and they'll still be at work. They could come and do it."

Fiona now put her head back, looked up to the ceiling and smiled broadly, before she said, "You mean you want to ask Bill to move you?"

"I . . . I am not going to ask him, but you can ask him. You can tell him to send his men."

"I can tell my husband nothing, Mother. He isn't the kind of man that you can order to do anything that he doesn't want to do, and I don't think he would be inclined to do anything for you after the way you have treated him."

"Girl!"

"I don't have to remind you again, Mother, that I'm not a girl."

There was a long pause; then the voice that came over was small: "Fiona."

"Yes, Mother?"

"I'm at my wits' end. Everything is packed up, every utensil, everything." The voice sounded tearful now. "It isn't all that far away between the houses. Fiona, please."

"Mother, I cannot ask my husband to do this service for you, but you could ask him yourself. Anyway, I don't suppose he has any men left on the site; they, too, will have started their holidays."

"Don't make me, Fiona. Please don't make me."

"I'm not making you, Mother, but he is more likely to accede to your request if *you* were to ask him, and put it politely, and tell him that you're in a hole."

"You're enjoying this, aren't you, Fiona?"

Fiona was still smiling but her voice sounded serious as she said, "No, Mother, I am not enjoying this. I only know, after all that's been said I couldn't ask my husband to go and move you, and at this late stage too. Anyway, I'll leave it to you. This is his number; he may still be at the works."

She now repeated the number, then said, briefly, "It's up to you, Mother; I can't do any more." And at this she put the phone down; but immediately picked it up again and rang Bill's office.

"Bill."

"Oh, hello, love. All right?"

"Yes, yes, I'm all right. Listen." Then almost word for word she gave him the gist of the conversation that had just taken place, and he replied with one word, "Never!"

"Yes, yes; you are her last resort. But I don't know whether she'll take it or not; she might prefer to sit on her boxes. In that case, dear, I would have to have her here for Christmas Day; I couldn't leave her there."

"Oh, no! Oh no, you don't. You're not spoiling Christmas Day."

"Well, if she phones, will you do it?"

There was a pause before he answered; then on a laugh, he said, "Aye, lass, I'll do it. Of course, they're open lorries, but by the sound of it a couple of trips should be enough. But the few lads here are finished at twelve. What time is it now? Ten to ten. Oh, well, lass, if she phones I'll get them goin'. But I'll go with them."

"Oh! Bill, you needn't."

"I wouldn't miss it."

"Don't be rough on her."

"You leave it to me. You remember me and me dinner jacket?"

"Yes. But what has that got to do with it?"

"Well, I'd like to give her a surprise. And it's a pity there's not a film producer goin' along of me, 'cos after the act I'll put on he might pick me for stardom; in fact, no might about it, a sure thing."

"Oh, Bill. Anyway, I must advise you, Mr Bailey, if you're going to put on an act, watch your aitches and sound your g's."

"Nark it, Mrs B. 'Bye, love."

He had hardly put the phone down when it rang again, and a voice said, "I'd like to speak to Mr Bailey."

"Mr Bailey speaking." The tone could have been attributed to Sir Charles Kingdom.

"Mr Bailey, the builder?"

"Yes. What can I do for you, madam?"

"This . . . this is Mrs Vidler."

"*Oh, Mrs Vidler.*"

He said no more. And the voice said, "Are you there, Mr Bailey?"

"Yes; yes, I am here, Mrs Vidler." His accent remained high-falutin but his tone slightly stiff. "What can I do for you?"

"I . . . I have been on to Fiona. I . . . I've explained to her about . . . about moving. They've disappointed me, let me down. My furniture and effects are all ready to be moved into the bungalow. There's not a great deal of stuff, and . . . and as it is the holidays the removal firm has closed. I explained to Fiona and . . . and" – there was a pause – "and Fiona suggested that you might be able to help me."

"She did?" There was surprise in the tone now.

"Well . . . well, she said as it was an emergency. . . ."

"What exactly are you asking me to do, Mrs Vidler?"

"Well, I thought you might have emp . . . empty lorries and such, and your workmen and you might oblige by re . . . removing me today."

He knew that this was the space where he should have put in, "I'd take great pleasure in removing you, Mrs Vidler, and as far away as you like," but what he said, was, "Well, well now. I just don't know about this. Most of my men finished on Friday. It's a holiday you know; I've only a few here who have come in to tidy up. . . . Where are you moving to, Mrs Vidler?"

"Oh, it isn't very far, not a long journey, just to Primrose Crescent."

"Oh, Primrose Crescent. Yes, yes; I know those bungalows. Well now, under the circumstances, I will see what I can do."

. . . "Thank you. When can I expect you?"

"Oh, now, now, let me see." He paused for a full minute before adding, "Let's say within the next hour."

"Thank you."

Hearing the phone being put down, he replaced his own receiver, sat back in the chair, and let out a bellow of a laugh. But it stopped abruptly as he thought: If Fiona had only been all right we'd have made a thing of this. It would have given us a belly laugh for weeks.

Barney McGuire, and Bert Ormesby, and Jack Mowbray all knew of the situation between him and his mother-in-law. In fact, Jack Mowbray seemed to have her twin sister as his mother-in-law . . . and living with them. So when Bill said to them, "What about it? Will you do it?" they said as one voice, "Anything you say, boss." And then he said, "Well now, I'll tell you something. It's like this. I intend to put on an act when I get there. You'll see what I'm at when I open me mouth, an' so I want you to fall in with it. Touch your forelocks, be sort of deferential like. You know what I mean. But don't overdo it." . . .

And they fell in with it. When, for the first time, Bill entered the house in which his wife had been born he realised yet again the wide difference in their upbringing. And when Mrs Vidler, standing amid the ordered chaos in the hall, which was as large as the sitting-room and dining-room put together at home, and he saw that she had difficulty in speaking, he opened with, "Good-morning, Mrs Vidler. Will you show me exactly what has to be removed?"

She stared at him. This wasn't the broad Liverpudlian, the big, raw, wisecracking individual who had spurned her. She decided that he was either acting, or Fiona had been working on him. Perhaps she had sent him to one of those speech therapists.

"Mr Bailey."

Her tone immediately pointed out to Bill that his facade could be blown at any moment, and so, still keeping up the gentlemanly pose, he swung round, saying, "Oh, excuse me; I'll tell my men to get on with it, because time is pressing. They are due to be finished at dinner-time you see." And now he called, "Mc-Guire!"

Barney actually bounced in, touched his forelock and said, "Yes? Yes, boss?"

"Get the men to start moving. Look round and see what has to go on first."

"As you say, boss."

Bill turned away now. He thought Barney was slightly overdoing it; and he was no actor. But Bert Ormesby apparently was, for, crossing the hall, he lifted his cap to Mrs Vidler and in a quiet voice he said, "Mornin', ma'am."

But Jack Mowbray coming in on Bert's heels completely ignored her, likely thinking of his own mother-in-law; and addressing Bill, he said, "How long is this likely to take, boss?"

Bill thought for a moment; then looking at the perplexed lady, he said, "You said a lot of your big stuff had been disposed of?"

"Yes, yes; it's gone to a sale."

Turning his head now towards Jack, he said, "Oh then, about a couple of hours I should say. You might have to make two runs each." Again he was looking at the perplexed lady, saying now, "Of course, you know, Mrs Vidler, I have only lorries not pantechnicons."

"Yes, yes, I understand."

"But we have brought tarpaulin covers in case it should rain. Thankfully it's dry."

"Yes, yes." Her head was nodding now as if it was on strings.

"Boss." Jack Mowbray stopped as he was on the point of moving away and in a low voice which was very carrying he said, as he thumbed across the hall towards an open door, "Mr McGuire tells me you've got a committee meeting at twelve. You forgot?"

"No. No, I haven't forgotten, but that's quite all right; I've already told them I might be a little late. They'll wait."

Now with a slight nod towards Mrs Vidler, he followed the man into the first room where the other two were already standing grinning widely, and when there was a slight splutter, he put up a warning finger to his nose; then quite loudly he said, "Yes, yes; I'd get this room cleared first."

And so it went on until the two lorries were packed high with furniture. And Bill wondered himself how long he could keep up the farce after handing his mother-in-law into his car and leading two lorries on the journey to Primrose Crescent."

He purposely kept silent in the car, all the while thinking, Wait till I tell her. She won't believe it.

The bungalow was well built, but with not half the accommodation of the house they had just left. And here the act became more difficult for he found that she was addressing him solely as to where the carpets and furniture should go. He then had to tell his men. Once or twice his natural tone came to the fore, but if she noticed it she showed no sign, although he knew, being Mrs Vidler, she would likely be thinking, What's bred in the bone will come out in the flesh no matter how thick the veneer.

In order to make a temporary escape, when one lorry was emptied he left Barney and Jack to see to the unloading of the other while he himself went back with Bert Ormesby to get the remainder of the furniture. And it was evident that Bert saw himself as an actor, for no sooner had they been seated in the cab then he said, "How did I do, boss?"

"You did so well, you could take it up; it'll pay more than bricking."

"Eeh! I've never enjoyed meself so much for I couldn't tell you how long. Is she as bad as all that?"

"Worse. And I can tell you it must have cost her somethin' to ask me to do this job. By, it must. Some women are the limit, you know."

Bert's voice had a serious note in it now as he said, "No, I

wouldn't know, boss; I've never been tangled up with them."
He glanced at Bill now, saying, "Scared, and that's the truth. I
only have to sit next to one and I become like a deaf and dumb
mute."

"You've talked to my wife."

"Yes, yes, but she's different, she's married."

"And you've talked to Nell. I saw you the other night when
you helped to bring the tree in. You were chatting away when
she gave you a cup of coffee."

"Yes, but she was easy. I mean . . . well she's married an' all."

"Not for long. Her divorce is coming through any time
now."

"Funny that: a man can have a woman like her and drop her.
She seemed nice."

"She is nice." Now he nudged Bert. "There's a chance for
you. We'll invite you round for the New Year."

"You'll do no such thing, boss."

"But I will, that's if —" he drew in a short breath now before
he said, "My wife's for hospital, Thursday."

"No!"

"Aye."

"Anything serious?"

"That's the point, we don't know."

"She seemed so bright and lively."

"Oh, that's just on the surface."

"Oh, boss, I'm sorry. But it'll be all right, you'll see. It'll be
all right. God looks after his own."

"Aye" – Bill's voice was sharp now – "and God takes them
young and good and beautiful."

"Aye He does because He's a jealous God."

Bill stared at this tough-looking individual by his side in something like amazement. He had worked with him for ten years
but he knew so little about him except as they all knew now, he
neither drank, nor smoked, nor apparently went with women.
But what was apparent, he believed in God.

It was a funny world. . . .

It was close on one o'clock when Mrs Vidler stood at the
door of her bungalow and, smiling at Barney, Jack, and Bert in
turn, she handed them a note, saying to each, "Thank you so
much. I'll always be in your debt."

And each man touched his forelock and said, "Thank you,

ma'am." And Bert, going one better, said, "Been a pleasure that doesn't come our way every day, ma'am. It's good to be of service."

Her smile was wide when, a moment later, she turned back into the small hall where Bill was buttoning up his overcoat. And looking at him steadily for a moment, she said, "I must be frank, Mr Bailey: I never thought the day would come when I would change my opinion of you. I . . . I am always one to admit my faults and I can see that I've judged you harshly. We all live and learn and I can see that you have learned over the past months. And I am grateful to you for the service you have done me today. It all augurs more favourably for our future."

Oh Gord! The words in his mind sounded like those issuing from a Cockney's lips. And he asked himself what would happen should she visit the house and find she had been the butt of a joke, because there was one thing sure, he couldn't keep this kind of patter up; it was too wearing. Another thing he had learned this morning: actors certainly worked for their money, whether it be in acquiring an accent or getting rid of one.

"I'm having dinner with friends tomorrow. But will you tell Fiona that I will call round to see her on. . . ."

He interrupted her here by saying, "I thought she may have told you, but she's going into hospital on Thursday."

"Oh, yes, yes. Anyway, if I can't call before I shall visit her in hospital."

"I'm sure she'll be pleased to see you."

Holy Harry! Let him get out of this. He made hastily for the door now, and she followed him, saying, "I'm sorry you'll be late for your committee."

He had forgotten about the committee business. Then, making one last effort, he turned and smiled at her as he said, "Oh, they'll wait. They're used to it by now. Goodbye Mrs Vidler."

He was half-way down the path when she called out, "Oh, you . . . you must send your bill in."

"Bill?" He turned round, his face screwed up. "There needn't be any talk of bills." His tone was pompous. He lifted his hand as if in final farewell, got into the car, started her up straight-away, and didn't seem to draw a breath until he had rounded the corner of the crescent. Then he let out a long, "Whew!"

Wait till he got back home and told Fiona. She wouldn't believe it.

As he entered the yard he saw Jack Mowbray and Bert Ormesby making for their cars, and Jack shouted, "She gave us a fiver each, boss. What did she give you?"

And when he answered, "Only the promise that she's going to call," they roared laughing.

He stopped the car outside the office, and as he got out said to Barney who was standing there, "I'll lock up, then I'm away." And Barney said, "You can't go home yet, boss."

"What d'you mean?"

"You've got a visitor; the watchman put her in your office."

"Who is it?"

"As far as I can gather, Mrs Brown."

"Mrs Brown?"

Why should that name disturb him? Whenever he heard it, it was as though his arm would go up as if warding off a blow. But her? What did she want?

He turned to Barney now, saying, "Well, get yourself away home. And thanks for this morning. Meself, if I was to speak the truth, I would say I enjoyed it, although it was a strain. My God! Yes, I'll say it was a strain."

"I hope the missis comes through all right, boss. Can I give you a ring?"

"Yes, do that, Barney. And thanks."

"Well try and have a good Christmas anyway. And my regards to the missis."

"Thanks. And you, Barney. And you. And thanks for all the good work."

"You're welcome. Oh, you're welcome."

On this they parted, and as Bill approached his office he straightened his tie and stretched his neck out of his collar. Then, pushing the door open, he said, "Mrs Brown."

He had forgotten for the moment to revert back to his natural way of speaking.

She rose from her chair, saying, "I hope I haven't called at an inconvenient time?"

"Well, you're lucky to find me." He motioned with his hand that she should again be seated. Then he sat down behind his desk, saying, "What can I do for you?"

"Oh, nothing in particular, Mr Bailey. I just called to ask if you have an estimate out yet for the damage done to your show house."

"No. It's too short a time. My accountant has already started his Christmas holiday and there won't be anything doing here until the New Year. I'll send the damage to your husband then."

"That is really the point I came to make: I would prefer that you send the bill and any future correspondence to me."

He narrowed his eyes at her as he said slowly, "You're comin' down hard on him, aren't you?"

"What do you mean?"

"Just what I say. If I'm to go by what you said the other night, you're removing him to London."

Her face became stiff as she said, "On that occasion I explained that I . . . we've many concerns in the South."

"And all of them under your name?"

Her face now slipped into a tight smile as she said, "You're a very discerning man, Mr Bailey."

His voice was somewhat grim as he replied, "It wouldn't take a very discerning man to realise who wears the pants in your household, ma'am."

"That's what I like about you, Mr Bailey, you don't mince words. You are what you are and you're not ashamed of it. You'll go places in the end, that is if you don't remain in the North. There are no real openings for men of your calibre here."

"You don't say!" That return was cheap but for the moment he couldn't find words with which to combat this woman. Yet he felt he already knew a number of things about her and one in particular he was refuting in his mind, while at the same time telling himself he was no fool where women were concerned.

She had her hand on the side of the desk now. It was long and slim and the only ring on it was her wedding ring. She had apparently noticed the direction of his gaze for she lifted her hand and, holding it before her face, she looked at it; and then twisting the ring around, she said quietly, "There should be a law passed to delete from the wedding ceremony this band of bondage."

He gave a short laugh now as he said, "You look on it as a bondage, Mrs Brown? Well, I think that can work both ways. But there's no need for anybody to put up with bondage these days, either man or woman; there's always the divorce courts."

"Yes, yes, of course. You've explained it."

"How d'you know that?" The muscles of his jaws were tight now as he stared at her.

"Oh, one moves around here and there, little bits of gossip you know. Most women's entertainment in life is made up of gossip. I know quite a bit about you, Mr Bailey. I know that you are an ambitious man. And that you'll be hard put to find work once this estate's finished. Money is very tight in the North. I don't have to point that out to you and I can't see the corporation stepping in. As for finance companies, apart from the present one, once your business is finished they'll be moving too. So I can't see where your next, at least substantial, job is coming from."

He was on his feet now. However, she didn't move, but she looked up at him where he was standing at the side of the desk, and her voice changed and her manner seemed to melt as she said, "Believe me, Mr Bailey, I am not trying to be nasty or rub it in. But honestly I think you, with your special kind of drive, are wasted here in this part of the country. And quite candidly the main object of my being here today is to offer you better prospects in one of my companies in the South."

He felt his jaw dropping just the slightest and he snapped it closed before asking quietly, "And does Mr Brown agree to your suggestion?"

She didn't answer; but rising slowly, she hitched the shoulders of her mink coat around her neck, turned up the collar at the back, wrapped the wide fronts of the coat over her slim body; then, looking directly at him, she said, "I am divorcing Mr Brown on the grounds of infidelity."

This time he couldn't restrain his jaw from dropping. His mind was yelling at him, he hadn't been wrong. My God! no, he hadn't. What lengths some women would go to. There was one thing he was sure of now, he was really sorry for Brown. Yes, he was.

What he said now definitely surprised her. His voice had a note of enquiry in it; it was low and his words were slightly spaced. "Are all business concerns in your name?" He watched her pencilled eyebrows move upwards. She looked slightly to the side; then she smiled and said, "There speaks the business-man. Yes, yes, Mr Bailey, they're all in my name, every one."

"Will he get a share?"

Her gaze was even wider now. There was a smile on her face.

"Very little. I've already told him if he takes me to court he will get less than I will allow him in redundancy pay. After all, he's only been a mouthpiece-manager; I have seen to the businesses from the back room, so to speak."

"You know something, Mrs Brown?" His voice was still and quiet.

Her face was bright and her lips apart in a smile when, looking at him straight in the face, she said, "No, Mr Bailey. You tell me."

Going to the door now, he opened it; then turning to her, he said, "I'm damned sorry for your husband. I've always hated his guts but I can understand his actions now, for, living with you, he had to take it out on somebody. And let me tell you, Mrs Brown, I'm wide awake to what you're offering me, and if you were the last woman on God's earth I wouldn't touch you with a barge-pole. . . . Have a happy Christmas."

When he had first seen her he had admired her pale alabaster-type skin, but now her whole face was scarlet, her eyes were blazing.

"How dare you!"

"I dare, Mrs Brown, because I'm a man who's had a number of women through my hands, so to speak. Like siftin' for gold dust, you know. And at last I've found a nugget. But my experience has taught me to recognise dross when I see it. One last word, Mrs Brown, if you go through with that divorce, you'll never get another puppet like the one you've got now." . . .

He watched her march to the car; and it seemed she couldn't even have taken her seat before it swung round, just missed a piece of heavy machinery, and sped out of the gates.

Sitting down once more at his desk, he held his head in his hands. He couldn't believe it. But yes, he could. And Brown. My God! What he must have gone through. No wonder he was the bastard he was. Wait till he told Fiona. . . . Should he tell her? No, no, he wouldn't, not now anyway. Sometime in the future. He'd make a big laugh over it.

But Madam Brown was right about one thing: when this big job finished there wouldn't be a similar one on his doorstep. That would mean sacking men. But sufficient unto the day the evil thereof, for he had enough on his plate to worry about at the moment. Fiona was his main concern. . . .

But that woman! If she had stripped off before him she couldn't

197

have made the offer more clear. And to him with his Liverpudlian voice and as brash as they came, because he knew himself. Oh aye, he knew himself, both inside and out. And he had no desire to change. He'd had a little experience of altering his image this morning, and that had been too much like hard work.

23

❧❧

Christmas Day started at six o'clock, at least for the children. There was no knocking, or "May I come in?" but a small avalanche descended on the bed. Apart from carrying things, Mark was wheeling a bicycle which he had found outside his bedroom door; Katie had a pair of ballet shoes hanging round her neck, a fur hat on her head, one hand in a fur muff, and both arms supporting numerous gifts; Willie was pushing a smaller bicycle, and over its handlebars was draped a space suit, and across its seat lay a large puppet; Mamie came in attired in an imitation fur coat and hat, nursing a doll on each arm. And bedlam came second best in the source of noise pervading the room for the next hour, until at last, shouting above the mêlée, Bill cried, "Get this clutter back to the playroom! Your mother wants a cup of tea."

"I can make it, Dad."

A silence came on the room, and they all looked at Willie's flushed face, and when he, tossing himself from side to side, muttered, "Well, 'cos you are in a way," Bill said, "Yes I am in a way, and it sounds . . . well, good coming from you."

"Better than Mr Bill?"

"Yes, Willie, better than Mr Bill."

"What's the matter, Mam?" Willie was addressing his mother now. "You're going to howl."

"No, I'm not." Fiona's voice was definite. "Howl? Why should I howl? But I'll tell you what, Willie, I think that's the best Christmas box I've had."

"You haven't had ours yet. They're downstairs around the tree. I spent a lot on yours."

"Did you Willie? Well, I'm sure I'll love it. But what I want most at the moment is that cup of tea, so away you go and make it, and take Mamie with you."

The other two didn't follow Willie but they stood rather sheep-
ishly looking at Bill, then with a rush Katie threw her arms
about his waist muttering, "Dad. Dad." But as Bill bent to kiss
her Mark grabbed her arm crying, "Come on, pick up your
things," and when surprisingly she obeyed him without any
comment and they were both scrambling from the room, Mark
who was now pushing his bike turned and grinning at Bill said,
"Be seeing you. . . . Dad." Bill didn't laugh but he stood by the
side of the bed and he nipped on his lip as he asked her, "Did
you put them up to that?"

"*No no. Honest.* I never dreamt of it."

"Well! Now I feel sort of established. And I can tell you this,
I'll never have a better Christmas box, no matter how long I
live. Happy Christmas, love." He bent and kissed her gently on
the lips. . . .

And that was the beginning of a long day. There was the
usual business of preparing dinner, and there were nine sitting
down at the table, for Nell and Mr and Mrs Paget had joined
them. After the meal, which went off with a great deal of laugher
and jollity, especially reading out the riddles from the crackers,
there was the usual chore of washing up. And this was done by
Bill, Mark, and Mr Paget, while Katie, Willie, and Mamie con-
tented themselves in the playroom, thus leaving Fiona in the
sitting-room with Mrs Paget and Nell.

It was when the conversation touched on Fiona going into
hospital that Nell, nudging her mother-in-law, said, "Tell Fiona
about the light."

"Oh, no, no . . . really!"

"Oh, Mam, go on." Then turning to Fiona, Nell added, "She
never swears, never. It's funny. I've never heard her, not once.
Here, take another sip of your port, Mam, and tell her. Go
on."

Mrs Paget sipped her port, giggled, then said, "Well, Fiona,
you know about this light they're using now for internal ex-
aminations; well, there I was in the theatre lying face down on
the operating table and Mr Corbit, the specialist, was talking to
me . . . as they do you know, not expecting any answers. 'Now I
am going to insert this light, Mrs Paget,' he said. 'It won't hurt,
it will just enable me to look around. . . . Just relax now. That's
it, just relax.'

"Well, there was a sister and a nurse present and a young doctor, and as the specialist pushed this thing up" – she giggled again – "he told them what he was looking for." She took another sip of the port before going on, "You know, as I said, he said it didn't hurt, well it didn't, not at first, it was just uncomfortable, but of a sudden he gave it a push and cried out, 'Ah! that's it. It's all lit up!' As you can imagine I let out a good imitation of a scream, but at the same time my mind, jumping back to the Review of the Royal Navy, at Portsmouth, I think it was, oh many years ago, when a B.B.C. announcer was describing the lights going up on the ships. He got excited and he said—" She almost choked now and she looked from one to the other and spluttered as she ended, "The whole bloody fleet's lit up!' Oh, that poor fella. He got the sack, I think, because, you know, language such as that was unheard of on the B.B.C. in those days."

Nell and Fiona were both laughing with her now as she went on, "You see it was because I thought about this that I began to shake, and the specialist, he pulled the thing out quick because he must have imagined I was having a fit or something. And when the nurses turned me over, there I was, my face running with tears, and when he said, 'You all right, Mrs Paget?' what do you think I said? and I hadn't had any" – she lifted her glass – "port that day. But I said, 'The whole bloody fleet's lit up!' Then, you wouldn't believe it, but he threw his head back, put his arm around me and he roared. You see, he was in his sixties and knew what I was laughing about, but the others didn't. And when he said, 'That was a night wasn't it, when the whole bloody fleet was lit up,' you should have seen their faces. Oh, dear! dear! it's many a year since I've laughed like that. I shouldn't, I really shouldn't drink port."

They had their heads together now and the tears were running freely down their faces, and Fiona thought how strange it was that you never really knew people, for who would imagine this refined and delicate-looking woman coming out with a thing like that. She was so genteel.

Oh, it was a nice Christmas Day. If only there wasn't tomorrow.

*

It was Willie's turn to keep them amused, and he did at tea-time and later on when there were charades. And the surprise of the evening, even to Bill and Fiona, was the appearance of Laurel and Hardy. Willie of course was Laurel, and Mark a pillow-stuffed Hardy. And their acting and the patter which must have been well rehearsed caused them all to laugh so much that when Fiona bent over double Bill bent too and whispered, "You all right?" And partly straightening up, she gasped, "Never better, Bill. Never better. The whole bloody fleet's lit up."

"What? The body's flattened up? What d'you mean?"

"Oh, Bill, be quiet. I'll tell you later."

"Now, give over; you'll make yourself ill."

Later, when Mr and Mrs Paget said their good-nights, they both confirmed they had never had such a happy Christmas Day that they could remember. Nell didn't say anything; she just kissed Fiona, looked at Bill, then punched him in the chest and went out.

And Katie expressed the thoughts of them all: when Fiona went to kiss her good night, she put her arms around her neck and said, "It's been a lovely, lovely day, Mam. Thank you."

It was all too much.

Like a child who had had overmuch excitement, she sat on the edge of her bed as she tried in vain to prevent herself from crying; but by the time Bill entered the room she had not only dried her eyes but creamed her face and was in bed awaiting him.

For a time they lay quiet, resting in each other's arms; then her voice low, she said, "Bill, I want to talk."

"Look, love, you've had a long day. Won't it keep?"

"No; there won't be any time tomorrow, no privacy."

"Well, what d'you want to say, love?"

"I'm frightened, Bill."

"So am I, love. But really there's not all that to be frightened of . . . or is there? Are you keepin' something back?"

"Yes. Yes, I've been keeping something back. I think I've got cancer."

The room was quiet, the house was quiet, the world was quiet.

"Did he tell you that?"

"Not exactly. When I asked him point blank, he said, 'It could be.' "

"Look. Look here." He pressed himself from her, raised his face from the pillow and, looking down into her eyes, said, "All right, let's say it's the worst, but they work miracles. Every day they're working miracles."

"Bill, I've got to say this. If . . . if it was my breasts, I . . . I would hate it, but I would likely face it, but if it's inside and what the consequences are after, I don't think I'm up to taking it."

"Now look here, you're up to takin'. . . ."

"Bill, please don't raise your voice."

"I'm not raisin' me voice, but you're scarin' the bloody wits out of me, woman."

"Well, you asked me to tell you the truth, and I don't want it to come as a shock to you after. It's better to know now I think. And so, I've thought things out and I've . . . I've talked to Nell. If anything happens. . . ."

"Shut up! will you."

"I won't shut up, Bill. Listen to me, please. If anything happens she'll see to the children, she's promise me. And she's a good woman, still young, so kind and nice. . . ."

"God Almighty!" He lay back from her, put his hands above his head and gripped the back of the bedhead. "I can't believe this. I just can't believe this. You've got it into your head if anything happens to you I'd jump at Nell."

"No, not that way."

"Not that way, be damned! Look, I haven't convinced you, all these months I haven't convinced you, you're the only one in me life. The only one I ever want in me life and nobody's ever going to take your place. I'll tell you something, and I wasn't going to tell you this, but I'll tell you something, that's the second offer I've had in the last two days."

"What do you mean, the second offer?"

"Well now, Mrs Brown called at the works. She offered me a job in London looking after her affairs or some such. And then she told me she's divorcing him. I tell you if she had stripped off naked and done a belly dance she couldn't have been more invitin'."

The bed started to shake. "Oh, Bill, Bill, stop it, stop it. I don't believe a word of it. Mrs Brown!"

He now pulled her round to him, his nose almost touching hers. He said, "I'm serious."

"You are?" There was amazement in her voice.

"Yes. She told me openly that he's just a kind of manager like he was in the brewery, as Sir Kingdom said. She's the power behind the scenes; she's the queen all right in that set-up. He isn't even a regent or consort; he's been a despised individual right from the beginnin'. And you know I can understand the man now and, as I told her, I told her to her face, I feel sorry for him. And you know what else I told her, Mrs Bailey?"

"No, Bill. What did you tell her?" Her voice was quiet.

"I told her that I had found a nugget, that's the word I used, and I was quick to detect imitations or something like that, and that if she was the last woman on God's earth I wouldn't touch her with a barge-pole. Now those are the very words I did use. I said straight to her face, I wouldn't touch you with a barge-pole."

"Oh, Bill, you didn't."

"I did, woman, I did."

There was a puzzled note in her voice now as she said, "But that's only the third time you've seen her, isn't it?"

"Yes, only the third time."

"And you were struck with her at first, weren't you?"

"Struck? No, woman, not struck in that way. I saw that she was class. And I remember pointing out to you that you had stepped down to take me but she had dropped a great deal further to take him. But now I take all that back, for what I saw the other day was a cold, ruthless, vindictive bitch. And I take back an' all what I said about him, because I do pity him. She must have treated him like a serf. And no wonder the lad has turned out to be like he is. So there you have it, Mrs B. Which one am I going to take after your demise?"

"Bill, don't look like that. I'm sorry, but I ... I love ... I love you so much, and I can't bear to think of you being lonely, because the children won't fill your life."

"I'm not goin' to be lonely; you're going to have the operation and, no matter what it is, you're going to get over it. Even if you have to go through hell and high water, you're going to get over it. D'you hear me?"

"Yes, Bill."

"Now go to sleep. Come on, snuggle up and go to sleep. Because this has got to last me for a week or ten days, for that's all you'll be there."

"Put out the light, dear," she said. And he put out the light.

24

❧

She was in at eleven o'clock, and he stayed with her till three, then returned home, promising to bring the children.

When he entered the house it was Mamie who came running towards him, sobbing, "Mammy B's gone on holiday."

He picked her up, saying, "No, no, she hasn't gone on holiday. She's got a pain in her tummy and the doctor's going to put it right."

Both he and Fiona had decided that in future the child must be told the truth, at least as near as possible. This business about her mother and father and brother going on holiday meant that they were never coming back. Although she never now mentioned her parents or brother the fear of loss through the word "holiday" had seemingly taken a permanent place in her mind.

"Look, I've just come from your Mammy B, and I'm going to take you and Mark and Katie and Willie to see her, as soon as I have some tea. You'll let me have some tea, won't you?"

"Yes, Uncle Bill. And we're going to see Mammy B?"

"Sure, sure as life, cross my heart." He didn't add, "Hope to die."

Nell, coming from the kitchen, said, "All settled in?"

"Yes, Nell, and very calm and composed."

"Good."

"What time are we going?"

"Well, as I've just said to this one here" – he humped Mamie further up into his arms – "I'd like some tea; I've never had a bite since this morning."

"No lunch?"

He smiled now, saying, "No. And the meal they brought her would have satisfied a navvy . . . She picked over it just to please them. She wanted me to finish it but I told her I wasn't doing any of her dirty work; if those dishes had gone out empty they'd have wondered why she was in there. Where are the others?"

"Up in the playroom. They've been at sixes and sevens all the time. Open war between Katie and Willie. I've suggested that they all write letters to their mother and give them to her when they go in."

"Good idea."

He put the child down on the floor now, and tapped her bottom, saying, "Go upstairs and tell the others they've got to be ready by five o'clock."

In the kitchen Nell said, "I've got a combination of hash-cum-shepherd's pie in the oven. Would you like that or some cold bits?"

"I think I'll have the hash. And, if you don't mind, I'd like you to come with them and bring them back. I'll order a taxi; they'll enjoy the change."

"I don't think they'd enjoy the Royal Coach today."

"No, perhaps you're right." He went and stood by the stove and, leaning his elbow against the wall, he rested his head on his hand as he said, "What am I going to do, Nell?"

"Well, like they say on the old flicks, keep a stiff upper lip."

"I'm serious."

"I know you are."

"If anything happens to her I'll go mad."

"No, you won't. You'll face up to it; you have four bairns to look after."

"Damn the bairns! Damn everything! Why should this happen?"

"Don't you bawl at me, Bill; I'm not Fiona."

"Oh, Nell, I'm sorry, but you know what I mean."

"I know what you mean, and I know how you feel, and I know how I feel at this minute. I want to sit down and howl my eyes out. Since you left the house this morning I don't know how I've kept a dry face, because, let me tell you, it's only her friendship that's kept me going over the past months. If I'd been on my own I know I would have taken a short cut out, because when you feel less than dust there's not much lower you can go. In a way I love her as much as you do. And you know something? I'm going to tell you this, likely she's put it to you too. She's got it all planned out if anything should happen to her that I'll see to the bairns. Well, I'll promise to do that at least for a time, but as regards seeing to you, that's a different kettle of fish, because Bill, I couldn't put up with you, not your type of man. And you couldn't put up with me, 'cos I'm not your type of woman. So, whatever she said to you, you can make your mind at rest, there'll be no pressure from this end."

His body suddenly began to shake. He turned his face to the wall and bumped his brow twice against it. Then, turning and looking at her, his eyes moist, he said, "Aw, Nell, that's done me the world of good. Yes, she had it all planned out on my side an' all. Anyway, now we know where we stand give me that stew-cum-shepherd's pie. Oh, now look, don't start cryin', 'cos I might be tempted to comfort you again. And what would happen if the two moles appeared at the door? Fiona would never believe it the second time."

They were both laughing now, and Nell said, "When she comes out and I describe these last few minutes to her she'll die."

The last two words brought them to silence until Nell had placed a steaming plate before him, and then she said, "The English language has got all twisted up, hasn't it?"

"It has, Nell, it has."

The night staff had taken over before he left the room. They held each other closely and the last words he said to her were, "See you tomorrow about three."

"Yes, dear, see you tomorrow about three. I love you, Bill."

"I'm quite fond of you an' all, Mrs B." He went out quietly, and she lay staring up at the shaded light above her head. And when the night nurse came in and said, "Would you like something to make you sleep?" her reply was eager: "Oh, yes please, yes." . . .

Everyone was so kind, but then she told herself they were always kind to people going on a holiday from which they might not return.

*

When Bill reached home he saw there was a light still on in the kitchen but not in the sitting-room, so instead of letting himself in the front door he went in the back. And on entering he was surprised to see Bert Ormesby standing at one side of the table and Nell at the other. And Bert began straightaway in a slight fluster, "I . . . I just dropped in to see how . . . how the missis was and everything like."

"Oh, thanks, Bert. Sit down then, sit down."

"No, I was just about to be off."

"How was she when you left?" This was from Nell. And he answered her, saying, "Apparently calm, you know, on top."

"What time will it happen the morrow?"

He looked at Bert again, saying, "She goes down at half-past nine and it all depends on how long she'll be there as to when she comes round. Would you like a drink?"

"No thanks, boss."

"Oh, aye, I forgot, man." He smiled weakly. "I don't know where I am."

Bill took off his outdoor things, and they all stood in awkward silence for a moment until Bert said, "Well, I'll be off then." And he nodded at Bill. "Don't worry about things back there on the site; I'll pop in now and again over the holiday. Good-night then. Good-night Mrs" – he paused on the name – "Paget." And Nell said, "Good-night Mr Ormesby."

At the door Bill suddenly said, "There was no car outside. Did you walk?"

"Oh aye; it's only a couple of miles. I often have a brisk walk at night; it helps me to sleep. Good-night then."

"Good-night, Bert."

He closed the door and looked at Nell who was coming in from the hall shrugging her arms into her coat, and he said offhandedly, "Very nice of him, don't you think?"

"Yes. He seems a good fellow, thoughtful."

"Yes; yes, he is, he's a good bloke." Then with a quirk to his lips he added, "He wouldn't bawl at you."

"*Bill.*"

"Aye, Nell; there's many a true word spoke in a joke, they say."

"Well, I don't think this is the time for jokes."

"Don't put me in me place, Nell, unless you want me to bawl."

"I'm sorry, Bill; we're both on edge . . . I'll be off. Try to get some sleep. Good-night."

"Good-night, Nell."

He now went into the sitting-room and to the drinks cabinet and poured himself out a stiff glass of whisky. but he didn't drink it there, he carried it up to the bedroom, laid it on the side table, got undressed, then he went out of the room and, gently opening Mark's and Katie's bedroom doors, he glanced in. The night-light in Katie's room showed the two girls fast asleep. But in Mark's room, although his bed was illuminated only by the light from the landing, he had the suspicion that the boy, although snuggled down under the clothes, was far from asleep. He did not investigate further, however, he just gently closed the door, then went back into his own room; but before getting into bed he threw off the whisky at one go. It was now eleven o'clock.

At half-past one he was sitting wide-eyed propped up against the headboard. The whisky had had no soporific effect on him whatever, apparently just the opposite, for he had never felt more wide awake nor his head more clear. Nor could he remember thinking along the lines on which his thoughts had travelled over the past two hours or so. When had he ever before felt emotion the like of which was filling him at this time? And he questioned it.

Before he had met up with Fiona his life had seemed free and easy. He couldn't recall any real worries except those connected with the job, and then they weren't in the same league as the worries that were besetting him at the present time. And all this had come about through falling in love. And what was love after all? Some people wrote songs about it; others wrote poetry extolling it; books by the million were written about it; films were made about it. But from whatever quarter it came, as he saw it now, it was wrongly represented. Because what did it consist of? What was it made up of? Anxiety. Worry. Pain. Fear. Dread. Yes, dread. Dread of losing all that anxiety, worry, pain, and fear. For what would his life be like without it?

He wished he could go back to just before the time he first saw Fiona in the newsagent's shop. *He did. He did.* . . . No, he didn't. He'd have to stop thinking along these lines or he'd go round the bend. He'd go down and have another drink. No, he wouldn't. He put his hand out and gently switched on the radio.

There was always somebody talking in the middle of the night. But what he heard now was someone singing in low deep melancholy tones. The voice appeared for the moment to be his own as it sang:

Do not go. Do not go, my love, from me,
For no blankets can warm my frozen heart.
Do not go. Do not go, my love, from me,
For the years ahead are stark.

He almost brought the radio from the side-table, so quick did his hand switch it off. Then with a heave he slid down the bed, turned on his side, pulled the clothes almost over his head and growled, "Go to sleep. God damn you! go to sleep."

He had been waiting in the hospital from eleven o'clock, but it was half-past twelve before she was wheeled out of the operating room. It was twenty minutes later when he confronted Mr Morgan and the surgeon told him the result of the operation. . . .

He had sat for hours by her side, during which time the nurses had popped into the room and popped out again. At one point the sister came and said, "Would you mind waiting outside?"

When he stood outside the door he was amazed to hear the sister saying, "Come along, Mrs Bailey, come along. That's a good girl." He heard a groan and a sound of vomiting. He closed his eyes tightly but did not move away from the door. When eventually the sister and the nurse appeared, the sister smiled at him and said, "I'm afraid you'll have a long wait. We've made her comfortable, but she'll sleep for some time yet."

"I won't be in the way if I sit with her?"

"No, no; not at all, Mr Bailey. But it could be some hours yet before she revives completely. Then, I must warn you, she'll be in some pain. You could go home and get some rest and I'm sure in the morning she'll be. . . ."

"If it's all the same to you I'd rather stay."

*

It was near eleven o'clock. The whole ward was quiet: there was no rattle of crockery from the kitchen, no buzzing up and down the corridor. He was sitting in an armchair near the bedhead. He had closed his eyes and when his head nodded forward he realised he had almost fallen asleep. He yawned and turned his head and looked towards the figure in the bed. Her eyes were open. She was staring at him. The jerk he gave not only pushed the armchair back and caused it to squeak on the wooden floor, but his hands on the side of the matress bounced it gently, and the movement caused Fiona to close her eyes.

"Love." He was bending over her. "It's adhesions."

"What?"

"It's all right. It's only adhesions."

"What . . . what d'you mean, adhesions?"

"That's what the mass was, the dark mass, nothing else, just a bundle of adhesions sticking your guts together."

"Oh Bill. Bill." She screwed her eyes up tight, opened her mouth wide, then again muttered, "Oh Bill. Bill. . . . Adhesions?"

"Aye. That's what it's all about. Never heard the word afore, but it sounds wonderful. How're you feelin', love?"

She looked at him tenderly. A smile spread across her face, then she answered simply, "All cut up."

He put his hand across his mouth to still the sound and stood away from the bed so his shaking body wouldn't again disturb the mattress.

When the spasm passed he sat looking down at her. His face was almost solemn now. This is what love was about too: besides the anxiety, the worry, the pain, and the fear, there was relief, and joy, and hope. But by God! he wouldn't like to go through these past few days again. And what he said now was characteristic of the Bill she knew.

"You've got no idea what I've been through these last few days, lass, so never do this to me again. I couldn't stand it. My God! no!" Then he was a little surprised to see her hands hovering over the counterpane above where her stomach was. And her face was almost contorted when she said, "Bill. Oh please Bill, don't make me laugh, it's, it's painful."

For the first time he really couldn't see that he had said anything funny. In fact, he had been very serious, very serious indeed: there was nothing funny about what he had gone hrough, but he had to concede that Fiona's sense of humour was at times a little off-key, especially as now when she was etting over the effects of anaesthetic, and this was proved when ext she said, "Oh Bill Bailey, you are funny. One day you'll be he death of me. . . . Oh! Oh!"

"Don't, love. Don't; you'll snap your stitches."